EVERYONE AND EVERYTHING

Nadine J. Cohen is a writer and refugee advocate from Sydney. Her work has featured in the *Guardian*, the *Saturday Paper*, the *Sydney Morning Herald*, the ABC, SBS, *Harper's Bazaar*, *Frankie* and more. She lives by the ocean with her cat, Blanche Devereaux, an overactive imagination and far too many shoes.

EVERYONE AND EVERYTHING

NADINE J. COHEN

Harriet, I hope you're enjoyin the UK. I loved meeting your lovely mum. Nadine

PANTERA
PRESS

PANTERA
PRESS

First published in 2023 by Pantera Press Pty Limited.
www. PanteraPress.com

Please send all permission queries to:
Pantera Press, P.O. Box 1989, Neutral Bay, NSW, Australia 2089 or info@PanteraPress.com

A Cataloguing-in-Publication entry for this book is available from the National Library of Australia.

ISBN 978-0-6452400-9-2 (Paperback)
ISBN 978-0-6457578-0-4 (eBook)

Cover design: Amy Daoud
Cover photograph © Ibai Acevedo / Stocksy
Publisher: Lex Hirst
Editor: Tom Langshaw
Copyeditor: Camha Pham
Proofreader: Bronwyn Sweeney
Typesetting: Kirby Jones

Printed and bound in Australia by McPherson's Printing Group

The paper this book is printed on is certified against the Forest Stewardship Council® Standards. McPherson's Printing Group holds FSC® chain of custody certification SA-COC-005379. FSC® promotes environmentally responsible, socially beneficial and economically viable management of the world's forests.

For Mum, Dad, Nanna, Zeida, Grandma and Ariella,
who made me who I am, though probably not on purpose.

Lifeline
Call 13 11 14
Text 0477 13 11 14

Each of us is an amalgam of all we have loved and lost and learned, our personal successes and failures, our particular regrets, and our singular joys.

Nick Cave, *The Red Hand Files*, issue 197

PROLOGUE

It's still dark as I walk through the park towards the water. I don't need to see, my feet have muscle memory. They quicken as I pass the children's playground, where the swings seem to oscillate no matter how still the weather.

When I reach the locked gate there are already two women waiting. We half-smile, in silent agreement that it's too early for chats.

I'm still new to this dawn business. A few months ago, I would have found the thought of getting up at fuck-off am to swim in the ocean laughable. I've always been a night person.

'You joining us, Miss Yael?'

A broad Australian accent. Cropped black hair and a red tracksuit.

Lynne, one of the volunteers, is standing at the gate waiting for me to come through.

'Sorry, Lynne.'

'Have a good dip!'

She's way too chirpy for this hour.

I walk along the concrete path and past the change rooms towards the ocean. I dump my bag on a patch of grass and peel off my shorts and t-shirt. I'm wearing one of my million black swimsuits, a gravity-defying one-piece with a low back. As I look down, it strikes me as ill-suited for a sunrise swim at a women's-only ocean pool.

In the crevices of the rock wall that buttresses the pool, a cast of crabs go about their crab business.

'Good morning, friends,' I whisper, before hopping in.

The other women do proper laps while I splash around like a child. My sunrise swims involve less actual swimming than the phrase implies.

'Here it comes!' Lynne shouts from her post and I look out to sea.

A rush of oranges and yellows roars up from beneath the ocean and slowly turns on the sky. Immersed in water as the sun announces its arrival, I feel weightless. I feel free.

It's how I imagine other people feel all the time.

And then it's over.

JANUARY

'So, what are our options?' Liora asks.

It's late. We're in my psychiatrist's office.

'There are three options,' Priya says. 'She can go to a private rehab clinic, she can move in with you or she can stay at home. I'm not sectioning her, so legally it's her decision.'

'Sectioning?'

'Remanding her to a public ward, or any ward, without her consent. I don't think it's in her best interests.'

I don't remember coming here.

'What are the pros and cons of a rehab clinic?' Liora asks, ever the pragmatist.

'The next week or so is going to be brutal. I'm stopping all her medications and starting her on new ones tomorrow. No weaning, we don't have time. This will probably make her quite sick physically as her body adjusts. At a clinic, she'd be cared for 24/7. She has private insurance, yes?'

'Yes.'

Usually, I hate being talked about like the cat's mother, but right now I'm hoping they don't talk to me at all.

I don't want to talk. I don't know if I can talk.

'The clinic is about an hour from here, but it's the best.'

Liora nods slowly, daunted.

'And what are the negatives?' she asks.

'Once she checks in, I can't have contact with her. The treating doctors can change her medication as they see fit. They generally don't, but it's a possibility. And there are people there for all sorts of reasons, many in far worse states than this.'

There are far worse states than this?

Priya tightens the shawl around her shoulders. She's always cold.

'I'm not sure it would be the best environment for her,' she says. 'It can make it hard to come back.'

'What about staying at my house?'

I close my eyes.

'That's an option. She wouldn't be leaving her normal surroundings, so she wouldn't have to reintegrate. But it would be a big strain on you and your family. I know you have small children. It would be confronting for them – for you and your husband, too.'

'And if she stays in her apartment alone?'

'I don't think she should.'

I open my eyes.

'What about Julia Louis-Dreyfus?'

They both look at me like they've forgotten I'm here.

I guess I can speak.

'Remind me again, who is Julia Louis-Dreyfus?' Priya asks gently.

'My cat.'

*

I love cats, but I had no intention of getting one when I accompanied my oldest friend Margot to the pet store after Pilates one day.

As an adopt-don't-shop kinda gal, I generally avoid pet stores, but Margot said this one had rescue cats, so I tagged along.

We walked past the display cases of designer dogs, with schnoodles, cavoodles and labradoodles as far as the eye could see. It's the Eastern Suburbs of Sydney – if you didn't have a poodle cross, what were you even doing?

I waved at the pretty pups as I followed Margot to the back of the store. There were three big cages, each with a few cats lolling about or trying to destroy each other.

'Look at the bubbas!' cooed Margot, a grown woman with a PhD. 'I love them.'

Margot's partner is allergic to cats, so this is how she gets her feline fix.

'Why don't you just dump Josh and get a cat?'

'Then who would make me ramen and put the kids to bed?'

That was when I saw her, in all her glory. A grey-and-white tabby with a hint of ginger and a Marilyn Monroe beauty spot, living her best life despite the micro-imprisonment. Her paws were wedged into the top of the cage and she was hanging off the bars like a gymnast commencing an uneven bars routine. She looked like an idiot. A tiny, beautiful idiot.

'Oh my god, come look,' I squealed at Margot. 'I love this one!'

'Of course you love that one,' she said. 'It's batshit.'

'Hey!'

'It's the cat version of your mate, he who shall not be named.'

'Please refrain from insulting my cat.'

'Oh, it's *your* cat, is it?'

'Maybe. Maybe? I guess I could get a cat. Could I get a cat?'

'Do you want me to ask if you can hold it?'

Don't do it. Don't do it. Don't do it.

'Yes!'

Margot got a stoned teenage pet store employee to come over and get Nadia Comăneci out of her cage. She started purring.

'She loves you,' Margot said.

'I love her. Is she a her? Are we still gendering domestic animals?' I looked at the baked kid.

'Totally.'

He didn't care.

'What's her name?' I asked.

'Beauty,' he said. 'You know, like, 'cause of the spot. On her face.'

'Yeah, I get it. Margs, I can't just get a cat. Can I?'

'Do it! Do it! Do it!'

She slow-clapped for emphasis.

'You're no help.'

'We can hold her for twenty-four hours if you want to think about it,' the teenager said slowly.

Oh boy.

'Okay, let's do that.'

The next day I officially adopted Julia Louis-Dreyfus, formerly Beauty, feline gymnast, tiny idiot, she/her.

Priya and Liora hesitantly agree I can keep living at home. Priya doesn't believe I'm 'a danger to myself' and Liora doesn't have anywhere to put me. Or Julia Louis-Dreyfus.

But there are rules:

1.   Liora comes over tonight and takes away all the pills.
2.   I check in with Priya every day, twice a week in person.
3.   I spend minimal time at home alone.

'I don't know how much time I can take off,' Liora says. 'What should she do when I'm at work or with the kids?'

I don't want to see people. I don't want to see people. I don't want to see people.

'Try and be at her apartment as much as possible while she adjusts to the new meds. She won't be able to do much. Beyond that, it's best she goes to places where she'll be surrounded by people, but not forced to interact with them. The beach, the cinemas. And gyms. Even if she just walks slowly on a treadmill or sits in the sauna. Yoga is great, too, if she's up to it – I know she likes it – and same for dance classes and that new ballet thing I don't understand.'

Barre.

'And when she's ready, she can see her friends.'

I can't imagine ever wanting to see anyone again.

Liora looks at me.

'Are you okay with this? Maybe you and Julia should just move in with us. We'll make it work.'

I hate it when she doesn't say Julia Louis-Dreyfus's full name.

'I want to stay at home,' I whisper.

Liora makes the face she makes when she's torn between two items on a menu.

'Let's see how it goes and reassess day by day,' Priya says. 'If it's not working, we'll reconsider your house or a clinic.'

'Okay, sounds good.'

We're nearly out the door when Priya almost shouts.

'Wait!'

We turn.

'No sad books, no sad TV, no sad films and especially no sad documentaries. Basically, none of the depressing crap I know you love. Also, no news. And absolutely no politics.'

I nod.

'Comedies and fluffy crap only. Rom-coms, sitcoms, all the coms. No documentaries. No *Four Corners*. Promise me.'

'I promise.'

'If I could control your Netflix, I would.'

Liora laughs and immediately looks like she got busted talking in class.

I just want to go to sleep.

Liora is panicking in her giant soccer mum car. I don't think I've ever seen her panic before. She's the most balanced person I know and not prone to public displays of emotion.

There are only three and a half years between us, and as kids we were pretty close, but once she went to high school we grew worlds apart and increasingly resentful of each other.

Before that, though, I remember wanting desperately to be just like her and copying everything she did.

Everything.

When Liora wanted to be a lawyer, I wanted to be a lawyer.

When Liora stopped eating fish, I stopped eating fish.

When she had a crush on Jason Donovan, I had a crush on Jason Donovan.

When she had a crush on Jason Priestley, I had a crush on Jason Priestley.

There were a lot of Jasons back then.

Every night for years, I wished on stars to wake up with hair just like hers. Her golden-blonde, dead-straight, beautifully thick mane was everything my dirty-blonde, curly mop was not. It didn't help that Mum called me Shirley Temple and Liora Barbie. I wanted to be Barbie. Barbie was pretty. Barbie had a convertible and a beach house. Barbie had Ken.

'I'm not sure about this,' Liora says, glancing at me as she drives. 'Maybe you should stay with us, even just for tonight. Julia Louis-Dreyfus will be okay. We'll feed her and come back in the morning.'

I shake my head.

'Okay. Should I stay with you? For a few days? Sean can deal with the kids.'

'I'll be fine,' I manage to get out.

'I could go home and get some things and grab us dinner and come straight back. Actually, I can live without my stuff for a night. I'll just order us dinner.'

'I don't want dinner.' It's taking all my energy just to speak. 'Go home. I won't do anything.'

She winces.

'Okay.' She sounds unconvinced, she doesn't believe me.

I'm not sure I believe me.

'But I'm going to put you to bed and stay till you're asleep and come back first thing in the morning. No arguments.'

I nod.

We pull into the driveway of my apartment building and she parks in a visitor spot. I hope none of my neighbours are around. There's just me and a bunch of septuagenarians living here, which I enjoy, but sometimes I want to journey from the car to my apartment without seventeen conversations about how the old gardener was better than the current one.

I walk up the stairs to my apartment and hear Julia Louis-Dreyfus crying at the front door. I've always wondered if she does this every time she hears the building security door open, or if she can somehow magically sense when it's me.

Inside I feed her and have a glass of water. When I turn around, I see Liora sitting on the couch holding something. Reading something.

Wait, is she crying?

Fuck.

Fuck, fuck, fuck.

I forgot about the note.

When I was a toddler, I saw a ferry sink. It was on some annual ferry day in Sydney Harbour that's no longer a thing, and by all accounts nobody was hurt, but I've had a problematic relationship with boats and open water ever since. This wouldn't have been a big deal if I hadn't grown up in a place where the quickest way to get many places was by ferry.

Mum and Dad managed to lure me onto a ferry when I was eight. We were going to the zoo with some family friends and they swore black and blue it wasn't leaving the wharf.

Those lying fuckers.

I cried and screamed from the minute the motor started to the minute we got off, which must have been fun for the other passengers. But it worked. I've been cautiously fine with boats ever since, as long I can see land at all times. This means cruises will forever be a hard pass, but that's no big loss – disease-ridden floating theme parks from hell.

So, we were at the zoo and we had reached the marine life section. Photos show I was wearing knee-length denim shorts, a yellow-and-white striped t-shirt and the white Apple Pie sneakers I'd begged for more than I'd ever begged for anything in my life.

Spotting my favourite animal friends, I yelled, 'SEALS!' and ran over to their pool enclosure, trailed by Liora and the two boys from the other family. Back then, the seals could swim right up to the bars and sit inches away, like a prison visit.

Actually, very much a prison visit.

I stuck my hand through the bars for a pat and then screamed like a hot girl in an '80s slasher film.

'What happened?' said Liora, next to me.

'He bit me!' I said through tears, raising a bloodied hand.

Now it was her turn to scream.

'Where's Mummy?' I yelled at her.

'I don't know!' she yelled back, standing on her tiptoes. People were gathering around us and we couldn't see past them.

'We'll find her!' one of the boys said and they both ran off, pushing their way through the crowd.

A nice lady in a floral dress crouched in front of us. I was crying hysterically and Liora was trying to comfort me.

'My husband's gone to find help, sweetheart,' she said gently. 'Do you think I could wrap my scarf around wherever he got you? It would help to stop the bleeding.'

'That's a good idea,' Liora said, sounding older than her eleven years. 'Can you show the lady where he got you?'

'I ... I ... I'm ... scared.'

'Of course you are,' the lady said. 'I promise I'll be very gentle.'

I looked down and saw my t-shirt covered in blood. I'd been cradling my arm, holding my hand against my stomach.

I held my hand out to her.

'Yael!' I heard Mum's voice. 'Where is she?'

'Mum! Mum! We're here!'

Liora jumped and waved.

Mum burst through the crowd, turning white at the sight of me, bloody and sobbing, a stranger wrapping a silk Ken Done scarf around my hand.

'Oh my god!' She rushed over. 'What happened?'

'I just wanted to pat him.'

'Oh, moosh,' she said, hugging me. 'He must have been hungry.'

'Where's Daddy?' I asked.

'He was a bit ahead of us,' Mum said. 'The boys have gone to find him.'

'Are all my fingers still there?' I asked the lady.

'Well, that depends. How many did you have before?'

I looked at Mum. I looked at my left hand.

'Five?' I said, not feeling confident.

'Then yes, they are all still there. He only had a nibble.'

Shock and adrenaline soon gave way to pain and I started howling, my swaddled hand held tight against my chest, turning Mr Done's pastel kaleidoscope into a crime scene.

Mum and Liora were crouching next to me, trying to comfort me.

'Who bit my Yael?' boomed a thick, ethnically ambiguous accent. 'Show me the culprit.'

Suddenly, Dad appeared and lifted me into his arms, careful not to touch my hand. I buried my face in his neck.

'Did a mean seal try to snack on you, shayna maidel?' he asked.

'YES,' I wailed into his t-shirt.

'Want me to try and snack on him right back?'

I giggled.

'I'll do it, I swear,' he continued. 'Nobody snacks on my maidel and gets away with it.'

A golf buggy pulled up and a man ushered Mum and me onto it. Mum thanked the lady and then turned to Dad, who was now standing with Liora, hands on her shoulders.

'We'll have you paged or something later.'

'Okay,' said Dad. 'I love you, chicken.'

'Make sure you get this lady's details so we can replace her scarf.'

'Oh, that's not necessary,' the lady said. 'I don't even like Ken Done.'

'Does anybody?' Mum said.

And then we were off.

Priya wasn't joking when she said it would be brutal. The withdrawal. The new meds. The withdrawal and the new meds. At the same time. Together.

There was shaking, there were headaches, there was vomit.

I couldn't sleep for more than a few hours at a time.

My body temperature changed every five minutes. I was either too hot or too cold. No tolerable medium, no just right. Was I withdrawing from medication or entering early menopause?

I wasn't heroin-withdrawal bad, but I wouldn't recommend it.

I kept thinking of the scene in *Requiem for a Dream* when Jared Leto detoxes in his childhood bedroom. I wonder if that movie holds up by today's everything standards. I'm gonna guess not, mostly because: Jared Leto.

I downplayed how bad I felt when Liora was there because I didn't want to go to rehab.

No, no, no.

*

For the record, I have nothing but respect for artist, icon and national treasure Ken Done.

'Welcome to the multicultural, semi-nude, body-positive utopia you never knew you needed,' my friend Romy announces, as we arrive at the women's baths. 'I honestly don't know how the fuck you've never been here.'

'I blame men,' I say quietly.

'That's the spirit!'

Romy insisted on taking me here after I told her about the thing.

'It's magical,' she said. 'Everyone says the water has healing powers.'

Ugh. She knows how I feel about pseudo-mystical wellness speak. She also knows how I feel about the ocean, but she promised there won't be waves.

She takes my hand and leads me down a concrete path. 'Oh, I forgot to tell you, entry is a gold coin donation. I've got you today.'

Romy and I worked together in media, but we had met long before that when she worked at a cafe around the corner from Liora's old house. We clicked immediately, bonding over fashion, *Gilmore Girls* and hating things – the backbone of any strong union.

At the bottom of the path, under a huge umbrella, sit two middle-aged women wearing yellow t-shirts with VOLUNTEER written across them in red. They have green zinc on their cheeks and noses.

I wonder if they've been here since 1987.

One of the be-zinced women holds out a bucket and Romy drops some coins in.

'It's her first time,' she says, motioning to me.

My heart high-jumps into my throat and I feel my cheeks getting hot. Maybe this is a bad idea.

'Welcome, love,' says the woman holding the bucket.

'Enjoy,' says the other.

Romy grabs my hand again and drags me down the rest of the path. I can see the full expanse of the baths now. There are what seem like hundreds of women, sunbaking, swimming, reading and chatting. I start to panic.

'Wait. Romy. Wait!' I say as loudly as I can manage.

She turns around and my mind goes blank.

'I … I don't know if I can do this.'

'Fuck, sorry,' she says. 'I forgot.'

'I just don't wanna see anyone I know.'

Not many people know about the thing. I only told Romy because she kept trying to commission me for stories.

'Why don't you put on that giant hat while we look for a spot? Please stay.'

'Okay. But can we sit away from everyone?'

Romy nods and we walk towards the water. The grassy areas on both sides of the path are covered almost entirely in half-naked women. We continue down concrete steps leading out to giant rocks, where more women are splayed, like Botticelli's wet dream.

Some of my friends' cool hippie mums took them to the women's baths as kids, but I can't imagine my shy, deeply self-conscious mother lying topless on a rock in broad daylight.

We reach the rocks and Romy pauses.

'How about over there, near that girl with the pink hair?' She points across the rocks.

Before I can say yes, a very Aussie voice yells, 'OI!'

I freeze.

One of the volunteers marches towards us with rage in her eyes.

'OI! YOUSE OVER THERE! WITH THE PICNIC BASKET! NO PHOTOS! YOU KNOW THE RULES! IF I SEE YOU POINTING THOSE PHONES AT ANYTHING BUT THE WATER, YOU'RE OUTTA HERE!'

Exhale.

'Oh yeah,' Romy says. 'You're officially not supposed to take photos, but the vollies don't mind if they're selfies or ocean only.'

'I don't think I'll be making content anytime soon.'

'Fair point.'

We make our way over to the spot Romy pointed out, jumping from rock to rock and trying not to step on anyone. After we lay out our towels, she gets undressed and takes off her lime-green bandeau bikini top.

'As you can see, free-boobing is allowed, nay encouraged, here. Get 'em out!'

'Baby steps.'

I am not in a topless sunbaking place. Or a swimming place. I don't know what place I'm in.

I apply sunscreen to every inch of my lily-white, mole-covered Eastern European skin, and suddenly feel very tired. This is my first social outing since the thing.

It's a lot, but at least it's beautiful.

'Thanks for bringing me here, Rom.'

'Any time.'

*

I started writing the note the minute I decided to do it.

I agonised over it.

There were several drafts.

Various fonts were trialled.

It had to be perfect.

Liora keeps trying to feed me solid food but the thought of chewing is mildly horrifying. I have no appetite. All I want are mango smoothies.

Normally I'd be thrilled about all the weight I'm losing, but I feel nothing. Not happy, not hungry. Not even sad.

I'm nothing.

Priya says it's dissociation, a trauma response, that an emergency wall has sprung up between my brain and my feelings. She says it's temporary.

I don't really care.

Which I guess means she's right.

'I'm going to send you to Priya Hoffman,' Dr Chandra told me about five years ago, when my depression escalated and I needed more care (read: drugs) than my psychologist was legally able to provide. 'She does talk therapy.'

'Don't all psychiatrists do talk therapy?'

'No, some strictly manage medication and leave the rest to psychologists.'

'Will she change my meds?'

'I assume so, but we'll see what she says. I think she's one of the best around, but she does have a reputation for being a bit tough. Some people don't respond well to her. If you don't like her, it's absolutely fine, just come back and we'll find someone else.'

I liked Priya immediately.

I was nineteen when I had my first depressive episode, or the first one that couldn't be readily dismissed as high school angst.

I was struggling. Not with uni work – it was a BA, basically tertiary kindergarten – but with being a person in almost every other way.

I was fighting with my family constantly, which to be fair was not a new development, and I felt emotionally disconnected despite an active social life.

One-on-one I was generally fine, but group situations could render me monosyllabic at best. On nights out, I'd often end up in the bathroom, crying or trying to talk myself out of my head, or just straight-up ghosting.

It all reached a bit of a head when I came home a mute wreck from a holiday in Byron Bay with my school friends.

'Did something happen?' Mum asked when I refused to leave my bed or eat for several days. 'Was someone mean to you?'

I'd just shake my head and roll over so my back was to her.

She'd return every so often, offering me food or trying to tempt me out of bed.

'What if I got you some hot chips? Or we could make popcorn and watch *Clueless*.'

'I'm not hungry,' I'd say. 'And I just want to sleep.'

I wish I could say it hurt to treat her like that, and I wish with my entire being I could take it back, but I was numb.

Eventually, she called in the big guns.

'Yael,' Mum said, knocking lightly on my bedroom door. 'Margot's here.'

'Can I come in?' Margot said.

I really didn't want to see her, but I was raised too well to refuse her request.

'Hey,' she said, sitting at the foot of my bed. 'I've been worried about you. Everyone's worried about you.'

I hadn't returned calls or texts since Byron.

'I'm fine.'

'Yeah, I really don't think you are, mate.'

I started crying and couldn't stop. Margot lay down, wrapped her arms around me and didn't leave till the next day.

Then Mum started again.

'Just tell me what you need, moosh. How can I help you? What can I do.'

I was a mess and my parents had no idea what to do about it. Actually, they did know what to do, they were just deadset against doing it. Mum's mistrust of mental health providers ran deep.

After a few weeks of this, Liora, who didn't live with us anymore, came into my room and practically hissed, 'What's so wrong with your life? Do you know how many people have it worse than you?'

Though I took umbrage with her tone – I love taking umbrage – a quick privilege check confirmed she was right; my life was objectively easy, semi-charmed even. And while self-awareness doesn't cure depression, it can give self-pity a good kick in the guts.

It was Liora who eventually convinced Mum and Dad to take me to therapy.

Turns out the road to treatment is paved with annoyed siblings.

I've been at the baths almost every day since Romy brought me.

I'm yet to brave the water, though. Just being here is enough.

The genius of the baths is that, despite sitting pretty between a very popular public beach and a very popular public ocean pool, it's built so deep into a cliff face that it can't be seen from either. The only possible vantage points are from the ocean and the sky, and if you go topless you just have to accept that ocean swimmers and helicopter pilots are gonna see your boobs. There's nothing anyone can do about it, so everyone just smiles and waves and hopes no TV crews are filming.

Somehow I manage to nab a coveted spot today on one of the big flat rocks closest to the pool. If I lay my towel lengthwise, I can stare out across the water and pretend nothing else exists.

I'm sharing the rock with three girls in skimpy bikinis I will never have the guts to wear. I haven't yet worked up the courage to go topless, but I love the aggressive self-confidence of the younger generations. All sizes, all genders, all sexualities, all loving themselves sick. In g-strings.

The trio are drinking Gatorade, eating hot chips and bemoaning their hangovers. They all had 'big ones' last night and they're debriefing.

I'm taken back to my twenties. Bloody Marys and big breakfasts with Margot.

I try to follow their conversation while pretending to doomscroll on my phone, but there seem to be two, if not three, men named Dan involved and it's all very confusing.

I realise I'm staring and quickly look away.

'Do you want some chips?' the blonde one asks, thrusting a giant bag of hot chips at me.

'Oh, thanks, but I'm okay.'

I must be sick.

I love hot chips.

'Are we going to talk about the note at some point?'

I'm on the after-school pick-up run with Liora. She and her husband Sean have three kids, known collectively as the squids. Ethan is nine, Lexi is eight and Hannah is five. They are my heart.

'Which note?' I say quietly, looking over at her.

She huffs and makes a face.

'You know which note.'

The squids go to a Jewish private school. It's not an oppressively religious or conservative school but considering Liora and I went to secular public schools, refused to attend Jewish social clubs in our teens and pretty much shunned the entire community, it's funny to me that all her kids go there now.

'Can't we just pretend you never saw it?'

'Nope. But we can leave it for now. Here come the kids.'

Three wriggly squids practically leap into the car, like clowns in reverse.

'Yay!' Hannah screams. 'Aunty's here!'

'If you love Aunty so much, why don't you marry her?' Ethan says, proving social progress is a lie.

'Yeah!' Lexi just wants to participate.

I lean my head against the window.

'Guys,' Liora says in a loud whisper. 'Aunty Yaya's still got a sore head so we have to talk quietly. I tell you what, whoever makes it the whole ride home without shouting gets a special Shabbat treat.'

Three little voices hiss, 'Yesssssssssss.'

I've been trying not to cry in front of them or be too despondent, but it's hard. It's only been a few weeks. The squids think I've been having a lot of headaches.

'I'm sorry your head is ouchy, Aunty Yaya,' Hannah says.

'Thanks munchkin.' I turn in my seat to see her beautiful face.

'Do you want to cuddle Shawarma when we get home?' Lexi says, referring to her toy llama, not the Middle Eastern meat dish. 'He always makes me feel better.'

'I'd love that. Thank you.'

'So,' Liora says. 'How was everyone's second day of school?'

I drift off, not fully asleep but not quite conscious either. It's a state I've found myself in a lot lately. A state almost entirely devoid of thought. I like it here.

We pull into Liora's garage.

'Were we good, Mummy?'

'Who was the goodest, Mummy?'

'What are the treats?'

'You were all very good. Now just be good until after dinner and you'll get treats.'

This was not part of the deal. The crowd isn't happy.

I really fucking love hot chips.

*

22

It's 11 pm and I'm in bed with Julia Louis-Dreyfus and self-pity when my phone starts ringing.

Margot.

I let it ring out.

She tries again.

I let it ring out.

She texts.

Pick up the phone, woman.

Margot moved to Tokyo two years ago with her partner and kids. She wanted them to experience more Japanese culture than she had growing up.

I miss her.

Sorry, very tired.

She texts again. Persistent bitch.

Liora told me what's been happening.

I told her not to tell you.

Well I'm glad she ignored you. I'm here. Love you x

x

Thank fuck this nightmare happened in warm weather. I must remember to have any future major life crises between November and March.

Liora and I had it pretty good as kids. Loving parents, a modest house, food and shelter, a cat. And unless I'm rose-tinting in my advancing age, we were quite fond of each other for our first decade together, give or take.

Random moments of sisterly harmony stand out to me from those halcyon days.

Choreographing what I now imagine were mind-numbing dance routines to songs by New Kids on the Block and Rick Astley, before forcing Mum, Dad and any other poor bastards who might have been present to watch us perform them, sometimes multiple times.

Playing Marco Polo, doing handstand competitions and riding inflatable bananas in our neighbours' pool, and any other pool we were allowed to dive-bomb into. I was afraid of the ocean, but pools were safe spaces.

Begging Mum and Dad to let us stay home for the few days each year that they'd make us go to synagogue, then having so much fun playing hide-and-seek and doing running races with the other kids that we'd beg them to let us stay longer when they declared it home time.

Gaining a warped and extremely premature sexual education giggling our way through countless '80s misogyny porn-lite films at our Nanna and Zeida's flat after they'd gone to sleep. Child-friendly classics such as *Bachelor Party*, *The Bikini Shop* and *Revenge of the Nerds* I through *IV*. Mum and Dad made them move the TV out of our sleepover room when they discovered the horrors of our viewing history.

Chopsticks fights at our favourite Chinese restaurant; non-scary rides at the Easter Show (we carry forth a long lineage of massive wusses); skipping ropes on our trampoline; falling asleep on each other in the car.

We had a good run.

Until we didn't.

It was an excellent note. I printed it at Officeworks.

FEBRUARY

Weekdays during work hours at the baths are the best now that most people are back at work. There's hardly anyone around, so I can cry on a rock to my heart's content.

Not that my heart's ever content at present.

'We should get you a loyalty card,' Lynne says when she passes me on a lap of the grounds. 'Every fifth visit is free.'

'Oh, you have those?'

'I'm pulling your leg, love.'

'Sorry.'

I'm not great with nuance at the moment.

'You're alright. You can buy a membership though, if you're planning on being here a lot. Saves you having to find a gold coin every time you come.'

'Oh cool, I'll get one next time.'

'No pressure, hon. Just an option.'

She wanders off and I pull out my brand-new Kindle, which I bought yesterday so I can read trashy novels without anybody knowing my secret shame. I probably don't need to be such an elitist arsehole about it – there's a book exchange shelf in the change rooms full of all kinds of reads.

I've never been into genre fiction, but with Priya's mandate about only consuming light pop culture, I remembered a podcast I once listened to called *The Allusionist.* Specifically, an episode on The Ripped Bodice, a specialist romance and erotica bookstore in Los Angeles. The two sisters who own the store explained how, historically, sales of romance novels spiked in times of economic, social or political upheaval. The same applied to other genres like fantasy and sci-fi.

It makes sense. In times of crisis, people want escapism, they need optimism, and genre fiction can provide both in abundance.

This is why I, a professional writer and bona-fide book snob, have resolved to read *Fifty Shades of Grey.*

Surely it can't be all bad.

Fifty Shades of Grey, page one, sentence one.
Oh dear lord, it's worse than I thought.

A phone call.
He who shall not be named.
Past tense.
'Hi.'
'Marry me.'
It was more a statement than a question.
'It's 4 am.'
'Time is stupid. Move to London with me.'
'You're wasted.'
'Correct!'

'I'm going back to sleep.'
'Marry me and move to London with me.'
Pause.
'Are you actually moving to London?'
'Yes. I love you.'
Pause.
'How long have you known about this?'
'A while. Marry me.'
Pause.
'When are you going?'
'Dunno yet. Can I come over?'
Pause.
Pause.
Pause.
'Okay.'

I set the Shabbat table while Liora is cooking. It feels good to have a task, to feel useful but not have to talk to anyone. It would feel better if her cats, two glorious ginger beasts called Pumpkin and Kumera, didn't keep jumping on the table and ruining everything.

I arrange plates, forks, knives, glasses and serviettes in their usual formation, adding condiments and jugs of water. Next, I hit the Jewish shelf in the pantry, where the Shabbat accoutrements live. I take silver candlesticks, candles, a silver Kiddush cup, shot glasses, grape juice, an embroidered challah cover, and yarmulkes for Sean and Ethan, and place them in their rightful spots.

I love the ritual of Shabbat, the ceremony. Liora and I did Shabbat with Mum and Dad every Friday night until our teens rendered such traditions unworthy of our precious time.

Sean arrives home with challahs and ice cream.

'You all good?' he asks, passing me a loaf to place on the table.

'Never better.'

He laughs.

'Excellent.'

He goes in search of the squids, who have been strangely quiet since we got home.

'Kids?' he calls out. 'I'm home!' There are only about three places they could be, it's not a huge house.

'Hi, Dad!'

'Hi, Dad!'

'Hi, Daddy!'

All three come bounding down the stairs carrying what look like drawings. They attach themselves to Sean at various heights and angles, clinging on and giggling as he walks slowly around the room.

'We made cards for Aunty,' Lexi says.

'Because she's not feeling good,' Ethan chimes in.

'And it's her birthday!' Hannah adds.

'It's not her birthday, dummy!'

'Ethan!' Sean scolds. 'Don't call your sister a dummy. It can be Yael's birthday if Hannah wants it to be.'

'Can it be my birthday if I want it to be?' a hopeful Lexi asks.

'Not today,' Sean says. 'Sorry, I don't make the rules.'

Lexi oddly accepts this without argument and they all give me their bespoke cards, which feature, in no particular order of calibre, a bus, a rainbow, and what I think is a penguin. 'Feel better soon' is written in large letters across all three with varying degrees of accuracy, the 'on' missing from one due to the apparent overconfidence of its scribe.

'Wow,' I say. 'You guys are the best.'

It's all a bit much.

'Which is your favourite?' Hannah asks.

'I love them all,' I stammer, and quickly excuse myself so the kids don't see me cry.

Two nosy felines follow me into the bathroom and we all sit in the bathtub like that's a normal thing to do.

I'm overwhelmed by a feeling I can't name, existing somewhere between guilt and regret.

'I just love them so much,' I tell the cats, who clearly just want me to turn on the bath tap so they can drink from it.

There's a knock on the door.

'Yael, it's Sean. Can I come in?'

I don't think there's any more room in the tub.

'Yup.'

He comes in and leans on the sink.

'You okay, mate?'

I wipe my face with my hand.

'Just having a moment. Sorry.'

'Nothing to be sorry for. Nobody's mad.' He pauses. 'Okay, Hannah's mad that you won't pick a favourite get-better card, but aside from that.'

I laugh.

I cry.

'I just love them so much,' I say.

'I know. They know.'

Pumpkin is aggressively rubbing his head on the bath tap. I get out of the tub and turn it on.

'I'll just wash my face and let these two drink,' I say. 'Gimme five.'

'No rush. Shabbat can wait.'

'Can Liora?'

'Solid point. But still, take your time. I'll stall her.'

He leaves me to powder my tear ducts and count my Sean-shaped blessings while I drift into an ASMR-style trance watching Pumpkin drink from the bath tap.

'Who's ready for Shabbat?' I ask when I come to and rejoin everyone.

'Me!'

'Me!'

'Me!'

In the dining room, Liora lights the candles and circles her hands three times, as if drawing the flames towards her, before cupping her face and covering her eyes. Lexi, Hannah and I do the same, and together we recite the blessing for the candles.

'Baruch atah, Adonai Eloheinu, mlech haolam, asher kid'shanu b'mitzvotav vitzi vanu l'hadlick ner shel Shabbat.'

'Amen,' Sean and Ethan chant.

Next, we hold up shot glasses of grape juice – kosher wine is gross – as Sean raises the Kiddush cup and reads the wine blessings from an ornate silver prayer book.

'Vay'hi erev vay'hi voker. Yom hashishi. Vay'chulu hashamayim v'haaretz v'chol tz'vaam. Vay'chal Elohim bayom hash'vi m'lachto asher asah. Vayishbot bayom hash'vi-i mikol m'lachto asher asah. Vay'varech Elohim et yom hash'vi-i vay'kadeish oto. Ki vo shavat kikoo m'mlachto asher bara Elohim la'asot.'

He takes a breath.

'Don't drink yet,' Hannah reminds everyone.

Sean continues.

'Baruch atah Adonai, Eloheinu, melech haolam, borei p'ri hagafen. Baruch atah Adonai, Eloheinu, echer haolam, asher kid'shanu b'mitzvotav v'ratzah vanu, v'Shabbat kodsho b'ahavah uv'ratzon hinchilanu, zikaron l'maaseih v'reishit. Ki hu yom t'chilah l'mikra-ei kodesh, echer litziat Mitzrayim. Ki vanu vacharta, v'otanu kidashta, mikol haamim. V'Shabbat kodsh'cha b'ahavah uv'ratzon hinchaltanu. Baruch atah, Adonai, m'kadeish ha Shabbat.'

'Amen!'

We drink.

Avowed secularism and atheism and any other isms aside, I love Shabbat. I love knowing that no matter what happens, no matter how much some may try and stop us, every Friday night as the sun sets, millions of people all over the world will fight hell and high water to light candles, drink terrible wine and eat challah, the greatest bread.

The kids fight over who's going to say the challah blessing, reluctantly agreeing to do it together on pain of no dessert.

'Baruch ata Adonai, Eloheinu melech ha-olam, hamotzi lechem min ha'aretz.'

'Amen!'

Sean breaks off a piece of challah, tears it apart and hands everyone a small piece.

'Good Shabbos, everyone.'

Nanna was seventeen when she married Zeida. They got married just days after they met. She wore her sister's school shoes to the marriage ceremony.

In postwar Europe, unwed surviving Jews of marital age coupled up and conceived fast in the countries the Holocaust hit hardest. Zeida was exactly double her age, and though she knew he was older, she didn't learn his age until after they married.

She was scared, but with no parents and her older siblings already married and starting families of their own, she wasn't in a position to cause a fuss.

I think Nanna and Zeida loved each other, but theirs was more a practical relationship than a romantic one. And with so much trauma between them, that might have just been all they could manage.

When Zeida died, Nanna was only in her sixties. She was too young and sprightly to simply hunker down and wait for death. Although that wasn't quite how we put it to her. We encouraged her to get amongst it, to join clubs, volunteer for charities and get involved with her synagogue. We hoped she'd have a social life instead of sitting in her apartment watching soap operas and drinking expired Coca-Colas from the milk bars she and Zeida had once owned.

Which, right now, sounds kind of awesome to me.

Over the years, a few suitors came a-courting. But Nanna wasn't interested and turned them all away, saying she could never be with another man.

Maybe she really was in love with Zeida.

Zeida never talked about the war. He never talked about anything.

He was kind and gentle and spoiled us with marzipan from the Polish deli he worked in after selling his own shops. But real-life monsters had robbed him of peace and haunted him into muteness.

Most of the time he was simply there, a strong but silent presence.

The bulk of my memories of him involve little to no dialogue, except when he bounced us on his knee and sang us Polish nursery rhymes. Nanna and I would sing one of them to the squids, a riveting tale about a man riding a horse.

Jedzie, jedzie pan, pan,
Na koniku sam, sam.
A za panem chlop, chlop,
Na koniku, hop hop!

Priya's receptionist changes every few months, sometimes weeks. I've always wondered if the high turnover is because Priya is horrible to work for or because she has impossibly high standards. Either way, it seems unconducive to operating a successful business.

Bill is the current receptionist and a bit older and a lot queerer than his forebears, at least since I've been coming here. He's also the only man I can remember holding the fort. We've bonded over hating the Liberal Party, loving Dries Van Noten, and wishing Oscar Isaac was our boyfriend.

Bill has actually lasted a while so I imagine he'll be gone any day now, which sucks, because he's been my favourite so far. He always finds something about my appearance to compliment me on, which on some days is no mean feat.

'Loving the nails, babe.'

'Did you get even prettier?'

'There's that arse that won't quit.'

In short, Bill's great.

Except for one thing.

Whenever I ask how he is, he'll complain about something without fail, usually something quite trivial. And theatrically. I'm against neither complaining nor hyperbole, but bear in mind where he works and why people come here.

'How are you, Bill?'

'Doll, I've been better. I've got a twitch in my eye and it's literally the worst thing that's ever happened.'

With no sense of irony.

'How are you, Bill?'

'Not good, hon. My mother-in-law has been staying for a week and I am losing my mind. She's seriously driving me insane. And *she's* the nutjob.'

It's quite something.

'Did you have a good weekend, Bill?'

'It was DREADFUL, sweets. We went to a wedding and the food was so bad I wanted to kill myself.'

I'm feigning sympathy for his struggle when Priya comes out of her office to greet me. She is always impeccably groomed, with good posture rarely seen in desk workers and the wardrobe of a royal – all high heels and feminine yet fierce dresses – like a British-Indian Princess Kate, with Queen Carrie Bradshaw's aversion to flats. I don't think I've ever seen her in pants. I doubt she even owns jeans.

She greets every patient in the waiting room, a nice touch that I especially appreciate so I can see her outfit from head to toe.

Today: Red dress, patent black Louboutins, perfection.

I follow Priya into her office and take my usual seat.

'So, how are you doing today?'

I really don't feel like talking. Maybe we can have a session like the one in *Good Will Hunting* where Matt Damon and Robin Williams just stare at each other until time is up.

'Yael?'

I guess not.

'I'm okay.'

I love that movie. Apparently the scene when Robin Williams talks about how he misses his dead wife's farts is entirely improvised and Matt Damon is actually properly laughing that hard.

'I know you're not feeling chatty, but can we find something to talk about?'

'You could tell me about you.'

'Nice try.'

I've always been unsettled by the therapist–patient relationship imbalance. I regularly visit this stranger, confess my deepest, darkest, most insane thoughts, and share intimate details of my sex life. But I know almost nothing about her. I know she likes Maltesers, hates rom-coms and shares my profound love of quality footwear. But that's it.

'We don't have to talk about anything heavy. What have you done since I saw you last?'

'Just going to the women's baths and Liora's.'

She sips from a giant mug.

In the five years I've been seeing her, Priya has never once been without a mug. I sometimes bring in a coffee or tea with me, so I can pretend we're just two pals having a chat. Except one's a total narcissist and they only ever talk about her.

'I'm so thrilled you've found somewhere you can hang out and feel comfortable. I must check it out sometime.'

The thought of Priya at the baths in her heels and finery almost makes me smile.

'You should.'

'And how's your cat?'

I feel bad for dragging her down to my level but not enough to stop. At least she's getting paid.

'She's good. Pets are weird.'

'In what sense?'

'It's like having a housemate who doesn't speak English,' I say. 'And who was raised by wolves.'

She laughs.

'I'd just love to know if she likes her life.'

'I'm sure she does.'

We continue this riveting exchange until Lady Time rescues her.

There were warning signs from the beginning. From before the beginning.

He was cocky, he was selfish, and he wasn't friends with any women – the biggest red flag of all.

We were on opposite ends of a vaguely connected social scene and we only saw each other at pubs and clubs. We had the odd drunken conversation, but I didn't pay him much mind except to note his low-key hotness, what Romy would call attainable hot.

'Everybody's attainable for you,' I always tell her.

'Yeah, but I'm not attainable for everybody.'

Then one day I saw him on the train home from work. I saw him as soon as I walked down the stairs to the lower level of seats. We made eye contact before I could avert my gaze or turn around, thus socially obliging us to have an awkward conversation until one of us got off.

'Hey,' I said, doing my best impression of a straight man on a dating app.

'Oh hi,' he said. 'Heading home from work?'

'Yeah, well, from the gym near work.'

I wished for death.

'What are you reading?' I asked, pointing to the book in his lap.

I'd never been so grateful for literature.

'*Shantaram*,' he said, doing his best impression of a straight man on a dating app.

Of course he was reading *Shantaram*.

I looked up famous people's notes for inspiration.

Sylvia Plath scrawled 'Call Dr Horder' before sticking her head in an oven. There's debate over whether she was being ironic or if her death was a botched cry for help. Either way, I laughed.

Beneath the words 'Football Season Is Over,' Hunter S. Thompson lamented the decline of his own jocularity and surmised that at sixty-seven, he'd stuck around seventeen years past his use-by date. Then he shot himself in the head and ruined Christmas for every toxic fuckboy who ever held a copy of *Fear and Loathing in Las Vegas*.

British actor George Sanders declared he was simply bored.

And comedian Tony Hancock summarised, with stunning brevity, how I'd come to feel about my own life:

'Things just seemed to go too wrong too many times.'

But it was Vincent van Gogh's scribbled swansong in which I found the most resonance in that particular moment:

'La tristesse durera toujours.'

The sadness will last forever.

It has been raining for what feels like months. A classic Sydney summer belter, not letting up for more than fifteen minutes at a time for days on end.

I don't mind it. Lying in bed with Julia Louis-Dreyfus, drinking hot chocolate and watching *Gilmore Girls* isn't a terrible way to while away the hours. It means breaking Priya's rule about spending too much time at home alone, but I can't help the weather.

The only downside is not being able to go to the baths. But today the sun is shining, so I hightail it to Coogee and nab a spot.

I lay my towel out on the concrete ledge overlooking the pool and continue reading the disappointingly vanilla adventures of Anastasia Steele and Christian Grey on my Kindle. The words 'inner goddess' and 'girth' should never be anywhere remotely close to a sex scene. And yet.

When Anastasia says 'holy cow' while being penetrated by a billionaire, I laugh out loud and lock eyes with the woman lying next to me.

'Sorry,' I say. 'Funny book.'

'What are you sorry for? Laughter isn't against pool rules.'

I smile.

'Have you read *Fifty Shades of Grey*?' I ask.

'No. Should I?'

I think I've made a friend.

'I'm Shirley, by the way.'

'I'm Yael.'

We're both lying parallel on our towels, looking over the pool. Shirley is wearing a white-and-navy nautical-themed one-piece and a straw hat with an emerald-green ribbon. Her hair is straight and silver, that bold shade of silver only a few women are blessed with, cut in a long bob down almost to her shoulders.

'Yael, what a lovely name. Where's that from?'

'It's Hebrew. I'm Jewish.'

I'm not sure why I needed her to know that.

'Well, it suits you. What are you drinking in that giant cup?'

'A smoothie.'

'I'm not sure I've ever had one of those.'

'It's from the cafe around the corner.'

'And they let you keep the cup?'

'It's my cup. I'm saving the world.'

'Oh yes, my son gave me one for takeaway coffee, but I never get takeaway coffee. Don't tell him that.'

'I wouldn't dare.'

I take my sunscreen out of my bag and start reapplying. I got burnt last time I was here so I'm trying to be diligent.

'Are you a regular here?' Shirley sits up on her towel, shielding the sun from her eyes. 'Sorry, I should stop bothering you and let you read. Don't mind me.'

'It's fine. I'm pretty new. How about you?'

'Oh, I'm practically carved into the rocks.'

She looks over at the giant rocks that kiss the ocean.

'How long have you been coming here?' I ask.

Her gaze returns to me.

'Oh gosh, at least thirty years,' she says. 'Maybe more. My memory isn't what it used to be.'

'Same.'

She laughs.

'You don't look anywhere near old enough for that.'

'I'm old inside.'

'Well, your outside tells a different story.'

*

39

Everyone assumed it was just another mild depressive episode. That I'd be sick for a while and then I'd get better with minimal intervention. That's what had always happened before.

Nobody knew this time would be different. Not even me.

I mean, I knew.

But I didn't *know*.

Don't make me explain how you can know and not know something, but I see now that the choices I was making were just red flag upon red flag upon really big red flag.

I rarely dressed, seldom showered and my hair was in the same bun for a hazardous stretch of time. My apartment was a mess, the fridge was mostly condiments, and I lived on muesli and carrots. Not at the same time.

When I ran out of cat food, I tried feeding Julia Louis-Dreyfus various canned human foods so I wouldn't have to go to the shops. She still hasn't forgiven me.

I missed deadlines more than usual and spent hours each day staring at my computer, trying to focus long enough to write more than a paragraph, lying to my editors about how I was going with this column or that. Then I just stopped replying to their emails.

I declined all social invitations, claiming to be swamped with work. I mean, I was swamped with work, I just wasn't doing any of it.

Most of the time, I was either asleep or watching *Roseanne*.

A text.

What in the ever-loving fuck is an inner goddess?

Margot is reading *Fifty Shades of Grey*.

*

We grew up in an idyllic cul-de-sac in a beachside suburb, with a small park and stunning rose garden that took up half the block.

It was a time when kids playing unsupervised on the street was still innocuous, encouraged even.

One day, when I was eight, Liora came outside to find me playing elastics in the driveway, two dining room chairs holding a long tied-up piece of elastic in place so I could jump over it. A common scene at the time.

'Wanna play?' I asked her.

'Elastics is for babies,' she said, a sharp knife digging into my heart. 'I'm too old to play with you now. I'm almost in year seven.'

The knife took a giant chunk.

I burst into tears and ran into the house to howl on my bed and scream for Mum. It was worse than when Liora had announced she'd grown too old for joint baths.

From then on, we struggled to find a connection, oscillating between arguing and ignoring each other. There was little in between, unless one of us was fighting with Dad, in which case we became instant besties, uneasy allies, united against a common enemy.

I don't remember the impetus for most of our fights, except that she constantly accused me of stealing her scoop-neck black top that made my boobs look amazing, because I constantly stole her scoop-neck black top that made my boobs look amazing.

Last night at dinner, I asked if she remembered what we fought about.

'That black top you used to steal all the time,' she said immediately, like she'd been waiting twenty years for the question. 'I knew you were doing it 'cause your giant boobs kept stretching it.'

My nieces giggled. My nephew looked horrified.

'Anything else?'

She paused, pondered.

'I think we mostly fought about pretty trivial things. I'm sure we had big fights too but I think we just genuinely didn't like each other. We were so different.'

'You're still so different,' Sean says.

'I'm different,' Hannah says.

'That's because you're adopted,' Ethan says.

'Ethan!'

Social media has been very good to me. I love to hate it but it's basically made my career. From a fancy advertising honcho finding my amateur-hour blog in the mid-noughties, to a fancy newspaper editor commissioning my first published story via Twitter. Plus, all the friends I've made.

'Nothing interesting has happened since you … took a break.'

I'm at the baths, on the phone with Romy and dangling my legs in the water like a big brave girl.

'I don't believe you.'

'It's super weird without you posting, dude. Are you tempted to come back at all?'

'Nope. Maybe I'll never go back.'

'I bet on Julian's life you will.'

Romy bets on her boyfriend Julian's life with disturbing frequency.

'How is Julian?'

'Alive. For now.'

I swear, if he ever dies mysteriously and the cops look through her phone, she's done.

'My phone's about to die.'

'Okay ciao, love you.'

'Love you.'

Sundays were my favourite days because Dad was at home.

He had his own real estate business and worked long hours, six days a week. Plus, his office was more than an hour's drive from home, so he left before Liora and I got up in the morning and usually returned after we'd gone to bed. I remember desperately trying to stay awake so I could see him.

On the nights he did make it home before I was asleep, he'd read to me, or tell me stories about Goha the Wise Fool, a Middle Eastern folklore character, kind of like an Arab Mr Bean.

Dad was Russian but grew up in Egypt. Mum was born in Poland but grew up in Israel.

'Do Goha! Do Goha!' I'd plead with him, never tiring of the tales.

'Okay, one Goha then sleep.'

He must have been so tired.

'Do the donkey one!'

He'd jump in bed with me and clear his throat.

'One day, Goha and his son were on their way to the next village. Goha was on foot, leading their donkey, his son perched on top. "How disrespectful of the child to sit while his father walks," said a lady on the street. Goha's son felt ashamed and insisted his father swap places with him.

'As they continued on, they passed a group of men. "Look at that selfish man, making his son walk while he rides." So Goha told his son to get on the donkey and they rode on together.

'"Look at those cruel people, making the poor donkey carry them both," said an old man to his wife.

'Then Goha had an idea – the two of them would carry the donkey! As they walked along, people laughed and jeered. "Look at those fools! Carrying the donkey instead of riding it!"

'Goha had had enough. He put his son back on the donkey. "You see, son," he said as he led the donkey on foot again. "You can never please everyone."'

I flash my shiny new membership fob at the volunteers on duty, smoothie in my other hand, as I head in for another dose of maritime therapy.

I think the baths might be helping more than Priya. No way I'm telling her that, though.

I plonk down on a spot and apply enough sunscreen to protect a small army.

Lying on my stomach, Kindle out, I'm deep inside the criminally unerotic world of *Fifty Shades of Grey*.

Holy cow, it's bad.

I feel drops of water on my legs. I look up to see Shirley towelling herself dry above me.

'I'm so sorry,' she says, retrieving a pair of glasses from her bag. 'Oh, it's you Yael,' she smiles. 'Did I wet you?'

'It's okay,' I say. 'I'm here to get wet.'

Somewhere in another dimension, Anastasia Steele giggles.

'How's the water?' I ask.

'Divine.'

Maybe I'll even get in today.

'Is that one of those Kindle things?'

Probably not, though.

'Yeah.'

'Do you like it?'

'It's okay.'

'My son wants to buy me one.'

'I think they're good for travelling.'

'Well my travelling days are over, but do you mind if I have a look at it?'

'Sure.'

I pass it to her.

'Ignore the terrible writing.'

'Why are you reading it if it's terrible?'

'You know how a movie can be so bad it's good?'

'I don't believe I've experienced that.'

She puts on her glasses and reads a bit.

'It is rather smart, isn't it? The Kindle. And you're right about the book.'

She hands it back and I start reading again.

'Can I ask you a question?' she says.

I turn the Kindle off.

'Sure.'

'So, it's midday on a Thursday and you're here.'

'Yup.'

'And you're here a lot.'

'Yup.'

I know what's coming.

'Well, I don't know the best way to put this.' She looks genuinely pained, searching for the right words. 'Do you not have a job?'

It's a fair question.

'You don't have to explain if you don't want to,' she says. 'I'm just wondering. And I'm nosy.'

'No, it's fine. Um …'

What do I say?

'I guess I'm in recovery.'

It comes out more like a question: recovery?

'Ah.'

I can see her mulling, deciding whether to probe further.

'May I ask what you're recovering from?'

Fuck it.

'I had a breakdown. A big one.'

A warning for anyone likely to have a mental breakdown: beware of blackout online shopping.

Otherwise you'll be going about your freshly destroyed life, trying to keep calm and carry the weight of the world, until one day you're at home, wearing a Korean sheet mask and no pants, when the doorbell rings.

'Hello?' you say into the crackly intercom, not expecting visitors.

'Delivery!'

I didn't order anything, you think, buzzing him up. Maybe someone's sent you flowers?

Nobody has sent you flowers.

You open the door to the DHL man, who you're on a first-name basis with because you may have a teensy emotional online shopping habit.

'Hi, George,' you say, eyeing the mysterious loot, instantly recognising the branding on the box.

'Hey, been a while,' he replies. 'I was getting worried.'

'I'm alive,' you assure him before he takes off down the stairs.

You open the box to find a dress you'd wear, by a designer you love, from a website you frequent. But you have no memory of buying it.

Did someone buy it for you? Who would do that?

You find your phone and open your banking app, scrolling to the date on the invoice.

There it is.

You scroll on to find several more transactions you don't recall, most done in the early hours of the morning.

Could this be fraud? you ask. Maybe it's fraud? But why would fraudy people send things to your apartment?

You think back to that time and realise it was the week you were extremely anxious and barely sleeping, adjusting to yet another change in meds.

Against your better judgement, you try on the dress. It's in your usual size but you've lost weight on The Breakdown Diet™. You know you should return it, you're not earning money, but it's so pretty.

Drunk on capitalism, you decide everyone deserves a treat, but vow to return all of the other mystery purchases.

You ignore the fingers crossed firmly behind your back.

The next time I saw him, we were at a mutual friend's house party.

I was in the living room with Margot and a few other friends, and he waved from his perch on a kitchen stool.

47

'Who are you waving at?' a very tipsy Margot demanded, following my direct eyeline to the kitchen.

'Nobody,' I said, hoping the interrogation was over.

'Oh my god, are you fucking Dave's flatmate?' she said, way too loudly.

Thankfully, louder music drowned her out.

'I'm not fucking him. I ran into him on the train and apparently now we're on waving terms.'

'He's pretty hot,' our friend Violet chimed in. 'I'd probably go there.'

'Same,' said Margot, who was about three drinks away from going anywhere.

'I'm getting another drink,' I said. 'Anyone want?'

Tasked with refills, I went outside to the ice tub.

'Hey,' said a deep voice when I was crouched down digging for wine.

I looked up and it was him.

'Oh hey,' I said, standing. 'How's *Shantaram*?'

Considering my recent reading habits, I won't be judging anyone else's tastes again. Also, as far as I know, *Shantaram* is great. Even if it is listed as every Tinder-using straight man's favourite book.

'Good,' he said. 'Finished.'

'Well done. What's next?'

'It's pretty nerdy,' he said. 'Come with me.'

What is happening?

As we passed the living room, Margot made sex signs with her hands, because she's always been a pillar of maturity. I really hoped he hadn't seen.

'Okay, in here,' he said, leading me into a home office. 'I don't know why I couldn't just tell you. I'm a bit drunk.'

48

He picked up a backpack and took out a book. A biography about Gough Whitlam.

I forgot about *Shantaram* immediately.

'So what happened in this breakdown? Tell me to bugger off if you want.'

I'm cold. The baths often become a wind magnet in the afternoon and it can get chilly even in the heat.

'I just broke. It is what it says on the box.'

'Ha, I like that. The box phrase, not that you broke. I don't quite know what that means.'

'Um, I guess I used to be a functioning person and now I'm, um, this.'

My hands trace the outline of my body.

'This,' she says, motioning to my body, 'looks perfectly fine to me.'

'Thank you. But I'm broken inside.'

I always imagined breakdowns as epic, seizure-like episodes with screaming, convulsing, maybe some light mouth-frothing. I pictured drama. I pictured violence. I pictured *The Exorcist*.

My sluggish descent seems woefully anticlimactic in contrast.

'Did something happen or was it completely out of the blue?'

She really is nosy.

'A lot of things happened.'

MARCH

From the day the doctor told us the cancer had spread, I started sleeping in Mum's bed.

Once it spreads, it's all over. Or back then it was, anyway.

I slept with her most nights for close to a year, bar her hospital stays.

I slept with her right up until the rental hospital bed arrived for her very last days. I didn't want to miss a moment with her, not even an unconscious one.

I also just needed my mum.

I tried hard not to cry, to be strong for her. To be the twenty-four-year-old woman I was and not the four-year-old child I appeared to be, sleeping in my mummy's bed.

To not make it about me.

Because it wasn't.

But the day we learned the cancer was in her brain, it was too much.

She was going to die.

Soon.

That night I lay next to her, sobbing. I couldn't stop. And she held me like she did when I was little, when I'd crawl into bed with her and Dad, scared of ghosts and monsters and the evil witch that Liora said lived in our toilet.

'I love you so much, Mummy.'

'I love you, moosh.'

There was nothing else left.

In what I can only assume is an act of vegan protest against my alarming dairy intake, the cafe's blender has self-immolated this morning and I have to get a juice instead of a smoothie.

The horror.

I'm feeling a bit strange today, a bit nervous, fragile, but I manage to get out of there before they see me cry over a milk-based beverage.

I hear Lynne yelling as I mosey into the baths.

'LADIES, IF I SEE THOSE CAMERAS POINTED AT ANYONE BUT YOURSELVES, YOU'RE OUT!'

At the volunteers stand, I wait to check in.

'Fucking backpackers,' she says when she sees me.

'I was a backpacker once upon a time,' I confess.

'I bet you weren't an arsehole, though.'

'I'm sure I was.'

'Well, have a good swim, love.'

I set myself up on one of the big grassy areas and listen to a podcast next to a diehard I've seen a few times.

She's hard to miss, maybe in her sixties, with a peroxide ponytail, a seemingly endless supply of fluorescent bikinis and a deep sun-rippled tan. She looks like the love child of Jane Fonda and a leather couch, and I'd bet good money she taught aerobics in the '80s. Today she's eating what looks like coleslaw from a worn Tupperware container and drinking Diet Coke from a can. After she finishes eating, she pulls suntan oil – which can't possibly still be legal – from her bag and starts lathering.

I'm staring again and she says something, meeting my eye. I take out my headphones.

'Sorry, I didn't hear you.'

'I asked if you wanted some oil.'

I'd be better off injecting cancer into my bloodstream.

'Oh no, thank you.'

'What're you listening to?'

I'm so not feeling chatty.

'A podcast.'

'Ooh, hubby's been trying to get me into those. What one are you doing?'

'Um, a comedy one called *How Did This Get Made?*'

'Nah, he likes all that, what do they call it – *true crime* – that everyone's into?'

'Yeah, that's pretty popular.'

Please stop talking to me, nice lady.

'Sounds pretty depressing to me.'

'This one always cheers me up.'

'I hope you don't always need cheering up.'

'Not always.'

Lies.

'Good, darl. Life's for living.'

'So they tell me.'

*

It started raining about twenty minutes after I got to the baths this morning, so I lured Shirley to the cafe for a smoothie.

'Well, this is an indulgent day,' Shirley says, perusing the menu. 'I have lunch with the ladies next.'

'Who are the ladies?'

'Three of my very oldest and dearest friends. We have lunch every Wednesday, been doing it for years. One of their daughters calls it "Sexless and the City".'

'You're clearly the Samantha.'

'Ha! I think I'm the Charlotte.'

We order smoothies and I briefly consider solids.

'What is ghosting?' Shirley asks, apropos of nada.

I laugh.

'It used to just mean leaving an event without telling anyone. Now it's also a dating thing. Like, if someone stops calling or messaging without explanation, they've ghosted.'

'Men did that in my day too.'

'I guess it just has a new name,' I say. 'It's big now because of dating apps.'

'I've never been so happy to be old.'

We silently ponder the passage of time.

'Have you been ghosted?' she asks.

'Yeah, once.'

'By someone you met in person?'

'Yup, but only a few times. Oh, and once by a friend.'

Twice. Same woman.

'That's awful. The end of a friendship can really sting,' she says.

'Totally. I've written about it.'

'I'd love to read it.'

She did it once, I forgave her. Then she did it again.

'It's not one of my best.'

'I'm sure it's brilliant.'

It's really not.

'Have you fallen out with friends?' I ask.

'A few times. I imagine most people go through it at least once.'

I can't imagine anyone having beef with Shirley.

'Were they recent?'

'That depends on what you call recent,' she says. 'Let me think.'

I haven't seen the friend ghoster since.

'I think the last one was maybe ten years ago,' she says.

Our smoothies arrive in giant stainless steel milkshake glasses.

'These are huge.' She takes a sip. 'I can see why you like them. But I am concerned for your stomach. Nobody needs this much dairy at once.'

She takes another sip.

'What happened with the friendship that ended?' I ask.

'Oh, it was very boring,' she says.

'I'd like to hear about it.'

'You tell me about this person you'd met who ghosted you. I'm sure it's much more interesting.'

She returns to her smoothie.

'It's not. He was just a random fuckboy.'

'I take it that's a bad thing?'

'Sorry, it means, um, womaniser?'

'Ah. And what happened with this fuckboy?'

I could listen to Shirley say 'fuckboy' all day.

'It was really nothing. We only went on a few dates. I didn't think we were soulmates or anything, but we had fun. And really good sex.'

Shut up, Yael.

'Sorry,' I say. 'Sometimes* I overshare.'

*Weekly, if not daily.

'You're fine,' she says. 'I asked.'

For a woman who comes across as quite prim and self-identifies as a Charlotte, Shirley is very easy to talk to.

'Okay. So after about a month, he suddenly went AWOL.'

'Did you ever hear from him again?'

'Only through the occasional dick pic.'

Shut up, Yael.

'I have so many questions.'

'About dick pics?'

'No. Well, yes, but I assume those are, what was it you said? "What you see on the box"?'

She slurps the dregs of her smoothie.

'Pardon me!'

'Only a Samantha would slurp like that.'

Admin is therapy.

Liora and I were in the kitchen of the house Mum and Dad had bought after selling our childhood home. A house I hated from the minute I saw it. A house Liora hated from the minute she saw it. A bad house. The bad house.

We were writing lists, one of our few shared passions.

Mum was asleep in the rented hospital bed in the spare room with Sheila, one of the nurses from the palliative care agency we had hired for those last weeks.

'Sheila's the best nurse we have,' the director of the agency told us. 'She's rough as guts but she's got the biggest heart. Everyone loves her eventually.'

Sheila was an angel sent from the heaven I didn't believe in to guide us through hell.

An angel of death but, like, in a good way.

'We're hired for the patients,' Sheila told me over a cheeky cigarette in the backyard when Liora wasn't around to yell at me. 'But it's the families that need us most.'

Sheila and a few other nurses made the unbearable more bearable and I will never forget their kindness. Some even came to the funeral.

Like I said, angels.

'Okay,' I said. 'So I'll call Anita and order sandwiches, fruit and breakfast pastries.'

Anita is a family friend and kosher caterer. Usually, when a Jewish person dies, there is no wake. We gather for prayers the night of the funeral – or for the next seven nights, for the devout – but it's generally rather sombre and often quite brief.

'How much do you think we need?' Liora asked. 'Actually, don't worry, Anita will know. Tell her it's for a hundred people. Does that sound about right?'

'Let's see when you've done your list,' I said. 'Not everyone will come.'

'Don't forget her teacher friends.'

'Yup, done. I think I've got them all.'

I checked the names under 'Colleagues' on my list. Everybody was present.

'We can get soft drinks and juices and we'll need urns for coffee and tea. Where the fuck do you get urns?'

I love it when Liora swears.

'I'll ask Anita,' I said. 'And I'll see if she'll bring disposable plates and cutlery or if we'll need to get them. We'll make a list of what she will and won't bring.'

'Good plan,' she said. 'More lists.'

Liora continued looking through Mum's address book while I went to check on Mum.

I braced myself in the hallway before I went in. I took several deep breaths and pictured what she'd looked like the last time I checked on her so it wasn't a horrible shock when I saw her again.

It didn't work.

She got worse every minute.

'Any change?' I asked Sheila when I went in.

'No, love,' she said, almost apologetically. 'No change.'

I kissed Mum's forehead and smoothed her hair.

She stirred but didn't open her eyes. Her beautiful hazel eyes.

I barely recognised that Mum on the bed. The Mum I knew was rosy and round and warm. This Mum was pallid and sunken and cold. She'd halved in size and doubled in age and almost all the Mum was gone.

'I love you, Mama. I hope you're not talking Sheila's ear off.'

Sheila smiled.

'Would you like some lunch or a cup of tea or anything?' I asked.

'A tea would be lovely, thank you. White with one please.'

After a cry in the bathroom, I went to put the kettle on and got a packet of Scotch Fingers from the pantry.

'Put biscuits on the shopping list,' I said to Liora. 'For when people come over. And milk. Normal and soy.'

This was before you needed thirty-six non-dairy milk varietals to cover every possible food intolerance and eating disorder.

I took the tea and biscuits to Sheila, had another cry, and returned to my lists.

*

Sleep evaded me for the most part last night. It's been playing hard to get all week and I do not care for it. That game sucks.

I've just been lying in bed all night, spooning Julia Louis-Dreyfus and worrying about money and the squids and nuclear war and climate change.

Before sunrise I get up and drive to the baths. If I'm going to be awake and agitated, I might as well be awake and agitated somewhere that might calm me.

I'm a bit early, so I sit in my car until I see Lynne walking towards the gates.

'Morning love,' she says when I catch up, opening the gates.

'Hi Lynne. Just me today?'

'Yeah, the sunrisers start to drop off as the mornings get chilly.'

I disrobe on my favourite ledge and walk straight down to the pool.

It's time.

It's too shallow to dive so I walk into the water. Slowly.

Ankles, pause. Knees, pause. Thighs, stomach, shoulders, pause, pause, long pause.

I don't even know what I'm scared of.

On the count of nothing I dive under the water, emerging victorious and proud of myself for doing something I've been doing since I was toilet-trained.

'You're in!' Lynne says, looking over the ledge where my stuff is.

'I am!' I say, looking up at her.

I submerge my head underwater again.

Alright water, heal me.

*

Driving home from the baths, my mind screams, 'RASPBERRY AND WHITE CHOCOLATE MUFFINS'. I can't recall ever having eaten a raspberry and white chocolate muffin, but the heart wants what it wants. Or the stomach does, anyway.

I drive around the Eastern Suburbs checking bakeries, cafes and other potential muffin vendors for the cakey object of my dissociated desires. Then I join the line at a beachside hipster deli.

I reach the front of the queue.

'Hi, what can I get you?' a multi-pierced girl with pink hair and pale green eyes asks.

'Hi.'

I forget why I'm there.

'Can I get you something?' asks the girl.

'Um, yeah.'

Stalling.

'Do you have smoothies?'

'We don't.'

Aware of the queue behind me, my heart quickens a bit.

'Oh, sorry.'

'All good. Do you want something else?'

This shouldn't be this hard.

'Um, do you have any raspberry and white chocolate muffins?'

'No, sorry. We've got rhubarb and apple or mixed berry and dark chocolate.' She points to a display of delicious-looking muffins that don't match my specific muffin needs.

'I have a craving for raspberry and white chocolate muffins,' I explain. 'I've been driving around trying to find one.'

As the words leave my mouth, I realise how stupid I sound.

'Why don't you make them?'

My first laugh in months.

Not once has this occurred to me.

At Liora's, I google recipes for raspberry and white chocolate muffins. *Easy* recipes for raspberry and white chocolate muffins.

I've baked three cakes in my life.

My family has a sketchy history with baked goods. Nanna made honey cake once a year for Rosh Hashanah and Mum never baked. She said our oven wasn't good for baking, and we believed her, even though it worked just fine for everything else.

We also believed that she made our birthday cakes but the ruse blew up on my seventh birthday, when I caught her friend John sneaking into the house with the coveted *Australian Women's Weekly Children's Birthday Cake Book* pool cake. Turned out John had ghost-baked all our cakes. The woman just didn't like baking.

'Why don't you ask Margot if she has a good recipe?' Liora says.

'Good call.' Margot's baking has reduced me to tears more than once.

Help! I'm having a muffin emergency.

The worst kind of emergency. Tell me.

Do you have a recipe for raspberry and white chocolate muffins?

No, but I can adapt one. Give me an hour.

I thank the good lord Rihanna for the negligible time difference separating me and my best friend. An hour later I'm walking to the shops to get the ingredients. Lexi tags along.

'Can I have an ice cream?' she asks when we reach the store.

'Sure. I'll have one, too.'

I find the white chocolate and scour the crowded freezers until I find frozen raspberries.

'What ice cream do you want, Aunty?' Lexi practically shouts across the store.

'Um ...'

The very basic question overwhelms me. My brain is playing a white noise concerto and my stomach is dancing out of time. I grip the pack of frozen berries so tight it burns my fingers. I can't move. I'm glued to the floor in the cold aisle of my sister's local corner shop. This is not ideal.

'Aunty Yaya? What do you want?'

I have to pull it together. I have to get back to the house without scaring Lexi. Tears tickle my eyes. I start doing yoga breaths. I'm desperate.

'Um, a Magnum?' I manage, spotting an ad above the ice cream fridge.

'That's what I'm getting! We're twins!'

She's oblivious to the fact I'm in the middle of a ... a what?

I don't know what this is.

I muster all the composure I can, pay for everything and walk home with Lexi. When Lexi asks if I'm liking the Magnum, I just nod.

'Did you get everything?' Liora asks as we walk through the door.

'We got Magnums!' Lexi chirps.

'Unfair! Where's mine?'

Ethan.

'I want ice cream!'

Hannah.

'Can I go to sleep?'

Me.

'Of course. Use our bed. Are you okay? Did something happen?'

'I just … I just want to sleep.'

'Okay. Whatever you need.'

I let Liora and Sean's super-comfy bed swallow me whole and recite Sheryl Crow's 'All I Wanna Do Is Have Some Fun' in my head until I fall asleep. It's been a habit for years, but the irony is not lost on me.

When I wake, it's starting to get dark.

I feel calm, back to normal. To my current not-normal normal. But what was that? I don't know what happened in that shop but I did not care for it one bit.

I go downstairs to find Liora and the kids in the kitchen, chatting and baking. They don't see me at first. Ethan is helping Hannah measure something and Liora is showing Lexi what buttons to press on the oven. I want to take it in.

Ethan clocks me.

'She's awake!'

'We're making muffins for you, Aunty Yaya,' Lexi says, covered in flour.

'Barsperry muffins,' Hannah confirms, forever renaming the best berry for our family.

'Wow, thanks guys. What a nice surprise to wake up to.'

'We figured you'd burn them anyway,' Liora says.

She's not wrong.

'How are you feeling?' she asks.

'Better.'

'When are you seeing Priya next?'

'Tomorrow.'

'Who's Priya?' Lexi asks.

'Priya's my doctor.'

'Are you still sick?'

'A little.'

'Is Priya a girl or boy?' Hannah enquires.

'I think she's a girl, but she's never told me for sure.'

'Do you have to tell people for sure?'

'Sometimes.'

'Well, I'm a girl.'

'Good to know.'

'Me too,' Lexi confirms.

And with an 'I'm not' from Ethan, all squids are gendered and accounted for.

A series of texts.

Him.

Past tense.

Hey babe, I'm sorry about the other night.

He was always sorry about other nights.

I worked late and I left my phone in a taxi.

He left his phone in a lot of taxis.

I promise I'll make it up to you.

He never made anything up to me.

Just when you think you've reached rock bottom … pantry moths.

Sometime in the last few weeks of Mum's life, as she slept the days away at home under the gentle watch of palliative professionals, I put a pot of water on to boil to make dinner.

It was late at night, our eating habits – all our habits – out of whack in this weird unreality we were living. It was like a depressing version of the period between Christmas and New Year's, when time loses all meaning.

When the water started bubbling like a jacuzzi, I got out a bag of penne from the pantry and a Tupperware container of leftover pasta sauce from the fridge. I tore open the pasta packaging, only to see two tiny moths rocket-man it outta there and ruin my life.

I shrieked, burst into tears and sank onto the kitchen floor. Liora, Sean and Sheila came running in.

'Are you hurt?'

'Did you slip?'

'Are you bleeding?'

'Worse,' I said, pointing at the pasta packet. 'Look.'

Liora took it and peered inside.

'I don't get ... oh fuck.'

She held the packet out for Sean and Sheila to see.

'Oh, you poor bastards,' Sheila said.

'Us or them?' Sean asked.

And that was the night we learned that if there's anything sadder than sitting around waiting for someone you love to die, it's cleaning out a moth-infested pantry while waiting for someone you love to die.

I rush into Priya's reception ten minutes late.

'All good, sweets,' Bill says. 'She's still in with someone. Fab t-shirt.'

It's a plain white t-shirt.

'I have exciting news for you,' he almost sings at me.

'Oh no.'

'You're our very first patient to reach the Medicare threshold this year!'

'And all I had to do was almost die.'

Bill looks horrified.

Too soon?

Priya appears at the door.

'Come through, Yael.'

I don't praise her incredible Alaïa dress and exquisite heels out loud but I think it, and it's the thought that counts, even sartorially.

'I think maybe I have bipolar?' I say as soon as I sit down.

She is visibly thrown and takes a few seconds to answer.

'Is that a statement or a question?'

'Um, both?'

'Okay. Why do you think you have bipolar?'

Suddenly, I don't think I have bipolar.

'This might sound stupid but I've been having, like, mania or something.'

'What do you mean by mania? Can you describe it for me?'

'A couple of times I've had this really overwhelming, stressful feeling. Stressful isn't the right word, but my head feels buzzy and my stomach knots up and I'm kind of paralysed and I have to take really deep breaths, and everything is in slow motion but also sped up. I can't really explain it more than that.'

Says the professional writer.

'Do you feel like your adrenaline is heightened? Have you been doing anything risky? Have you spent a lot of money?'

'Not really. I've barely bought anything except mango smoothies and blackout purchases, which don't count. It may be the only upside to all this. That and the weight loss.'

Oops, shouldn't have gone there.

66

'Your weight was fine before.'

'Was it?'

'Yes. I'm more than a little concerned that this lapse in appetite and drop in dress size is going to reignite some old patterns you've worked hard to overcome.'

'Noted.'

She takes a deep breath. Pauses.

'So, it sounds like you're having anxiety attacks.'

'Do I have anxiety now?'

'No. You have melancholia and you're experiencing anxiety as a symptom of that.'

The word 'melancholia' makes me feel all romantic and ye olde, like Virginia Woolf, or a Victorian-era painting. Or like I'm in a Lars von Trier film. It's so much better than 'major depressive disorder', which just makes me feel depressed.

'I've had melancholia forever,' I say. 'Why have I never had anxiety attacks before?'

'You've never been this unwell before.'

What else is going to happen now that I've reached peak sad?

'How do I make it stop?'

'I'll give you some diazepam,' she says. 'Only take it if you feel an attack coming on. Hopefully the new meds will kick in properly soon, and once we have the melancholia under control, the anxiety will likely stop.'

'I hope so.'

'Why did you jump straight to bipolar?'

'Family history, I guess. I thought maybe I could have developed it late, like the thing set it off or something.'

'Ah,' she says. 'No more self-diagnosing, okay?'

'I'll only diagnose others.'

She laughs.

'That's the closest you've come to a joke in a while.'

Mum didn't want to die at home.

Mum didn't want to die at all, but especially not at home.

In her mind, after she was gone, we'd all live together in the bad house while adjusting to our new reality. She had to believe we'd stick together after she died. And we did stick together, just not there.

We played along while researching palliative care agencies and how to hire a hospital bed. We weren't going to let Mum die alone in hospital and we had no intention of spending a minute more in that cursed abode than was absolutely necessary.

But she didn't need to know that.

The night she died, our rabbi came to our house and prayed next to her for hours.

We were probably among the least devout families in his congregation, but Rabbi Memmi is deeply rooted in our history. He officiated both Liora's and my bat mitzvahs, conducted Liora and Sean's wedding, and Ethan's bris.

A stocky man of average height with olive skin, a full head of greying black hair and a beard to match, Rabbi Memmi was loud and overbearing and he pinched my cheeks way too hard well into my teens. But although I had decided from an early age that religion wasn't for me, he showed me the good that spiritual leaders could do.

And then there he was, in our house, in the early hours of the morning, ensuring the smooth passage of Mum's soul to wherever it was going.

A true mensch.

'Jesus, what does he do for families who actually go to shul?'
I asked Liora.

We were in the living room, waiting. We'd left Mum's room
for the last time a few hours earlier.

Dr Samuels, a GP and family friend who'd been by her side
for the better part of twenty-four hours, another candidate for
Jewish sainthood (not a thing), had said Mum was hanging on
because we were there.

'She's fighting it,' he whispered in the corridor. 'Are you girls
ready to say goodbye so she can be at peace?'

We weren't. But we went back in, kissed her one last time
and told her it was okay to go.

'I love you,' Liora said. 'Thank you for being our mum.'

'I love you, Mummy,' I said. 'You can stop fighting. We'll be
fine. Let go.'

And we left.

Years later I learned that Sean had gone in to see Mum after
Liora and I had said goodbye.

He knew leaving me alone was her biggest fear and he
promised to always look after me.

A very good egg.

A week ago, Romy sent me an earwax removal video.

You've gotta get in on this, mate. For your anxiety. xxx

I watched the video. Then I watched another and another
and another and I felt calmer and calmer and my brain went
quiet. Like, almost mute.

It was the most at peace I'd felt since the thing.

Who knew watching magnified close-ups of wax and dead skin being scraped and suctioned out of people's ear canals was a visual benzodiazepine?

I guess Romy did.

As it turns out, earwax videos are a gateway to the hard stuff. A few days later, I dipped a tentative toe into dermatological YouTube and got totally hooked.

Now, one glimpse of two cotton tips pressing on a comedo – that's a posh word for blackhead – and I go into a waking coma.

Romy's really been coming through with the post-thing goods. I'm gonna send her a pot plant. But, like, a fancy one.

Anxiety gives zero fucks about when and where it presents itself.

In the morning.

In the night.

On the toilet.

At the movies.

It might be funny if it wasn't the worst.

Sometimes it's sudden, sometimes it's slow.

Sometimes lengthy, sometimes quick.

Sometimes shaky, sometimes still.

Sometimes low-key, sometimes epic.

It's like a fucking Dr Seuss book.

I've lived with death my whole life.

When you grow up in a Holocaust family – probably in any Jewish family – death is a constant. Death is in our homes, in

70

our synagogues and in our schools. It's in our minds, in our hearts and in our bones.

Jewish children aren't sheltered from death like other children, neither in the abstract nor the flesh. We go to funerals from infancy, and where it might be a taboo topic in other communities, death's omnipresence in ours somewhat normalises it.

We learn that while the most successful of its kind, that particular event is not marked in the annals of history as the sole attempt to kill us en masse, to eradicate us entirely.

We learn that it could happen again.

We know our nannas always have a bag packed in case it does. They showed us. We absorb their trauma. We were born with it; it's in our genes.

Jewish children observe the rituals of death from birth. We observe them as we grow. They seep into our core, become instinctual, reflexive, like clapping, like crying.

Chop wood, carry water.

I find great solace in that.

I invited Shirley over to meet Julia Louis-Dreyfus after the baths today. She loves animals and her dog, a corgi named Duchess, died last year.

We're watching the sun set from my balcony, drinking tea and eating almonds. My mother would be horrified by this shameful display of hospitality, but my recent lack of appetite has left my kitchen almost bare and this was an impromptu visit. It's impressive I even have almonds.

Shirley makes me order us pizza, insisting on seeing me eat more than almonds before she leaves.

'So, how is a lovely young woman like you single?'

It's quite the non sequitur; we'd been talking about floorboards.

Also, I hate that question.

'How is a lovely young woman like *you* single?'

'I'm not young! Or single!'

'You have a partner?'

'I'm a widow.'

'Oh, I'm so sorry.'

'It's okay.'

Julia Louis-Dreyfus wanders out onto the balcony and announces herself with a series of meows.

'Was it recent?' I ask, giving her a pat.

'It wasn't. But we're talking about you now.'

'Do we have to?'

'Yes,' she says with a wry smile. 'Have you ever been in love?'

I also hate that question.

'Maybe? Sort of. Not properly.'

'What does that mean?'

The cat rubs against Shirley's legs, fishing for pats.

'I thought it was love but I don't know. It was twisted and wrong, not something I'm proud of.'

I sip my tea. Maybe she'll just leave it there.

'Who was he?'

Dammit.

'He was a friend of a friend. I thought he was a total dick until I saw him reading a Gough Whitlam biography. I still thought he was a total dick, but one I felt compelled to sleep with.'

She laughs.

'Big mistake,' I say, scooping Julia Louis-Dreyfus onto my lap. 'Huge.'

The *Pretty Woman* reference floats high above her head, unnoticed.

I really don't want to talk about it. Just thinking about him exhausts me.

Shirley can see I'm going to a bad place.

'We don't have to talk about it, Yael.'

She puts a hand on my arm.

I take a deep breath.

'He was just very cruel. Lots of lies and games and gaslighting. It was super toxic.'

'Gaslighting, toxic. I'm going to start carrying a notebook around to remember all these.'

'Sorry. Basically, he was selfish and unkind ... but he was there. Maybe if I'd been drowning in dick it would have been a different story.'

'Drowning in dick!' Shirley practically squeals. 'I'm going to use that.'

'I'm sure the lunch ladies will love it.'

'They'll spit out their salads!'

Shirley's phone starts ringing.

'Sorry, I have to take this. I won't be long.'

'I'll give you some privacy.'

The cat follows me inside, my loyal shadow.

When the food arrives, Shirley comes in and we eat pizza on the couch.

'Have *you* ever been in love?' I ask. 'Oh wait, you were married.'

'I was in love once before I met my husband, though it was more of an infatuation. I was just a girl.'

'Who was he? Or she? They?'

73

She half-chokes while taking a bite. There's something delightfully comical about Shirley eating pizza. Despite her liberal disposition, she's quite proper and proper people don't eat pizza.

'*He* is ancient history. You don't want to hear my boring stories.'

'Yes, I do. I've just been banging on about myself like an arsehole.'

'Hush, you're not an arsehole. I've been firing questions at you. Also, I'm not sure I can even remember my stories.'

I make an 'I don't believe you' face.

'Yes you do,' I say. 'And it's my turn to fire questions. May I ask about your husband?'

'You may.'

'What was his name?'

'Peter.'

'He must have been young when he passed?'

'Oh no, he was in his eighties. He was a fair bit older than me. It didn't matter in the beginning, but then he was old and I wasn't and now I've been alone for a decade.'

I couldn't have chosen a worse moment to have a mouthful of pizza. I chew faster.

'I'm sorry,' I say once my mouth is free. 'That must have been really hard.'

'Losing anyone is hard, but it's part of the deal.'

'That's true. But it doesn't make it easier.'

I hope she doesn't make me eat any more pizza.

'How did he die?'

'He had emphysema.'

'Was he a smoker?'

'No, just unlucky. It was reasonably quick as far as these things go, which was lucky, awful as that sounds.'

74

She closes the pizza box, much to a lurking Julia Louis-Dreyfus's chagrin.

'I totally understand. Once someone is really sick – dying-sick – the quicker they go the better. Long, drawn-out suffering benefits nobody.'

'Yes, exactly.'

Time for a subject change.

'You said you have a son in Melbourne?'

She smiles.

'Yes, Andy. He's about your age, a tad older.'

'Why is he in Melbourne?'

'For work.'

'Oh, what does he do?'

'He does a few things, like everyone these days. He's an academic and a session musician. Don't ask me what that means.'

I laugh.

'I know what it means. What instrument does he play?'

'He plays a few. He's a bit of a musical whiz, which he certainly didn't get from me.'

'I'm rubbish at music, too. I tried to play the saxophone in primary school and I was so bad the teacher told me to pretend to play in the Christmas concert. My family have never let me live it down.'

'And nor should they.'

'True. So, just Andy?'

'Yes. We wanted more, but it wasn't to be.'

I feel a vibe shift. Something in Shirley's face politely says to back off.

'I'm sorry. We can talk about something else.'

She looks at her watch.

'Oh my, I should get going,' she says. 'It's long past my bedtime.'

'Do you want me to walk you to your car?' I ask as I'm leading her to the front door.

'Don't be silly! It's right around the corner. I'll be fine.'

'Okay, but can you let me know when you're home?'

'You're sweet to worry,' she says. 'But I'm a big girl. I'll see you soon.'

Grief is having to process a death over and over.

Forever.

She's been gone for a decade and every so often I still have to accept that I'll never see her again, as if it's new information.

It's a real drag.

That first time, at his place after the house party, he surprised me.

There was no sex. There was no attempt at sex.

We talked and kissed and fell asleep clothed.

In the morning he made me coffee and eggs and we did the *Good Weekend* quiz. Badly.

'How am I supposed to know where the Sea of Marmara is?' I protested.

And he drove me home.

'That was fun,' he said when we pulled up outside my building. 'Can I get your phone number?'

I didn't think he'd ever use it.

Then he did.

*

'Can we take the squids for ice cream?' I ask Liora one afternoon.

We're in Liora's black SUV in the car pick-up line for the kids' school – the very long car pick-up line – surrounded by a million other black SUVs.

Girt by SUV.

'We took them yesterday. They can't have ice cream every day.'

'Who says they can't have ice cream every day?'

'It's the law.'

I used to love picking them up in my ancient, beat-up Toyota Corolla hatchback, surrounded by the giant new off-roaders that never left the Eastern Suburbs. I liked to imagine all the mums texting *Who is she?* at each other and taking down my numberplate.

'What happens if we break the law?'

'We probably won't get arrested.'

'You never know in this unceded penal colony.'

I pause.

'I made a friend at the baths.'

'That's great. Who is she?'

We inch forward a whole half-metre in the car queue.

'How do you know it's a she?'

'Does the women's baths allow men now?'

'There are more than two genders, Liora.'

'Noted. Are they letting trans women in yet?'

'Yes! Finally. Wait, how do you know about that?'

'I know about a lot of things. I'm very informed.'

'No, you're not.'

'Clearly I am.'

We spot three squids, but they're not allowed to get in the car until we're at the front of the queue.

'Anyway, my friend's name is Shirley.'

'What does she do?'

'She's retired ... I think.'

'What? How old is she?'

'I don't know. Seventy? Seventy-five?'

She rolls down her window to talk to another mum about mum things. I watch a kid wearing giant headphones dance with abandon and think there's hope for the world yet.

'I swear,' Liora says. 'You and your old-people thing.'

I may have an old-people thing.

'You'd like her. She came over yesterday and made me eat dinner.'

Old people have good stories, and sometimes I just want someone to call me 'dear'.

'She came over to your apartment?'

Oops. Probably should have kept that quiet.

'Briefly.'

'Yael!'

'What?'

'You can't just invite strangers to your flat!'

'She's not a stranger!'

I've never wanted to get to the front of a line more.

'What do you know about her?'

'I know she's a widow and she has a son in Melbourne.'

'Do you know her last name?'

'Maybe ...?'

'Yael!'

'She's really nice.'

The dancing kid is still vibing. I wish I knew what he was listening to.

'It's well established you're way too trusting.'

'I know, but she's, like, seventy! What could she do to me?'

'Your last random stray conned you out of $3000.'

I may also have a random-stray thing.

'She was twenty-five!'

'I don't think con artists age out.'

'She wasn't a con artist. She was damaged.'

'You're damaged!'

Rude.

'I promise I won't give her any money.'

Dance boy boards an SUV and I wish him well.

'Hmm. And please don't make her your new cause. You need to focus on yourself.'

'I think if anything I'm her new cause. But yes, okay, I hear you.'

We hit the front of the line. Ethan, Lexi and Hannah clamber into the back seat, a three-part harmony of chatter and cuteness.

'Who wants ice cream?'

'Yael!'

One day, she may actually murder me.

Oh, the Anxiety You'll Have.

Oh, the Places You'll Panic.

Green Eggs and Diazepam.

Oh, the Thinks You Can Overthink.

One Fish, Two Fish, Red Fish, YOU'RE GOING TO DIE ALONE.

*

A text.

    Liora.

    I wanna meet Shirley.

    Oh god.

    Unnecessary.

    Very necessary.

    I hate this for me, but I know she won't give up.

    Fine. Let's all have a coffee.

    Or I could come to the baths.

    LOL.

    LOL.

    Shut up! I can go to the baths. I'm going to the baths.

    You're gonna hate it so much.

    She really is, though.

    Bathtub. Female sign. Party popper.

    Oh god, Mum's discovered emojis.

APRIL

On a random day when I was in year three, Robert James Lee Hawke, the twenty-third Prime Minister of Australia, popped by my public primary school smack bang in the middle of a federal Liberal safe seat and put a down payment on my future voting habits and potentially those of every child present that day.

How?

Ice cream.

The Honourable Mr Hawke, a man of whom my father was very much not a fan, showed up with a Paddle Pop for every single kid, teacher and admin worker at the school – lactose intolerance be damned!

I pledged allegiance to Karl Marx on the spot.

'When will I be allowed to vote?' I asked at the dinner table that night.

'When you're eighteen,' Mum said. 'Why?'

'I wanna vote for Bob Hawke,' I said, confident he'd be on the ballot in a decade.

'Hawke!' Dad banged the table. 'That man's a charlatan. A communist charlatan.'

'No he's not,' I said, unaware of what any of those words meant. 'He's nice.'

'How do you know about Bob Hawke?' Liora asked, smirking.

'He came to school today and gave everyone ice creams. I got a rainbow one.'

'That bastard!'

Dad was so annoyed he threatened to pull me out of school.

When Dad was angry, he'd go bright red, swear in Arabic and yell until he was unable to form words. Then he'd storm out of the house, threatening to throw himself off the cliffs a short walk away.

This terrified me as a child. I'd become hysterical, crying and clinging to Mum until he inevitably came home. As I got older, I understood that these were hollow threats – he'd never do it.

My father was older than all my friends' dads. He was forty when I was born, which was old to have a baby back then. Now men are having kids in their fifties; seventies even, if they're in The Rolling Stones.

Dad was also very old-fashioned, having grown up in mid-twentieth-century Egypt. When he and Mum got married, he told her he didn't want her to work. She told him to get stuffed. When he told Liora and me that he'd disown us if we married gentiles, we both told him to get stuffed.

Poor guy was outnumbered. He never stood a chance.

Over the years, his temper became more volatile, and by my mid-teens, Daddy's little girl was gone and we were constantly fighting. I became politically aware (and super annoying), and my grunge-costumed journey to full-blown leftism seemed to parallel Dad's road to centre-rightism.

Dad and I fought constantly, and it hurts now to think about what our battlelines did to Mum. Her 'no politics at the dinner table' rule was broken almost nightly.

We were two angry peas in a pod.

'I know I banned you from politics,' Priya says as I take my seat for today's session, 'but it's strange not hearing you rant about the government.'

At least twice a year, Priya and I will spend an entire session talking (arguing) about politics.

It will start with me saying that some social issue or proposed new legislation is upsetting or angering me. Then she'll call me a bleeding heart, I'll call her heartless, and forty-five minutes and $350 later we'll realise we've done it again.

I get most of the money back on Medicare, but sometimes I wonder whether I need therapy or a seat in the Upper House.

'Is there anything I need to know?'

'Nope. All the politicians have been getting along, nobody is being racist or sexist or homophobic, and everyone's getting all the welfare payments they need.'

'Phew.'

I haven't even thought about politics since the thing. It's a bizarre alternate reality but one in which I'm not angry all the time, which is nice.

'How have the last few days been? Since our last appointment.'

'Okay and bad.'

'Any good in there? Even a sliver?'

'Good would be a stretch. Would you take mildly pleasant-ish?'

'I would.'

'Okay, we'll go with that.'

I take a sip of water from the bottle in my bag. The new meds make my mouth uncomfortably dry, to the point where I can't talk properly because there's no lubrication on my gums. Now I'm pretty much drinking water or chewing gum all the time.

'So, what was mildly pleasant-ish and what was bad?'

'Sunrise swims at the baths were mildly pleasant-ish.'

'Are you going all the way in now?'

'Yup.'

'That's wonderful news! I'm so pleased.'

The woman has a low bar.

'Was anything else more than okay?'

'Um, hanging with the kids. Oh, and I did a yoga class.'

'Oh, that's good. Do as much yoga as you can handle.'

'Maybe I'll finally nail a headstand.'

'Small goals are good for you right now. You conquered the ocean pool, headstands are next.'

After that: washing my hair.

'Dare I ask what was bad?' she asks.

'I was super anxious all of yesterday. I was supposed to go to a movie with Romy but I felt so wired and nauseous I couldn't leave the apartment. I barely left the bed.'

'Was there a trigger?'

'No, same as the others. It arrived without warning and then wouldn't leave. Like the Kardashians.'

She laughs.

'I might steal that line for lectures.'

'I might charge you for it.'

*

84

Liora is at the baths. I can't believe it. She hates swimming. And nudity. And anything vaguely bohemian.

I lead her down the path to the volunteers stand.

'Miss Yael!'

'Hi Lynne, this is my sister, Liora. It's her first time.'

Lynne looks Liora up and down and makes a silent decision.

'Welcome, Liora. Beautiful name. Where is it from?'

'It's Hebrew,' Liora says.

'Ah, of course,' Lynne says. Then to me: 'Make sure she knows the rules.'

'Briefed her in the car.'

'Excellent. Enjoy, ladies!'

'I like her,' Liora declares.

'You like rules.'

We head towards the water, stopping at the top of the concrete steps to survey the land. Thankfully the place isn't packed and there are lots of options for once.

'Patchy grass or rock?' I ask.

She surveys the land with abject horror.

'Is there a third option?'

'Hey, you wanted to come.'

'Sorry, yes I did. I do. That's quite the Sophie's choice, though.'

'Let's go grass. There's a good bit over there.'

We stake a claim with our towels and set about undressing and applying sunscreen.

'I've never seen so many boobs in my life,' Liora says.

'You need to watch more porn.'

'I've never watched any porn.'

'I'm shocked.'

'Have you? Actually, I don't want to know. Are you going to take your top off?'

'Are you?'

She cocks her head and raises one brow.

'Nah,' I say. 'I haven't done it before and it's probably too much for your first day.'

'So considerate.'

'I know, right? Wait till you see what I brought you.'

I pull corn chips, hummus and a *Marie Claire* out of my bag and put them on Liora's towel.

'You know me well.'

I unbutton my mandatory white-lady white linen shirt and tuck it into my bag.

'What's that?' Liora points to a small medical plaster that's poking out of my bikini top on my left breast.

'I don't know. I think maybe Julia Louis-Dreyfus scratched me in my sleep. When I woke up this morning there was blood there.'

'What a bitch.'

'I know, right?'

Liora opens *Marie Claire* and I check in with Christian and Anastasia on my Kindle. I'm on book two now. I took a break after book one because I thought it was making me stupid but Margot demanded I keep going.

Hell no! You got me into this and you're going to see it through with me.

'When will Shirley be here?' Liora enquires, not looking up.

'She said around midday.'

I hope this isn't a giant mistake.

Liora and I began noticing odd behaviour in Dad when I was about sixteen. It's one of the only things we agreed on back then.

As well as his worsening temper, there were other tells, mental and physical. He fell over a lot, his forehead was often bruised from bumping into things, his driving skills deteriorated so much that none of us would get in a car with him, and after losing his business – a huge shock in itself – he couldn't hold down a job.

People think dementia is just about memory loss. If only.

All my life, Dad had been a smart, strong, agile man. A good driver and a competent businessman who worked his arse off for us. Affable, generous, the life of every party.

Now he was like a confused child.

Liora and I tried to talk to Mum about it.

'Don't you think it's weird he keeps falling over?'

'He's just getting older, Yael. This is what happens. I'll ask him to get his eyes tested. It's been a while.'

'What about his temper? It's getting worse.'

'Well, you two have to stop provoking him and learn to walk away.'

It didn't work.

It's 12.30 pm and Liora is getting narky.

'Are you sure she's coming?'

'She said around midday. It's still around midday.'

'Hmm.'

'Eat your snacks. Or go for a swim.'

'Never.'

'Why do you hate salt water when all it does is love you?'

'Says she who's literally terrified of the ocean.'

'I go in now!'

'Excuse me, young lady, is this grass taken?'

Shirley's here.

'Hi,' I say, standing up to meet her.

'Sorry I'm late,' she says. 'I got held up at the bank.'

'No problem. Shirley, this is Liora. Liora, Shirley.'

'Hi, it's so nice to meet you,' Shirley says, offering her hand to Liora.

Liora stands, dusts corn chip remnants off her hands.

'Sorry,' she says. 'Yael's been plying me with savouries. It's good to meet you, too.'

They shake hands. It's all a bit formal and awkward.

'So, Yael tells me you're in education?' Shirley addresses Liora, laying out her towel.

We all sit down.

'Yes, I do fundraising and development for a university.'

This is good, Liora loves work talk.

'That must be tough with all the government cuts. Horrendous what they've done to unis.'

Oh no, Liora hates politics talk.

'Yeah, it's been a challenging time and there's certainly a lot more pressure on my team. But I feel mostly for the teaching staff and the students. They've all lost out.'

'My son's an academic at Monash in Melbourne. The last few years have been quite stressful for him.'

'Oh, what's his field?'

'Environmental science and policy. Don't ask me what that actually means, I like to think he teaches people to save whales and predict the weather.'

Liora laughs.

'At least he's in a faculty unlikely to downsize any time soon,' she says.

Liora offers the corn chip bag to Shirley.

'Oh, no thank you. They get stuck in my throat. The things they don't tell you about getting old.'

'Oh god, don't say that,' Liora says. 'Not being able to eat chips is Yael's worst nightmare.'

'I've already repressed it,' I chime in. 'Please tell me hot chips are fine. Otherwise, what did I live for?'

They both shoot me looks.

'So, Shirley, what do you do?' Liora asks. 'Or what did you do? Yael says you're retired?'

'Nothing exciting, I'm afraid. Before I had Andy, I was a seamstress, and then I helped my husband with his business.'

'Our nanna was a seamstress,' Liora says. 'When she first came to Australia.'

'Oh, really? When was that? Do you know where she worked?'

'It would have been the mid- to late fifties into the sixties. She did shifts and outwork for a few sweatshops. We don't know where exactly, but it was around Kippax Street and Central Station.'

'Oh yes, there were a lot of sweatshops there back then. I dare say there are still some. But I think most are now hidden out west or offshore.'

'Don't start Yael on the fashion industry,' Liora teases. 'Actually, don't start Yael on any industry. We'll be here till midnight.'

'I'm sorry I care about workers' rights and sustainability. And shoes.'

'You care about everything!' Liora says, laughing.

I look at Shirley.

'She says it like it's a bad thing.'

Shirley laughs.

'Nothing wrong with passion,' she says. 'And standing up for your values.'

'Thank you, Shirley,' I say loudly.

'Wait till you've received your seventh lecture on the British monarchy,' Liora says to Shirley.

'They are evil, land-stealing, publicly funded leeches and it's weird their wealth hasn't been seized and redistributed to those peoples colonised, raped and murdered by their gross lineage.'

'Wow,' Liora says. 'I think that's the longest sentence you've said since January.'

'Harry's still hot, though.'

'Oh, I do like Harry,' Shirley agrees. 'And I loved his poor mother. A class act.'

'An icon.'

'A goddess.'

We ponder the people's princess.

'Hey,' Liora says, looking at me. 'What do you want to do on the twenty-eighth?'

'What's on the twenty-eighth?'

She looks at me like a disappointed parent.

'It's Mum's birthday.'

'Don't look at me like that. I don't even know today's date.'

I do the maths in my head.

'She would have been sixty-six this year,' I say. 'It's officially been a decade.'

'So,' Liora says. 'Sour cherry pancakes at Monty's, or fish and chips at the beach?'

'You pick.'

'Pancakes it is.'

'I don't believe I've ever had sour cherry pancakes,' Shirley says.

'Mum loved them,' Liora explains. 'She loved cherry anything.'

'She had good taste,' Shirley says. 'What was her name?'

'Sara.'

'And your father?'

'Aleks. But with a k-s not an x.'

He always clarified when he introduced himself.

'May I ask how old they were when they passed?'

'Dad was sixty-two and Mum was fifty-six,' Liora says.

'So young. Was Sara sick for long?'

'Just under two years.'

Twenty-one months, to be exact. Twenty-one god-awful, precious months.

'And it was breast cancer?'

'Yeah,' I say, 'but it spread all over.'

Overachieving bastard.

'Did she have a mastectomy before it spread?'

'A double,' Liora says. 'And chemo and radio. It bought us a few months of thinking she might beat it.'

'Dreadful. I'm so sorry.'

'It's okay,' I say. 'We're used to it now.'

I hope we stop talking about this soon.

'I haven't told you this, Yael, but I actually had cancer in my late twenties, soon after I had Andy.'

Well, that was unexpected.

'Oh, fuck,' I say. 'That's awful. Breast cancer, too?'

'No, endometrial. A horrible business, but we got through it.'

'It's amazing that you did,' Liora says. 'So lucky for your husband and son.'

'Extremely lucky,' she says. 'Though we wanted more children.'

'I'm so sorry,' I say.

We're all silent for a moment or ten.

'Alright.' Shirley swiftly rises. 'I'm going for a swim. Who's coming?'

'Me!'

I jump up and look down at Liora.

'Come on.'

'I'll hold the fort,' she says. 'Mind our stuff.'

'Nothing's been stolen here since 1973.'

'Well, today could be the day.'

'You're coming.' I offer my hand to help her up. 'You don't have to get in, just come dangle your legs in the water and meet the crabs.'

I regret my words immediately.

'THERE ARE CRABS?'

'Yes, there are crabs. Fish too. It's the ocean.'

Liora glares at me.

'You know how I feel about sea creatures.'

'You two are a treat,' Shirley says.

I grab Liora's hand and drag her to the pool.

Mum kept Dad in the dark about my considerable teenage shenanigans, made easy by his six-day work week and colossal, and rather endearing, naivety.

'Your father will ground you if he smells alcohol on your breath.'

Fair.

'Your father will disown you if he sees that hickey.'

Less fair.

'Your father will throw you out of the house if he sees you wearing that.'

Unfair.

He didn't know about the time I'd been suspended from school for drinking in class or busted smoking weed on holiday with a friend's family or any of my other clichéd acts of adolescent rebellion. I mean, at one point he didn't even know his own name, but you get the gist.

At my sixteenth birthday dinner, he actually believed the toast he made:

'Sweet sixteen and never been kissed!'

Even Nanna laughed.

The weekday morning after my year twelve formal, I rocked up to the house with ten friends – ten very high friends – thinking it would be empty, only to find Dad hosing the front garden.

'Sorry, I thought you'd be at work,' I said, panicking on the inside while trying my very best to look like a person who hadn't ingested enough MDMA to power the sun. 'Is it okay if my friends hang out for a bit?'

'Of course!' he declared emphatically. 'The more the merrier.'

Then, compelled to explain our collective state yet too high to craft any more proper sentences, I said: 'We're very drunk!'

I was eighteen by then so boozing was officially kosher, and what he said next is one of my favourite Dad memories. It helps if you imagine a deep French-Arabic accent, but a Russian or Greek accent will also suffice.

'May you always be drunk!'

He even threw his arms up in celebration.

My friends and I then sat in the backyard for many, many hours, barely talking, randomly giggling and with pupils the size of our hands. Dad had no idea and kept bringing us food that nobody ate.

It wasn't until afterwards that I learned he was home that day because he'd lost his job.

Mum kept me in the dark sometimes, too.

I've secretly connected to the bluetooth in Liora's car on the drive back to her house after the baths. We have very different music tastes – shocking, I know – and I like to annoy her through the medium of sound when I can.

'So, what do you think?' I ask her.

'About what?'

'About Shirley. You clearly hated the baths, but what about her? Is she going to rob me blind?'

I start playing something she loves, to lull her.

'Ooh, Adele!'

She sings.

'I didn't hate it. I'm just never going back.'

Then, in her best Taylor Swift 'We Are Never Getting Back Together' voice: 'Like, ever.'

I laugh.

We both sing.

'It's okay to hate it. I knew you would. But I appreciate you giving it a go.'

'You know I don't cope well with anything alternative.'

'You're a complex and uncompromising woman.'

'And pretty.'

'And pretty.'

Adele's reaching a crescendo. We're invested.

'So, Shirley. Thoughts? Feelings? Judgements?'

'Hold on, this is the best bit.'

We belt out the last few choruses of 'Someone Like You' in off-key harmony, arms flailing wildly, and I line up the next song.

'She's nice,' Liora says once she's regained her post-Adele composure. 'I like her. But that doesn't mean she hasn't got ulterior motives.'

'Is it so hard to fathom that someone might simply enjoy my company?'

'Of course not. Although right now you're a bit of a downer.'

'Bitch.'

'Whore.'

'You can't say that anymore.'

'I just did.'

I press play on 'Informer' by Snow.

'OHMIGOD,' she shrieks. '"Informer"! Remember how much Mum loved this?'

It's true. For some inexplicable reason, our Joni Mitchell–loving mother was obsessed with the 1992 surprise chart-topper from Canadian rapper and one-hit wonder Snow. A song he wrote in prison. The single was the only CD she had in her cobalt-blue third-generation Ford Laser.

'I can't believe they're still playing it,' Liora continues. 'Did we ever work out what he was saying?'

She still thinks it's the radio.

'Not the exact words. A lot of it was in Jamaican Patois, but apparently it was about him being in jail for a knife fight murder or something.'

'Now it's even funnier that Mum loved it.'

'She loved a bad boy.'

'And Harrison Ford.'

We both sing along in gibberish to the chorus.

'Can you at least try to give Shirley the benefit of the doubt? You're so judgey.'

'And you're not judgey enough. I'll try to give her the benefit of *some* of the doubt.'

'That's big of you.'

'Yael, listen.'

Serious voice.

'I love that you want to see the best in people, but you've been hurt before. A few times. You're extremely fragile right now and you have a history of missing or outright ignoring red flags. A woman Shirley's age spending all her time with someone your age is a tad strange, don't you think?'

'Nope.'

Okay, maybe. But I'm not admitting it now.

'Have you seen where she lives? Have you been to her house?'

'Nope and nope.'

'So she could be homeless and you wouldn't know.'

'She's not homeless!'

I think.

'How do you know?'

'I just do. But what if she is? Being homeless isn't a crime.'

'I'm not saying it is, I'm illustrating a point. We know nothing about her and she doesn't seem to want to share a lot about herself.'

'She probably just couldn't get a word in.'

'She got lots of words in. They were mostly questions, particularly about Mum.'

'How dare she! The very nerve.'

Liora hits my arm.

'Look, I'll back off. But please don't hide anything from me. If you start lying to protect her, please try to recognise you're doing it.'

'Deal.'

As Snow lickies his last boom-boom down, I line up 'Lay Me Low', one of my all-time favourite Nick Cave songs.

'And for the love of Hashem, do not give her money.'

'I won't. I'm too scared of running out.'

Liora hates Nick Cave. ('It's so depressing.')

'Yeah, we need to talk about that.'

'I know, just not now.'

Deep inhale.

'Okay, no money talk today.'

Deep exhale.

'Thanks.'

Nick Cave is singing about how everyone is gonna celebrate when he dies. What's depressing about that?

'Honestly, between you and Sean,' Liora says, 'I may never be allowed to mention money again.'

'What? What's going on with Sean?'

'Oh nothing serious. He's fine.'

'I don't believe you. What's happening?'

I can see the scales in her head, weighing up whether to tell me.

'Okay, I wasn't going to tell you, but Sean lost his job.'

'Oh fuck! When?'

'About a month ago.'

'A month! Why?'

'Nothing bad. The business is closing. His boss is over it.'

Sean works – worked, I guess – for a lovely company that runs sports programs for kids, in particular those living with social disadvantage and/or disabilities. They do – did? – great work.

'Is Sean okay?'

'He's fine. He's looking. He'll find something. He can always go back to teaching. We just have to tighten the budget until he's earning again. We can't survive on one income for long.'

'And all this has been going on and you've had to take care of me, too? I'm sorry.'

I'm the worst.

'It's not your fault.'

'Yeah, but I've been a major time-suck. Don't worry about me. You need to be with Sean and the kids.'

'I can't not worry about you. But I'm glad you know now.'

'Me too.'

Nick's about to crescendo.

'What's for dinner?' I ask to distract her.

'We're having pies with leftover bolognese. I can make you a few vego ones. Will you eat?'

As I consult my stomach, Liora hears the music.

'Wait, is this Nick Cave?'

A text.

Margot.

Have you read the third book yet? We need to discuss ASAP.

I've created a monster.

Packages keep arriving, full of questionable purchases I have no memory of making.

Among them:

—Winter thermals (it's never that cold)

—Reading glasses (I have 20/20 vision)

—A leash for Julia Louis-Dreyfus (no way she'd let me put it on her)

Sticking to my promise, I send everything back immediately.

Except one teeny-tiny pair of not-even-that-expensive Simone Rocha sandals that were definitely on sale, I swear.

It seems blackout me has some taste, after all.

Shirley and I are eating gelato on the Coogee Beach steps, looking out across the sand to the water, where a few surfers are kidding themselves about the meagre swell.

I've a scoop each of pistachio and coconut, my forever faves, while Shirley's gone classic with chocolate and French vanilla.

'If I keep following your every food whim' – Shirley scoops a bit of vanilla off her blouse – 'I'll be double my size by Christmas. And probably diabetic.'

'Sorry,' I say, not meaning it. 'I'll crave salad next time.'

We eat our treats in comfortable silence.

'I wonder when you'll get your proper appetite back,' Shirley says when her cup is empty.

'It's happening a bit. But to be honest, there's a big part of me resisting it.'

'Why's that?'

'I've never been this thin and it's hard not to like it.'

'Ah. Is that something you struggle with?'

'Yeah, since I was a kid. I don't think it's possible to grow up female in the Eastern Suburbs and not struggle with it. But it hasn't been bad for a long time.'

I return to my ice cream, which is melting fast in the heat, the unseasonable, middle-of-April, 5 pm heat. Thanks, climate change.

'That's one good thing about old age. It doesn't matter what I look like anymore. I'm invisible.'

'You are not.'

'You'll see when you're my age. Most people ignore old people, which does have its upsides. I could walk around naked or rob a bank and nobody would notice.'

'We should definitely test those hypotheses.'

'Imagine.'

I tip my cup and drink the rest of what is now basically pistachio-and-coconut soup.

'I've been meaning to ask – how did you find out about the women's baths?'

'The same way you did. A friend told me about it when I was recovering from the cancer and coming to terms with not having more children.'

I hope I've thanked Romy enough for doing that for me. Maybe I'll buy her new swimmers.

'That must have been a rough time. Was there any support available back then, like counselling groups?'

'Not that I knew of. Nobody talked about medical issues in those days, especially not women's medical issues. It was private family business. And only "crazy" people went to therapy.'

'But the baths helped?'

'Very much. Having somewhere beautiful and peaceful to go when Andy was in preschool was everything. I believe it saved me.'

A common claim, I'm discovering.

'Was Peter supportive?'

'He was.'

I wait for her to go on, but she doesn't.

'Would you ever consider another relationship?' I ask, realising how insensitive it is as I say it.

'Oh Yael, I'm much too old for you.'

'Wow, look who's learned to rib.'

'Are you proud?'

'I am, but if you start swearing like me, I'm gonna ghost you for your own good.'

'Deal.'

A dad and what I assume is his kid are trying to launch a kite on the sand, but the kid keeps letting it go too soon.

'So, back to my question,' I prod.

'I suppose I've never felt ready for a new partner. The lunch ladies used to try to set me up with every divorced or widowed chap they encountered, and Andy's been at me for years, but I think that's from guilt over moving away.'

'He probably just wants you to be happy.'

'Can't I be happy on my own?'

'You absolutely can, but the majority of people don't understand that.'

'That is true.'

The dad and kid have swapped kite roles and now the kid keeps letting go of the kite handles when he's running with it.

'Are you happy on your own?' I ask.

She tilts her head and rolls her eyes up in thought.

'Sometimes I'm ecstatic. Sometimes I'm not. I'd be the same with a man around.'

'Yeah, that's how I feel.'

The sun is fading fast. Daylight savings ended last week and I don't love it.

'Do you want a partner?' Shirley asks.

'I guess?' I say. 'I mean, yes. But not desperately. Anyway, we should go.'

Kite dad hoists the kid over his shoulders, and they head off up the beach, kite held high.

'Sometimes I think the company would be nice,' Shirley says as we walk to our cars. 'But I've made peace with dinners for one.'

'Same.'

'You're much too young for such resignations.'

'So are you.'

'Lies! And it's futile anyway.'

'Why?'

She pinches the top of her nose.

'Where would I even meet someone?'

'The lunch ladies sound hooked up. Or I'm sure there are apps for all ages.'

'You haven't exactly sold those to me. I don't want to get ghosted.'

I snort.

'Unless you're planning on dating millennials – or younger – I think you'll be fine.'

'You never know. Maybe there are eighty-year-old – what do you call them, fuckboys? – out there.'

I laugh so hard I startle two cavoodles.

Like a neglected child, or a member of a cult, I lived for Miss Jenny's attention.

Miss Jenny, of Miss Jenny's Dance Academy, was a towering, intimidating presence with a permanent top bun and a shriek instead of a voice. Her wardrobe was a highly flammable rotation of drapey pink or black chiffons and she was never without a poorly applied red lip, no liner. As a child, I thought she was ancient, a relic from olden times. But she could only have been forty-five at most.

She was perhaps best described as Enid Blyton-y: presenting to parents as a kind, fun and nurturing friend to children, but in truth a joyless, sadistic misopedist. She'd laugh if you struggled to master a routine, call you names and physically force your body into shapes it had no business being in.

'I don't believe in "can't", Melissa,' she'd say, pushing down on some poor girl's shoulders to force her into the splits. 'You can, you will and you'll thank me for it.'

While certainly not the only dance teacher before or since to practise ritual torture and recreational humiliation, she was particularly skilled at both. I craved her approval and, much of the time, I got it.

I was good. I was very good.

Miss Jenny would put me at the front of routines and in the older eisteddfod group, and for years my talent largely spared me her wrath.

Until one day when we were all crammed into the windowless church hall that was our dance studio, to hear who had made it into the eisteddfod groups for that year.

I was quietly confident, having been chosen the past two years, and I listened patiently as Miss Jenny called out the names. Some were expected, some a surprise. When it seemed like she'd been reading out names forever and mine hadn't been called out, I started to panic. But then …

'And of course, our little Yael.'

Yay!

'Though, she's not so little anymore, is she? We're going to have to put you on a diet, Yael. Nobody likes a fatty in a leotard.'

Boo.

I bit back tears and willed home time to come quick.

'Nu?' Mum said, after I got in her car. It's Yiddish for 'out with it'.

'I made it.'

'That's wonderful! I'm so proud of you. But I knew you would.'

At first she didn't notice my lack of enthusiasm but when I was silent for a few minutes, which was almost unheard of, she started sneaking glances at me.

I pretended not to notice.

We hit a red light.

'Moosh?' she said.

'Yeah?'

'What's up?'

'I don't want to do it anymore.'

'Don't want to do what? The eisteddfod group? But you love it.'

'I don't want to do any of it anymore. I don't want to go back there.'

Even though we were close to home, Mum pulled over and stopped the car.

'Did something happen, moosh?'

'She said I have to go on a diet.'

'Who said?'

'She said I'm fat and nobody wants to look at me.'

'What? WHO?'

I started crying.

'Sweetheart, can you tell me who it was?'

I tried to calm myself.

'Miss Jenny.'

'WHAT?'

The rage that flashed across my mother's face in that instant made her almost unrecognisable to me. I'd seen her mad before, mostly at me, but this was new. This was primal. Her hands gripped the steering wheel so tight they drained of all colour.

'Did she say it just to you or in front of the other kids?'

'She was on the stage in front of everyone.'

'How dare she.'

'I didn't know I was fat.'

'You're not fat. But even if you were, it wouldn't be okay.'

'Please don't make me go back there, Mummy.'

The following afternoon, my quiet, sweet-tempered mother stormed into the church in the middle of a class and apparently gave the red-lipped despot what for, and I never saw Miss Jenny again.

I don't know if Melissa ever mastered the splits.

Two packages arrive and I learn that blackout me thought I needed a set of (quite beautiful) new wineglasses and three books I already own.

Priya jokes I should give her access to my bank account so she knows when I'm spiralling. It's not the worst idea.

I keep the glasses.

Of all the illnesses and deaths, one moment haunts me the most.

It's very brief, a two-second mental gif, but it always gets me right in my core, like I've been punched in the feelings.

I'm with Liora in what was in reality a doctor's waiting room, but which my mind has since transformed into a European ski chalet. I don't know why. There's even mounted taxidermy.

Memory is weird.

My parents emerge from a room with Dr Simons, who's been running all manner of tests on Dad.

'Take your time,' he says. 'You're my last appointment for the day.'

He goes back into his office and nobody says anything for what feels like days.

Then Dad crumples onto a tan leather sofa that was definitely not a tan leather sofa and folds himself over his knees, head in hands.

'Girls,' Mum says in a tone I've never heard before. 'Sit down.'

She sits next to Dad and puts her palm on his back.

'Girls. Your father has ... well, Dr Simons believes he has ...' I can see how hard she's trying not to cry. 'It's called Lewy body dementia.'

She probably said more but that's all I got because at the exact instant she gave it a name, Dad sat up and looked straight at me.

I think I could live a thousand years and never again see anything as harrowing as my father's face in that moment. It's impossible to convey the look of sheer terror in his bulging, tear-stained eyes. I felt it in my bones, in my soul.

Right then, I vowed to be a better daughter. To stop fighting with him and be nicer to him and spend more time with him.

I don't remember what happened after that, but I'm fairly confident we left the chalet before daybreak.

*

Romy pulls into my driveway and rolls down the passenger window.

'Get in loser, we're going swimming.'

'Harsh,' I say, getting in.

'Wow, you missed a *Mean Girls* reference. You really are fucked.'

'Nice to see you, too.'

Sydney is having a freak April heatwave and we're kidding ourselves we'll find parking in Coogee.

'Do you have a permanently reserved patch of grass at the baths now?' she asks as we drive around in search of a spot, low-key stalking beachgoers who might be leaving.

'Only on weekdays. Thanks again for introducing me to the place. I owe you one.'

'You owe me nothing. But I'll take a few stories when you're ready to write again. I'll even pay you for them.'

'Quick!' I shout. 'That guy's leaving!'

Romy almost kills the dude, but we finally have a park.

Inside the baths we dump our bags on a rock and head straight to the pool. The crabs are out in force and I nod to them in silent salutation.

'How is work going?' I ask. 'Any better?'

'It's been slowly improving. They finally agreed to hire me a deputy and it took a while to get him up to scratch but he's on it now, commissioning up a storm.'

'That's great.'

'Yeah, now I only work sixty hours a week instead of seventy. Feminism was right, you *can* have it all.'

She disappears under the water.

Two women are kissing and chatting on the ledge. They look so in love and I hate myself for thinking about him.

'Stop staring, creepo,' Romy says, resurfacing.

'I just love love.'

'No, you don't.'

'I love it for other people.'

'Dare I ask if you've heard from him?'

Ugh, she knows me too well.

'I told him to leave me alone when he moved to London.'

'Yeah, but has he?'

'I don't really wanna talk about it, Rom.'

'Sorry, mate. I'll shut up.'

I disappear under the water.

We agreed it would be casual. No strings. No emotions.

We made rules.

Nobody needed to know.

Never two nights in a row.

No 'couple stuff'.

I wasn't worried about getting attached. I'd done the fuck-buddy thing successfully in the past, plus I still thought him a bit of a dick, albeit a bit less so.

He was nice to me in the beginning, sweet even. He called me The Bard, Bard, sometimes Shakespeare. I liked it. I'd never had a cute nickname before.

He'd text me random thoughts or ask how my week was going, not every day, but enough to keep him front of mind, and if he saw one of my stories online, he'd tell me he liked it or give his thoughts on the subject.

Tried that Thai place you raved about. Best green curry I've ever had.

In struggle town this week. You?

Tony Abbott sucks balls. Nice article.

We had a lot of fun and crazy-good chemistry in an enemies-to-lovers rom-com sort of way, but nobody ran through an airport or climbed through a crowd to declare eternal love at the end.

Not even close.

MAY

In the early hours of 21st October, Rabbi Memmi and Dr Samuels emerged from the room where Mum lay dying.

'She's gone. Long life.'

When someone dies, we say to the mourners 'long life' or 'I wish you a long life', often followed or subbed with 'May their memory be a blessing.'

I had been pacing and kind of forgot how feet and gravity worked, and so I half-fell, half-crumpled to the floor. I'd been watching her die for days, for months, and it still shocked me. Like a part of me still believed she'd be eating All-Bran in the morning and nagging me about finishing uni.

Sean and Dr Samuels tried to help me off the floor, but I decided that was where I needed to be. I didn't want to be comfortable. Not without her.

What could have been minutes or hours later, the rabbi spoke.

'Welcome to the orphans club, girls.'

A pause.

Everybody looked at everybody else.

Then Liora and I laughed.

He went outside to organise for her body to be picked up and when he returned, he sat opposite me and Liora.

'I'm amazed I remember this,' he said. 'But isn't your father's yahrzeit the 18th of Tishrei?'

The yahrzeit is the Jewish calendar anniversary of a person's death. It falls on a different date of the mainstream Gregorian calendar every year for complicated reasons you can google yourself.

'Yes,' Liora and I said in unison.

'Do you remember what time he died?'

'About 3 am,' Liora said.

'Well, it's about 3 am on the 18th of Tishrei.'

'Oh wow.'

Liora.

'Holy fuck!'

Me.

'Sorry, Rabbi.'

Also me.

Even though Dad had died on 14th October, two years and one week before Mum, they have the same yahrzeit, their Hebrew calendar anniversary. I'm not superstitious and I'm pretty convinced about post-life nothingness, but this comforts me. They're together, in some form, or no form.

Which means everything and nothing.

At twenty-two, I was the same age when my father died as he was when his father died.

At sixty-two, my father was the same age when he died as his father was when he died, killed on impact when a drunk truck driver hit his pushbike.

It's like a really depressing riddle.

I didn't realise this symmetry until long after Dad died. Nor did I truly appreciate how young Dad was when Grandpa Isaak died, and how much that must have shaped him.

It gives context to how old-fashioned he was, how much older than his years he seemed. At twenty-two, as the only child of a migrant widow who had never worked, he was suddenly responsible for the both of them.

My twenties were no picnic – what with all the caring and grieving – but I also managed to have a lot of fun. I'm not sure he did.

Dad was fiercely devoted to Grandma Ruth. She was a sweet woman, with a great warmth and a beautiful French-Arabic accent. Even as a kid, I could see how strong their bond was, how much he loved her.

I don't remember a whole lot about her but when I was sick or sad, I'd lay my head in her lap and she'd stroke my hair and tell me everything was going to be alright.

During sleepovers, we'd make popcorn and hot chocolate and watch *Are You Being Served?* She loved that show.

She was also obsessed with *The Price Is Right* and wanted me to marry Larry Emdur, a man twenty years my elder. I told him this once at a work Christmas party.

'Aw, what's your gran's name?'

'Oh, she's extremely dead now.'

Silence.

In my defence, what was Larry Emdur doing at my work Christmas party?

Grandma Ruth died in hospital, five days after her eighty-fourth birthday. Mum, Dad, Liora and I watched the life ebb out of her after the flipping of a switch.

I was fourteen.

It was the first time I had seen my father cry and it destroyed me. He looked so lost.

I held his hand.

I stroked her hair.

In her final moments, she spoke French, saying 'Maman' and 'Papa', as if having a conversation with her very much dead parents. I like to think they came to take her, even though I don't believe that's a thing.

Witnessing this peaceful, seemingly painless death was a godsend, easing many of my fears about my own mortality and preparing me to process that of others.

Merci, Grandmère Ruth. Je t'aime.

There exists a series of photos of actor and intrepid motorcycle enthusiast Ewan McGregor in the middle of London, dressed as a giant tomato.

It was for some sort of promotion for the Film4 TV network.

Dame Judi Dench, a living queen, is in some of the pictures, dressed as a giant lobster.

Margot and I send them to each other when one of us is having a rough time.

Because you cannot possibly be sad looking at a handsome Scottish man dressed as a nightshade.

It's just science.

Sometimes I walk into a session with Priya knowing exactly what I want to talk about, but mostly I just sit down, open my mouth and take us both on a little adventure.

Today, it was this:

'I just wish I didn't think about him.'

She makes her sympathy face, which I'm never entirely sure is genuine.

'But even after everything, I still want him to make me feel better.'

She backs it up with a lazy nod.

Sometimes I think she hates me.

'And the worst part is, he never made me feel better. If I was down, he'd feign care and then find a way to make it about him or turn it into a sex thing. And I'd let him. I'm such an idiot.'

I'd hate me.

'You're not an idiot. You know all this. You knew it then. If you didn't, you'd be in London with him. Your intelligence isn't the problem. He isn't even the problem. The problem is that your lack of self-worth and your very normal desire to be loved are a terrible combination.'

We've had this conversation a thousand times. She must be so sick of it. I'd be sick of it.

I *am* sick of it.

I resolve never to talk about him again.

LOL.

'Before I go, can I quickly get your medical opinion on something?'

'My medical opinion? Maybe.'

'Okay, it's a bit gross.'

I pull down the neck of my top so she can see my cleavage.

'I don't know what this is.'

I lift up a side of the plaster sitting at the top of my left breast.

'It just randomly started bleeding a few weeks ago and the pus started this morning.'

There's a sentence I never want to say again.

'Ouch.'

'It doesn't hurt.'

'Well, that's something,' she says, leaning in closer. 'It looks like it could be coming from a pore. You have no idea what caused the bleeding?'

'Nope. Just woke up one day with blood on my boob.'

'What does it feel like when you press it?'

'I haven't tried.'

'Can you gently apply pressure and see if you feel anything? Put the plaster back on first, your hands aren't sanitised.'

I do as I'm told. For once.

'It feels like maybe there's a little lump or something?'

Lump.

'Look, I imagine it's nothing, but can you go see your GP? Who do you see again?'

'Dr Chandra.'

Lump.

'Oh yes. How about I call her office and see if I can get you in tomorrow? Do you have time to see her?'

'I don't know, I'm pretty busy with all the lying in the sun reading pseudo-erotic literature.'

'How is *Fifty Shades of Grey*?'

'So bad. Comically bad. But also kind of endearing?'

'That's not what I expected.'

Lump lump lump.

'I know. I think E. L. James has Stockholm-syndromed me.'

'Remind me to tell you why you shouldn't joke about Stockholm syndrome.'

'Oh no.'

'Oh yes.'

'Well anyway, I've read the whole trilogy and now I'm on the one from the man's perspective.'

LUMP.

'Priya?'

'Yes?'

'This is how they found Mum's tumour.'

After seeing Priya, I drive to the baths, a bit rattled.

There I find Shirley on a lush patch of grass, a rarity around these parts. I guess cooler weather and fewer bodies give the place a chance to breathe.

I haven't seen Shirley for over a week. She hasn't been feeling well and wouldn't give me her address when I offered to drop food in.

'Beautiful Yael,' she says, patting the grass next to her. 'Come join me.'

'Hey, how are you feeling?'

I don't sit down.

'Much better. How are you?'

'I'm okay.'

'Are you staying?'

'Um, I just I need to be alone for a bit. If that's okay?'

She looks up at me with obvious concern.

'Of course. Is everything alright?'

Do I tell her?

'I'm sorry, I don't want to be rude.'

'You're not being rude. But did something happen?'

'Um, sort of. Remember that gross thing on my chest?'

'I do. I was going to ask about it.'

'I showed my psychiatrist, and we felt a lump underneath it.'

She's taking it in, considering what to say next. I've heard about this, about people who think before they speak. I would like to learn their ways.

'That must be scary,' she says. 'What did your psychiatrist say?'

'She made me an appointment with my GP tomorrow.'

'Okay, that's good. Will Liora go with you?'

I hesitate.

'Um, I haven't told her yet,' I say. 'She's got her own stuff going on.'

She's choosing her words again.

'Forgive me, Yael, it's not my place, but I think she'd want to know.'

'I'll tell her if I'm dying.'

Classic disapproving mother look.

'Don't say that,' she says. 'Not even as a joke. You're not dying.'

'I might be dying.'

'Are you sure you won't sit down?'

I consider my words. I'm learning.

'I don't want to be rude,' I say. 'But if it's alright, I'd like to be alone.'

'I understand. If I don't see you before I leave, I'll check in tomorrow.'

'Okay, thank you. Bye.'

I lay my towel on a rock, dunk myself in holy water and tell the crabs the latest.

Three days after Dad died, I came home from a coffee run and found Mum cooking.

'What the fuck are you doing?'

'Please don't swear, moosh. I'm making lasagne. I just heard [insert name of vague acquaintance I can't remember] died.'

'I don't know who that is.'

'He's [insert name of another vague acquaintance I don't recall]'s cousin. You met him once at a picnic when you were seven.'

She kept chopping the onions.

'Mum,' I said gently, hoping to kill the cooking with kindness. 'Dad just died. Nobody expects you to cook for other mourners. Especially not ones you barely know.'

She tipped the contents of the chopping board into a saucepan, which hissed and sizzled.

'I'm happy doing something for someone else. It's better than sitting around feeling sorry for myself.'

'Okay, fair enough. I get it. But you could just give them one of the ninety-three lasagnes people have brought us. Nobody would ever know.'

She gasped.

'Wash your mouth out.'

I'm in Dr Chandra's waiting room, reading an ancient copy of *Who*. How did I not know Delta Goodrem dated a Jonas brother? What else have I missed?

The room is textbook medical practice. Light blue walls, navy carpet, uncomfortable black chairs, a box of mutilated children's books, semi-functioning toys and myriad germs.

A tired young mum is cradling a sniffly baby while her toddler runs around in circles. I smile at her, half-sympathy, half-envy. She smiles back.

I've been coming here since I was born. This is where my measles was diagnosed; where the ukulele strings were pulled out when they snapped and went right through my thumb; where they stitched my head all three times I cracked it open.

In this hallowed building. Between these sterile walls.

I don't see the two male doctors I did growing up. Mostly because I'm pretty sure one of them started rubbing his gross old man crotch under his desk when I asked him for birth control as a teenager.

I've never told anyone that. Not even Mum. I didn't think she'd believe me. We weren't getting on much at the time. I was a messy seventeen-year-old and she was … doing her best. But she didn't argue when I said I only wanted to see women doctors from then on.

'Mama.' The toddler has abandoned his circular marathon and pulled out every book in the toy box. 'Mama read me.'

'I will very soon, my sweet,' she says while breastfeeding. 'Henry's just having a drink.'

'No! Now! Now! Now!'

'Can I read to you, sweetheart?' I offer.

I look at the mum to check if it's okay.

'I'm not sick,' I say, remembering where we are.

'Gabe, honey. Can the lady read to you until Mummy's ready?'

Gabe decides to roll with it but just as I sit down next to him, Dr Chandra appears.

'Yael?' she says. 'Come through.'

'Oh no! I'm sorry, Gabe,' I say, standing up. 'We'll have to read together another time.'

'Sorry,' I mouth to his mum.

'It's okay.' She does up her maternity bra. 'I can take over now.'

I follow Dr Chandra into her room.

'So, tell me, what brings you here today?'

I've been seeing Dr Chandra for about twelve years. She's petite, South Asian and maybe a decade or so older than me. She's always in silk shirts with slacks or pencil skirts and ballet flats, her wavy hair tied in a neat bun at the nape of her neck.

I don't see her very often, I have a famously robust immune system, but if during an appointment she senses I'm struggling mentally, she'll call to check up on me in the days following.

I show her the crime scene on my chest.

'Yeah,' she says, pressing on the lump. 'There's definitely something there.'

'Awesome.'

She makes a face.

'Yael,' she says in her kindest voice. 'I know you're thinking about your mum, but most of these things turn out to be benign, especially at your age. Please try not to panic.'

'I'll try,' I say, panicking.

'Do you have time to get an ultrasound done today?'

'I have nothing but time.'

There was a woman at the baths a few weeks ago who looked very familiar. She was about Shirley's age, with a shock of tinted blonde frizzy hair and a brightly coloured swimming costume covered in birds-of-paradise flowers, Mum's favourite.

I thought she might be one of Mum's old friends, a woman named Agi. They weren't close, so her likeness isn't etched into my mind.

She busted me stealing glances at her.

'Hi, um, is your name Agi, by any chance?'

'No, sorry, I'm Flora,' she said, swimming closer. 'But I do know someone named Agi.'

A strong, familiar accent soothed my soul.

'Sorry,' I said. 'I thought you might be a friend of my mother. Can I ask – is that a Polish accent?'

'It is,' she said, delighted. 'Are you Polish?'

'My mum's side of the family is. Dad's side was Russian-Egyptian. I was born here, though.'

She waited a beat.

'Are you Jewish?'

'Yup!'

She looked around the pool, as if playing spot the Jew.

'And tell me,' she said. 'What shul do you go to?'

'I don't really go anywhere, but I grew up in Maroubra Synagogue.'

'But this is my shul,' she said.

Oh wow.

'Do your parents still go there?' she asked.

I hate this bit.

'They died a long time ago.'

She looked me up and down.

'What is your name?' she said after several genres of thinking face.

'Yael Silver.'

'And your mother's name?'

'Sara.'

I felt like I was trying to cross a border.

'And your father was Aleks?'

Eeep.

'Yes!'

'My god, I did know your parents! Not well, but we were in the same circles. You have a sister also, yes?'

'I do.'

'Such a shame about your parents. Wonderful people. May their memories be a blessing.'

We talked a bit about the salad days before she got cold. And as she swam away, a multicoloured, Eastern European vision, I whispered to the crabs.

'Of all the ocean pools, in all the suburbs, in all of Sydney, she waded into mine.'

I called Liora on the drive home that day.

'Hey.'

'Hi.'

'What's up? Where are you?'

'In the car. Triple M just stuck "Scar Tissue" in my head without consent.'

'Is your car still doing that?'

So, sometimes my car does this thing.

Every so often, I'll turn it on and BOOM! Dad rock will spew out of the speakers really loudly, forcing god-awful quasi-music on my ears.

Somehow, the digital radio will be set to Triple M.

I don't listen to Triple M. I have never listened to Triple M. None of my frequencies are pre-programmed to Triple M.

And yet, Triple M.

'Yup. Anyway,' I continued, 'something amazing happened.'

I relayed my conversation with Flora.

'Her husband's name is Ezzy and they have a daughter and son around our ages.'

'I know who you mean,' she said, her pristine memory unravaged by illicit substances and psychiatric episodes. 'They were good friends with the Sterns.'

'She said we should have coffee sometime. Maybe with Sue Stern.'

'Here we go.'

'What?'

'How many seventy-year-old friends do you need?'

'Heaps, obviously.'

A pause.

'Any news on the Sean employment front?' I asked.

'Not really. There's not a lot out there. He's pretty down.'

I feel so bad for him. Job-hunting blows.

'Can I do anything?'

'Not unless you can give him self-confidence and a decent salary.'

'I can't even give that to myself right now.'

She laughed.

'He doesn't know I told you, so please don't mention it.'

'I won't.'

It was after my parents' deaths that I realised how Jewish I am. Or rather, how much Jewish culture informs how I relate to the world, even though I don't practise the religion. You can take the girl out of organised monotheistic religion, et cetera.

Dad's was the first parental death among my various social circles, not counting Margot's dad, who died when she was one.

And in the immediate aftermath of Dad's passing, my grief was compounded by the almost wholesale absence of my friends. They all came to the funeral, but then I didn't see or hear from all but a handful for some time.

I'd always been taught that when a friend loses a loved one, you make a lasagne, take it to their house and stay there until they all but kick you out. I took it for granted that everybody abided by this rule, so when my mates didn't, I thought they just didn't care.

Exacerbating this was the fact that Liora's friends were always around. As were Mum's and Dad's.

I felt like the biggest loser in Grief City until Liora pointed something (frankly, glaringly obvious) out.

'It's because almost none of your friends are Jewish.'

She was right. My social circle has always skewed gentile, and unlike Jews, most white Australians have no idea what to do when someone carks it.

Beyond wearing black, sending flowers and drinking a lot, the guiding tenet of dominant Australian culture seems to be stand back and stand by. Give mourners privacy and space, let them come to you.

They wait to be invited over; we wait to be asked to leave.

Once I understood this, I told my friends. And when Mum died two years later, I couldn't get rid of them.

George dropped off a package this morning.

I thought it was another blackout purchase, but there was wrapping paper and a card.

Imagine if he'd played Christian Grey.

Inside was a hoodie with a photo of a certain Scottish actor in a giant tomato costume printed on the front.

I hope Margot got one for herself, too.

I'm lying down in a back-to-front medical gown, arms up over my head. A young guy with spiky black hair and an eyebrow ring is running a jelly-coated scanner over my boobs and trying not to look at me.

Shirley is in the waiting room. She called and insisted on coming.

'I'm an old hat at these,' she said when we met outside the building.

'Can you see anything?' I ask the technician.

'Sorry, I'm not allowed to comment on the scans.'

When I get home, I feed Julia Louis-Dreyfus, have a shower and settle into bed to dull my brain with pimple-popping videos. I've added cyst excisions to my roster of earwax removal and blackhead extraction content, and I don't know who I am anymore.

I bring up Dr Pimple Popper's page and click on an epidermal cyst removal. Whoever first thought of putting this veritable torture porn on the internet should be canonised and thrown multiple parades. That, or incarcerated.

As the woman cuts a leaf shape into some poor bastard's skin, something is different. I imagine it's my skin being sliced open. Instead of my mind going numb and my body melting into the bed, I become super anxious and tense. When she cuts through the layers of skin and cells, trying to free the cyst, I picture my own, possibly cancerous, cyst being excised. It's my blood pouring out of the incision and my body being sewn back up. Pain even manifests in my chest.

I'm paralysed, staring at the screen, as if having an out-of-body experience. A really bad one.

Halfway through another video, I close YouTube as my phone starts vibrating.

Liora.

If I ignore it, she'll just keep trying.

'Hi.'

'Hey, what are you up to?'

'Nothing. Just in bed, a bit anxious.'

'Did something happen or just because?'

'Nothing happened.'

Don't do it. Don't do it. Don't …

'But something might be happening.'

'Are you going to explain or is this a riddle?'

I give a dry laugh.

'Now I wish I'd made up a riddle.'

'Next time.'

'Okay, so remember that scratch on my boob at the baths? It got all gross and I showed it to Priya and there's a lump there.'

'Are you sure?' she asks.

I press on it again.

'Yup.'

'What did Priya say?'

'She said to go see Dr Chandra.'

'Okay,' she says, 'I'll come with you.'

I pause.

'Um, I kind of already went.'

'What? When? Why didn't you tell me?'

'This morning. I was trying to handle something myself. Be a big girl again, a proper functioning adult.'

'I really wish you'd told me.'

She sounds hurt.

'I'm sorry.'

Way to go, Yael.

'What did Dr Chandra say?' she asks after a minute.

'She said I should have an ultrasound, so I had an ultrasound.'

Silence.

More silence.

'It's okay, Shirley came with me.'

I regret it as soon as it's out there.

'So, you went for an ultrasound for a lump in your breast and you took someone you've known for five minutes and didn't tell me?'

'You've got enough going on with Sean and the kids and everything. I didn't want to bother you. I'm always bothering you with my melodramas.'

'This is hardly a melodrama, Yael. I can't believe you went to fucking Shirley before me.'

Fuck, she's swearing.

'It wasn't intentional!' I say. 'I ran into her at the baths right after I saw Priya and she asked about the wound. Should I have lied?'

'That's not fair.'

It's truly not.

'She actually insisted I tell you. She said you'd want to know.'

'She was right.'

'I'm sorry. I knew you'd feel obligated to come and you've already missed so much work because of me.'

'That's my choice to make, not yours. This is serious and I need to know about serious things. I promised Mum.'

'Promised Mum what?'

'That I'd take care of you.'

I don't know why that stings so much.

'So you're just doing it out of loyalty to Mum, or guilt or something?'

'That's not what I meant.'

'But if you hadn't promised Mum, it would be different.'

'No it wouldn't.'

It occurs to me that I might be being an arsehole.

'Are you still there?' Liora asks. 'Yael?'

'I was just trying to give you space to focus on Sean and the kids.'

She clears her throat.

'I appreciate that. It's just that this is exactly the kind of thinking that led to … it was in your note.'

'What was?'

'The stuff about not wanting to be a burden. You're not a burden.'

'I'm a massive burden.'

'Okay, you're a burden *right now*. But you won't always be. If something's wrong, I want to know.'

'Okay.'

Julia Louis-Dreyfus comes into my room to find out who's crying, sees it's me and goes right back out again.

'When are you getting the results?'

'I don't know.'

'Will you call me straight after?'

'Yup. It'll be pretty funny if I'm dying.'

'Yael!'

'What? You have to admit, the irony would be worth at least a few laughs.'

She admits nothing.

'Do you want to come over?'

'Nah. I'm gonna watch *Dawson's Creek* until I pass out.'

'Is this the eightieth or ninetieth watch?'

'Shoosh. It soothes me.'

Pacey Witter cures all ills.

'I just don't love you being alone in this state of mind.'

'I'm always in this state of mind.'

'I don't love you being alone ever.'

'That's because you hate being alone.'

She really does. Always has. Not to phobia levels, but enough that it's a thing.

'Okay,' she says, 'I have to cook dinner. Are you gonna eat something?'

'I'll consider it.'

'Say hi to Pacey for me.'

It's mostly that she doesn't like sleeping in a house alone, which never happens anyway.

'No. He's mine.'

With Dad, we had no choice but to watch him slowly die in hospital. His needs were too high. That none of us were there in his final hours was a bitter pill that still hasn't fully gone down.

The next morning I do a yoga class, hoping it will help me stay zen.

I've been coming to this studio since I was nineteen. It's peak Bondi, squeezed between a juice bar and an activewear shop (which will set you back $325 for a pair of leggings), and like most studios outside India, everyone acts like we're downward-dogging by the Ganges with Shiva himself.

It's cringe.

But it's mine.

'Yael, sweet angel, where have you been? We've missed you.'

It's Richard, one of my favourite instructors.

'I tore my rotator cuff.' It's technically true as I did once tear it. 'My doctor says I'm good to practise again.'

'Well, take it easy and use child's pose whenever it gets too much.'

'Thanks, Rich.'

After the class, I check my phone and find two missed calls from the doctor's office.

I call back.

'Yeah, hi. I missed some calls from you. It's Yael Silver.'

'Okay, let me see. Oh yes, Yael. Dr Chandra wishes to see you urgently. Are you able to come in this morning?'

There goes my zen.

Pacey bought Joey a wall for her art.

This has long been the lens through which Margot and I scrutinise all love interests.

'He's great, but is he *buy-you-a-wall* great?'

So far, only her partner has passed this test.

*

Nanna loved soap operas. She watched them religiously. Namely *The Young and the Restless, The Bold and the Beautiful* and especially *Days of Our Lives*.

On sick days and school holidays, Liora and I would often be parked on our grandparents' couch, watching aesthetically blessed people backstab, double-cross and cheat on each other, with two Holocaust survivors who'd experienced far worse.

I always thought it odd that Zeida watched them too. I imagine he developed a mindfulness-adjacent white-noise practice in which he saw the pretty people on the screen but absorbed none of their melodrama. I think he applied the same practice to Nanna.

There they sat for years, side by side in matching blue reclining armchairs, drinking milky instant coffees and eating tinned fruit, rarely speaking and perhaps not needing to.

Always together, forever alone; sometimes happy, forever haunted.

During one particular school holidays, I watched so much *Days of Our Lives* that I became deeply emotionally invested in the plight of two beautiful, beleaguered characters.

Aryan lovebirds Jack Deveraux and Jennifer Horton were just your average cis hetero couple. He was a man; she was a woman. He had short hair; she had long hair. He was secretly adopted by a sociopathic killer, survived Hodgkin's disease, married (and raped?) his biological brother's soulmate, tormented the same brother who still gave him a kidney when he fell off a roof, ran for government, bought a newspaper, helped a woman escape from an insane asylum, kidnapped Jennifer on her wedding day, and murdered his own father; she was a virgin.

Jack and Jennifer's star-crossed will-they-won't-they-ness hooked a ten-year-old me right in and set some lofty goals

132

for my romantic future. They had sex for the first time while shipwrecked on a tropical island, and the second time on the set of a game show, and I determined to settle for nothing less.

Spoiler alert: I settled for much, much less.

When they got engaged, I read a *TV Week* at the supermarket and learned with horror that I'd be at school when their wedding was going to air.

The *Wild West–themed* wedding.

I. Had. To. See. That. Wedding.

Now, this was the early 1990s. There were no on-demand streaming services, there was no timer-based TV-recording technology. Well, there was, but not in my chronically late-adopting household. I couldn't even set a long-play VHS tape to record all day because there wasn't one long enough. I either had to watch it when it aired or never at all.

So, I chucked a sickie for the first time in my then fledgling life, school-loving little nerd that I was.

I set it up days before, just to be sure.

Day one: 'Mum, my throat's a bit sore.'

Day two: 'I don't feel very good.' *cough cough*

Show day: *whimpering* 'Do I have to go to school, Mummy?'

My blemish-free school attendance record worked as I'd hoped. I didn't even have to go to Nanna and Zeida's. Mum let me stay home alone. It was almost too easy.

Except for one thing.

The fucking wedding went over two episodes. I was too young to know that TV weddings were always dragged out for maximum drama. Someone would get cold feet or rip their dress or get taken hostage by a murderous international drug cartel hell-bent on revenge.

I had to keep the lie going for another twenty-four hours.

Suddenly racked with guilt, but not enough to miss the second episode, I did what I had to do.

Am I proud of it? No.

Do I regret it? No.

Suffice to say, I didn't chuck another sickie for a long time. Probably less out of remorse and more because I learned to truant in high school instead.

So were the days of my lies.

Liora bursts into the waiting room about ten minutes after me.

'I may have run several reds on my way here,' she announces, plonking herself down next to me.

The old man nodding off in the corner, whose arrhythmic snoring has just begun to pacify me, bolts upright, chokes on a breath and says 'excuse me' in Yiddish before nodding off again.

'Would have been funny if you'd died on the way to find out I'm dying,' I deadpan.

'Stop it, you're not dying.'

'I mean, I might be.'

She forfeits.

My victory is unfulfilling.

A door opens and a young woman walks out, tossing a hasty 'thanks so much' over her shoulder as she exits.

After a beat, Dr Chandra leans out of the doorway.

'Come in, Yael.'

As we enter, I realise she and Liora have never met before.

'I don't think you know my sister, Liora? She sees Dr Weinberger.'

I'm suddenly overcome with embarrassment, a grown woman needing her big sister to accompany her to the doctor.

'Nice to meet you, Liora.'

'Likewise. Yael speaks very highly of you.'

Dr Chandra turns to her computer and what I assume is my ultrasound appears on the screen.

'Now,' she exhales, turning back to us. 'The ultrasound came back and I'm not going to beat around, it's showing that the lump could be cancerous.'

Liora inhales sharply and reaches for my hand.

It feels strange. Close as we are now, we're not really touchers.

'I want to emphasise the "could". This isn't a diagnosis, it's a possibility.'

The possibility hangs in the air for a bit too long.

They're waiting for me to speak. I look at my feet.

'Okay,' Liora says. 'What do we do now?'

I guess I really do need my sister to accompany me to the doctor.

'I've called a surgical oncologist and he can see you first thing Wednesday.'

It's Monday.

'You'd have to have a mammogram tomorrow. Can you do that, Yael?'

I nod.

'Of course,' Liora says. 'Whatever we need to do.'

I never came clean to Mum about that first sickie.

I confessed to a few sins in those last years with her. Sneaking boys in and out of my room, getting busted smoking joints by my friends' parents, hitchhiking to raves.

She was always torn between judgement and amusement, ultimately settling somewhere in the spaces between.

'I'm sorry I was naughty,' I'd say.

'No, you're not.'

'I'm a bit sorry.'

'You're a bit forgiven.'

I fell in love with him like the frog in the pot of boiling water.

It was so gradual, so subtle, I had no idea it was happening. And by the time I realised, it was a done deal, and it didn't matter how much he lied or how selfish he was.

I was all in.

I just didn't know she was too.

Nobody's ever going to buy me a wall.

JUNE

'I don't think you should drive right now,' Liora had said as we left Dr Chandra's office on Monday. 'I'll drive us to the radiology place and we can get your car later.'

I nodded my agreement.

'Have you eaten? Do you want to grab food or coffee on the way?'

I shook my head.

'No you haven't eaten or no you don't want food?'

'Both.'

'Okay, we'll go straight there.'

In the car, I stared out the window while she called Sean and told him to get the kids from school and sort out dinner.

'So,' she said when she hung up. 'I know you don't want to talk, but can you tell me what's going on in your head?'

'Not a lot.'

'Okay, but what?'

'You're not going to like it.'

'Go on.'

'You can't get mad.'

'I won't.'

'I think dying slowly and painfully will be super annoying when I could have topped myself super quick months ago.'

'Jesus.'

'I warned you.'

'You can go back to not talking now.'

The summer after Dad died, Mum, Liora and I set off on a road trip to Adelaide for my great-aunt's birthday. Liora and I wanted to get Mum out of the house, out of the city, to do something fun after the horrors of the recent past.

'Can you believe the state government is trying to sell off part of the national park?' I asked, bringing the fun as always.

'The first rule of road trip is there's no politics on road trip,' Liora said.

'Have you even seen *Fight Club*?'

'Have you?'

'Yes.'

'Is this what you two are going to be like the whole time?' Mum said.

'Sorry, Mum.'

'We'll be good.'

'Good,' said Mum. 'Because the first rule of road trip is there's no fighting on road trip.'

But the fun was fleeting.

On New Year's Eve, we set up camp, and by camp I mean hotel, in the tiny town of Echuca on the banks of the Murray and Campaspe rivers. We were getting ready for dinner when we heard Mum screaming in the bathroom.

We rushed in to find our beautiful mother, standing topless in front of the mirror, holding one breast.

There was blood.

A lot of blood.

Her nipple was bleeding.

That's how we found out Mum had breast cancer.

Dad had been dead less than three months and Mum had breast cancer.

A lot of it.

A few minutes into the mammogram, I start crying and don't stop.

The technicians are lovely.

'Oh love, are we hurting you?'

They actually are – who knew mammograms were painful? – but that's not why I'm crying.

'No, well a bit, sorry. I'm just having a bad day.'

I imagine they're used to women crying in this room.

'It's more uncomfortable with big boobs like yours. There's more to squash.'

'The banes of my existence.'

'Big beautiful banes. We'll be done soon, promise.'

God, I love Irish healthcare women. They've mastered the perfect combination of comforting and direct, but also know when to stop talking. They should teach classes.

When I'm dressed, the older nurse gives me a disposable cup of tea and asks how I'm getting home.

Above and beyond.

'My sister's here.'

'Oh good.'

She walks me to the waiting room and hands me over to Liora. I feel like a kid travelling alone, being escorted off a plane by a flight attendant to a waiting parent.

'Thank you so much. And sorry for making it weird.'

The nurse laughs.

'Oh, honey. I look at tits all day. It's always weird.'

I'm still crying as we walk through the car park, which Liora interprets as a sign of my restored commitment to living.

'Hey,' she says, when we're seatbelted in her mum-mobile. 'At least we know you don't want to die anymore.'

I decide against telling her I just don't want to die from cancer.

When we found out Mum's cancer was terminal, she decided she wanted to get tested for the hereditary BRCA gene fault, which exposes carriers to a high risk of breast and ovarian cancer. Breast cancer is disproportionately prominent in Ashkenazi Jews and the discovery of the BRCA gene finally explained why.

Liora and I didn't want Mum to get tested and tried to talk her out of it.

'Why do you need to know?' Liora asked when Mum brought it up for the millionth time. 'What good is it going to do?'

We were having breakfast at Mum's favourite cafe. Every time I went there with her, I was conscious that it could be the last time. Every time I did *anything* with her, I was conscious it could be the last time.

'I want you two to know if you have it. I want you to be prepared.'

She thanked our waiter as he put a bowl of porridge in front of her. Her appetite was almost entirely gone by then.

'Okay,' I said as my own porridge was delivered. 'So, what if one of us gets tested and we don't tell you the results? Then we'll know and we can deal with it and you won't have to worry.'

'Yes!' Liora said, who was heavily pregnant with Ethan. She poured syrup on her hot cakes. 'That's a great idea.'

'I'll think about it,' Mum said unconvincingly, after three tiny spoonfuls of her food. 'Now, who wants the rest of my porridge?'

'Do you want to come to ours for a while?'

'Can I just go home?'

'Of course, whatever you want.'

'My car's still at the doctor's.'

Liora mulls.

'I don't think you should drive right now. It's in untimed parking, right? Let's worry about it tomorrow.'

We drive in silence for a while and she keeps stealing glances at me, as if fearful I might jump out of the moving vehicle.

As we go past my gym, I make a mental note to cancel my membership.

'I'm sorry,' my mouth says without consulting my brain.

'What are you sorry for?'

My brain catches up.

'For being sick and maybe now more sick and having nobody else.'

'You don't have to be sorry. You didn't do anything on purpose. I know that. I'm not mad at you.'

'I made some pretty bad choices.'

Liora pulls over, turns off the car and turns to me.

141

'Do you remember when you first got sick?' she says. 'When you were at uni, and I thought you were being a brat?'

'Yup.'

'And I basically told you to suck it up and check your privilege?'

'Yeah?'

Is she going to tell me that again?

'I get it now,' she says. 'Not fully, but I get that you can't control it, that it's not rational. I get that it doesn't matter that your life is arguably blessed and I get that you have that perspective anyway. Yes, you've made mistakes, but who hasn't?'

'Um, you?'

She laughs.

'I've made mistakes.'

'Name three.'

Silence.

The cancer went to Mum's liver before travelling on to her brain, and having just watched helplessly as a truly grim disease robbed one parent of his mind, I was now watching helplessly as a different, equally grim disease robbed the other.

Mum went – to use a word I would never throw around lightly – mental.

First came the compulsive spending. We couldn't leave her alone in a shop for even a minute because she'd buy everything in sight. It got to the point where I had to hide her wallet and lock her inside the house so she couldn't go on a shopping spree. In a period dominated by low points, holding my mother hostage was right up there.

Next, there was the gardening. Mum loved gardening, and the fact that Liora and I didn't share her passion was a source of upset. Don't get me wrong. I love flowers. I love trees. I love gardens. Just as long as someone else deals with them. In recent years, I got better at keeping house plants alive, but when I stopped trying to keep myself alive, there was a flow-on effect.

I called it inplanticide. Priya had laughed.

Anyway, the act of gardening in and of itself wasn't so much the problem as when Mum wanted to do it. She started waking me earlier and earlier and demanded I join her in the back garden. I tried reasoning with her, but reason was no longer part of her skillset, and so it was easier to just get up and do it.

We gardened at 5 am; we gardened at 4 am; we gardened at 3 am. It certainly didn't aid her lifelong campaign to make me a green thumb.

At that point, I had been trying to work and do at least one uni subject – activities I attempted sporadically and with limited success throughout those years – but this new obsession with nocturnal floriculture and the prompt decline of Mum's faculties in general put a stop to that.

Somewhere in all that landscaping, Liora and Sean came to stay for a week while their bathroom was being fancied up. They knew that things were bad, but I had been trying to keep the full extent of Mum's escalating delirium from them. My sister was five months pregnant with Ethan and I didn't want to put any more stress on her. So, when they moved in, they got a bit of a shock.

'How have you been dealing with all of this?' Sean asked when he found me and Mum out gardening at 5.30 am.

Badly, it would seem.

To top it off, at the same time that all of this was happening, the smoke alarm started going off at random intervals. The malfunctioning little prick would suddenly start beeping in the middle of the night – and only in the middle of the night – when I was getting the few hours of sleep afforded to me by my tyrant mother. I'd grab the broom I kept nearby for such occasions and push on the button until the beeping stopped, as you do.

But one night, it all got too much and when I grabbed my trusty sweeper, the beeping bastard copped it. Two years of grief and rage came flying out of me as I knocked the plastic arsehole off the ceiling, smashed it to pieces and threw it in the bin.

Then, with a new, very temporary sense of calm, I went outside and gardened with my mother until the sun came up.

Liora ordered us a new smoke alarm that same day.

A text.

Hi Yael, I'm just checking in to see how you're going. What did the doctor say? From Shirley.

She's never texted me before.

Mum got the BRCA test. Sneaky bitch got a friend to take her, telling me they were going for a drive.

Thankfully, and really more for her sake than ours, she tested negative.

Years later, when it was discovered men could also carry the gene fault, Liora also tested negative, which means I'm negative too.

So, that's something.

*

'Where will I and Julia Louis-Dreyfus live if I have cancer?'

Liora and I are in the surgical oncologist's waiting room with takeaway beverages, filling out forms.

Liora started drinking coffee recently and will only have it iced with one and a half sugars in a paper cup with a straw. I refuse to order it for her.

'You'll move in with us.'

'You don't have any room.'

'We'll move.'

Well, that's lovely.

'I don't want to upend your lives. I should hire a carer or something.'

'Let's not do this now. We'll work it out if we have to.'

I've never felt so single and pathetic in my life.

'The squids shouldn't see me sick. Remember Mum during chemo? We're scarred and we were adults.'

'Let's get a diagnosis before we decide how much to scar the kids.'

I finish filling out the new patient forms and sit quietly, trying to decide what songs I want played at my funeral. That's not really done at Jewish funerals, but I'm leaving a Spotify playlist anyway.

'Yael?' the receptionist says, looking at me. 'The doctor will see you now.'

Liora and I walk into a giant office with floor-to-ceiling windows and views of the city. A sexagenarian man with white hair and kind eyes sits behind a large mahogany desk.

'So, who's the patient?'

'Me. I'm Yael.'

'Thank you, I was wondering how to pronounce it. And who's this?'

'This is my sister, Liora.'

'I gather you've had a scary few days?'

'Just a tad,' Liora says.

'The note from your GP said there's a family history of breast cancer?'

Liora informs him Mum died from metastasised breast cancer.

'Are you Jewish?'

'Yes,' we both confirm.

'Have you had the BRCA test?'

'Yes,' Liora says. 'Mum and I both tested negative.'

'Okay, well I'll get right to it. You don't have cancer. They've worried you for nothing.'

Liora and I exchange looks.

'Are you sure?' she asks him.

'Two hundred per cent. I've been doing this a while.'

I giggle.

'There have been a few legal cases in the last few years where patients have sued radiographers for missing things. So now they're saying every tiny spot might be cancer and scaring the hell out of people, just in case.'

Well, that's not a great solution.

'We just thought because Mum had it ...' Liora starts.

'Of course. But here's the thing, the hereditary link has been blown way out of proportion. Yes, your chances of getting it increase slightly, and being Jewish puts you at higher risk, but without the BRCA gene, that risk is still low.'

'Oh wow,' I say. 'But if it's not cancer, what is it?'

'A cyst of some sort, almost certainly benign. I won't know exactly until we cut it out and do a biopsy.'

'I still have to get it cut out?'

Damn.

'Unless you want your chest to look like that forever, yes, you have to get it cut out. But at least it's not going to kill you.'

A text.

To Shirley.

Hi, sorry for not replying yesterday. It was all a bit much. Turns out the lump is a cyst of some sort. I'll explain when I see you.

Almost as soon as I send it, the animated little dots that herald a forthcoming response appear on my phone.

That's wonderful news! I'm so pleased. You must be relieved.

I don't know what I am.

I'm going to the baths for the afternoon if you're around.

I'm sorry, I can't. I have a meeting.

Shirley has meetings?

The dots appear again.

But I'm so happy for you. I'll buy you a smoothie next time.

When I was sixteen, Mum's friend Tova died of cancer.

Mum and Tova had been friends since high school. They were each other's bridesmaid. And though they were about an hour and one iconic bridge apart, they were always in touch.

I really liked Tova. She was beautiful and kind, a genuine soul with a pure heart and a calming presence. I can still summon the sound of her voice. I can't remember half of my childhood, but I can still hear Tova.

Tova and her husband Geoff were more liberal than my parents, more bohemian, which granted wasn't hard, and I sometimes envied their kids that. Mum's spirit did become considerably freer over the years; Dad's, not so much.

Tova's death really shook Mum. Of course, one of her best friends dying in her early fifties was awful. But it went beyond grief. She was possessed by it, tormented. She tortured herself for not seeing Tova more, as if the onus of their friendship had rested entirely on her.

I'd never seen her like that before. I'd never seen anyone like that before.

In Tova's passing, I saw for the first time the very specific type of grief that accompanies untimely deaths. A grief bursting with lost experiences and milestones. A grief for a life as well as a death.

Mum kept talking about Tova's son and daughter, Jeremy and Nessie, about how Tova would miss their graduations, their weddings and their children. My assurances that Jeremy and Jessie were probably too progressive for weddings didn't mollify her.

She was particularly obsessed with Nessie not having a mother anymore.

'She's only nineteen,' Mum kept saying. 'She's so young. She needs her mother.'

It's like she sensed what was coming for us.

Not long after Tova died, Mum had to have surgery on her thyroid. It wasn't life-threatening, just an underactive gland. Or maybe overactive? Definitely not right.

Tova's death was clearly causing her anxiety about her own mortality, which didn't seem to ebb after the successful operation.

With Mum on strict bed rest orders, I went to the video store, which was a thing that existed once. I loved going to the video store because a cute boy worked there. Several, in fact.

Advances in audiovisual technology have robbed the pubescent of prime flirting locations.

I got four movies that looked Mum-ish, based solely on their titles and covers, and went home to commence the moviethon.

It was a disaster.

In every single movie, a mum died of cancer.

Stepmom: a mum dies of cancer.

One True Thing: a mum dies of cancer.

I can't remember what the other two were, but a mum died of cancer.

I don't know if it was a coincidence, a particularly common plot point in that era or if we were just more sensitive to it.

'Why are you torturing our mother?' Liora asked, only half-joking.

'I didn't know!'

Thankfully, Mum found the whole thing morbidly hilarious, but I was never allowed to choose movies again.

After the surgical oncologist, my sister drops me at my car, which is still near Dr Chandra's office.

I start the engine.

'FUCK!'

Triple M.

My disgust fades fast as I recognise the song playing.

I call Liora.

'Oh my god! Listen to what was playing when I started the car.'

149

I put my phone on speaker and turn the radio volume up as far as it will go.

We both sing along to the chorus. Poorly.

'Oh my god! It's a sign.'

'A sign of what?'

'Um,' she says. 'That Mum's happy you're not dying?'

'You think our dead mother is sending me a subliminal message via the runaway '90s hit "Informer" by Snow?'

'Maybe.'

'Sweet. I hope this becomes a thing.'

'Same,' she says. 'Maybe that's why your car keeps playing Triple M. Maybe Mum's doing it.'

'I really hope Mum doesn't hate me that much.'

'She's getting back at you for all the depressing grunge music you forced her to listen to.'

'Fair.'

'We really should have played it at her funeral.'

I start driving.

'Are you still going to the baths?' Liora asks.

'Yeah, but going home to change first.'

'Did Shirley get back to you? Is she meeting you there?'

'No, she has a meeting.'

'What kind of meeting?'

Oh, for the love of Gaga.

'I don't know. I didn't ask.'

'Does she often have meetings?'

'I have no idea. She's mentioned one before but I haven't hacked into her iCal.'

'I just wonder what her meeting was about.'

I pull over.

'Alright, Nancy Jew,' I say. 'Calm down.'

'What?' she says in her best innocent voice. 'She doesn't have a job.'

'People have meetings outside work all the time. With lawyers, accountants, whoever they want. Maybe she's on a charity board or does volunteer work, who knows. You're being ridiculous.'

'I'm not being ridiculous, I'm being cautious.'

'And I'm hanging up.'

At home I find what looks like a wedding invite in the mailbox.

Poppy and Jack would love you to save the date.

More details to come.

I didn't even know they were engaged. I wonder what else I've missed.

I try not to get anxious at the thought of attending a function and mentally commit to messaging them mazel tov.

I do love a fun wedding.

Dad really loved weddings. Bar and bat mitzvahs too. Anything with free food and a band. He dominated dessert tables and dance floors, living his best life, especially when Mum would dance with him.

We have great footage of him dancing at Liora and Sean's wedding. He was diagnosed by then and still very lucid, but he did stumble a bit walking Liora down the aisle.

He was so happy that day, completely in his element, king of the conga. It was the last family milestone before he died and I'm so glad for Liora that he was there, that they both were.

Some of my favourite photos of Dad capture him mid-hora or YMCA. But there are many iconic photos. Dad lying on the grass with baby me on his chest. Dad cuddling with Toffee, the cat he fought tooth and nail not to get and swore he'd never love.

In one particularly excellent photo, Dad and Sean are standing on the street draped in Sydney Swans scarves, on their way to a game. It was after his diagnosis, when his beloved first cousin, an AFL devotee, was in town from Adelaide, and she and Sean, a lifelong Swans fan, took Dad to the football and then to Harry's Cafe de Wheels for pies.

Dad looks so happy, which is hilarious considering he had zero interest in sport. Ours was not a sporty household, bar a few years of netball for me and Liora. The sportiest Dad got was saying, 'Mate against mate, state against state', if he happened to know the State of Origin was on.

His giant smile in this photo clearly had nothing to do with sport and everything to do with bonding with his son-in-law, spending time with his cousin and the promise of a pea floater after the game.

I love it so much I'm smiling.

It was an ingrown hair.

It was an ingrown fucking hair.

I have a scar running the interior length of my left breast because of one little hair.

Bodies are so weird.

Overcast days always feel suspenseful to me, like the third act in a thriller.

Like the sky has secrets.

When I get to the baths, the ocean is dark and choppy, but there are still a few die-hards swimming.

A sign near the volunteers station says the baths will be closed for a few weeks in July for renovations. How dare they.

On the pool steps, I exchange pleasantries with the few brave crabs not in hiding, as is my ritual. I'm enamoured with the semi-camouflaged little creatures. They calm me, like crustacean diazepam.

Romy said it's because my rising sign is Cancer. I pretended to believe her.

The water is surprisingly warm.

For a minute, peace.

But then it gets rough.

The sea is having a panic attack.

As I swim back towards the steps, a huge wave throws me sideways, pushes me under and slams me against the rock wall.

When I surface, six or so women are swimming towards me.

'Are you okay?'

'Are you hurt?'

I don't actually know.

'I, I think I'm okay?'

I hope I didn't hit any crabs.

'Quick love, let's get out before it happens again.'

My saviours follow me out of the pool, hovering. My right side is sore and I scan my body for blood, but it's all still inside me.

'Thanks so much. I think I'm okay.'

I don't want to be fussed over.

As the women disperse, I notice that my heart is racing.

Why does the ocean hate me?

*

The phone wakes me. A photo of Liora's cats fills the screen.

'Hey.'

'Mum and Dad say hi.'

'What?'

'Did I just wake you? It's 11 am.'

'Um, not sure if you've noticed, but I'm kinda going through some shit.'

'Lazy. Anyway, Mum and Dad say hi.'

'Huh? Where are you?'

'Rookwood.'

Mum, Dad and three of our grandparents are buried at Rookwood Cemetery.

'Did you just call your chronically depressed sister to make dead parent jokes?'

'Yep. I had a funeral and now I'm with the parents.'

'Can you put stones on the graves for me? And the grandparents?'

'I did and I will.'

Jews don't do death flowers. Not at funerals and definitely not on graves. Something about how flowers die and stones are forever. And like ten other possible reasons people who actually practise the religion would know.

'How are they?'

'Same old. Mum's annoyed at Dad. Dad's annoying Mum. Both are worried about you.'

'Ask them if I can borrow some money.'

'They say get a job.'

'Fair.'

*

'I'm having a hard time with something,' I say, after Priya and I have spent a good ten minutes on blackout shopping. 'Okay, I'm having a hard time with everything, but this specifically.'

'What is it?'

Gripping her mug.

'Why now?' I ask.

'Why now what?'

'Why did all this happen now, in January to be exact? How did I get through all the illnesses and deaths relatively intact but break now?'

She straightens her posture, moves her chair closer to her desk, and picks up a pen. Her classic 'this is deep / important / deeply important' move.

'This is why I hate the term "breakdown",' she says. 'You didn't break. You're not broken.'

'How else would you describe it? I used to be highly functioning. Now I can't work, I could barely speak a few months ago, and everything gives me a panic attack. I broke. I'm broken.'

Never argue semantics with a writer.

'Yael, this isn't permanent. You will get better. You're already so much better. You'll work and you'll speak and you'll rant about the government and make fun of my body temperature again. Even if you are broken, you won't be forever.'

'But why did it happen now? Nothing that happened in the last few years even vaguely compares to watching everyone die. Why now and not then?'

'For lots of reasons,' she says, waving the pen around. 'Firstly, mental health isn't rational, you know that. You've got through plenty of rough times without crashing and you've had down times when things have been going objectively well.'

155

This is true.

'But I also believe you got through everything with your parents and grandmother because you didn't have a choice. They needed you, and when somebody relies on us that much, we're taken out of ourselves. We live for them. It's primal. You were in survival mode.'

I wonder what mode I'm in now.

'But also,' she continues. 'This *is* because of everything you went through with your parents and grandmother, not just a product of your recent past. It's been building and building over time. It's all of it. It's everything.'

JULY

The anxiety has evolved (devolved?) into singularity, sparked by and entirely focused on one subject.

Money.

Specifically my ability, or lack thereof, to support myself financially.

I know how privileged I am to have been able to take an extended break from working, but it can't last forever.

I'm not filthy rich; I had some rainy-day dollars from my parents and Nanna but they're almost gone, and I have to start earning again soon.

How?

The thought of trying to write something – anything – is laughable. I can't work like this. Not with permanent brain fog and the attention span of a goldfish.

Could I get government payments?

I'd probably have to sell my apartment, but after settling the mortgage, that money wouldn't last long. I should be grateful I have an apartment to sell. I *am* grateful I have an apartment to sell.

Where would I go?

I could move in with Liora and Sean for a while, but I can't sponge off them forever.

What if Pumpkin and Kumera hate Julia Louis-Dreyfus?

Would I have to rehome her? Surrender her to a shelter? Maybe one of my friends would take her.

Who likes cats?

And on and on until I have to take a Valium and crawl into bed and watch *Gilmore Girls* until I fall asleep.

It's an unseasonably warm day and I'm hoping Lynne's at the baths.

'Oh good, you're here,' I say when I get there, handing her a paper bag. 'I got you something.'

'What? What's this for?'

She pulls a giant muffin out of the bag.

'Just 'cause you said mine looked good the other day.'

'Oh, aren't you a doll?'

'I hope you're not gluten intolerant,' I say.

'I'm everything tolerant.'

I laugh.

'Except of people taking photos here.'

She laughs.

'Thank you, love. I'm so chuffed. You've made my day.'

I make the most of what I know will only be a few hours of sun, if that. I sunbake, I read the silly books. I consider swimming, but I'm a bit shaken from the ocean trying to kill me last time.

I text Margot.

Do you reckon Christian Grey's into pegging?

Ooh excellent question.

Thanks. Y/N?

The guy's a control freak with mummy issues and a Madonna/ whore complex. He LOVES it.

This is why we're friends.

Lynne comes and sits with me after she finishes her shift. She's never done this before.

'No Shirley today?' she asks. 'Or was she here before I started?'

'No, she's coming less now that winter's hit. And she has lunch with her friends on Wednesdays.'

'Such a lovely woman. She's been comin' here for donkey's. Long before my time.'

'Yeah, she's great. I'm glad I found her.'

'I'm glad you did too, love. It's not my place, so tell me to rack off, but there's a bit more light in you than when you first showed up here. I mean, you still look miserable sometimes but less miserable. Sorry if that's wrong of me to say.'

'No, it's fine.' I smile. 'I've wondered how obvious my ... state has been.'

'Oh, us vollies see everything, and it looks like Shirley's put some colour back in your face. And she seems all the better for meeting you, too.'

We gaze out to sea and I wonder how I could have had a positive influence on someone when I've been feeling this low.

'How long have you been coming here?' I ask her, digging around in my bag for lip balm.

'Well, let me think. I moved to Sydney in '91 for a job and a friend brought me here probably not long after.'

'Where did you move from?'

'Tamworth, love. I'm a country girl. Don't let all this sophistication fool ya.'

She gestures down the length of her body, clad in a yellow volunteer hoodie, long baggy denim shorts and navy Crocs with socks.

I laugh as my hand grasps what I think is lip balm in the depths of my bag.

'I love country music,' I tell her. 'Some of it, anyway. Townes Van Zandt, Patsy, Hank, Johnny. Dolly, obviously. And some new stuff.'

'Well, well,' she says. 'Miss stylish black swimsuits loves some country.'

'I'm full of surprises.'

I realise what I thought was lip balm is a random battery.

'What was the job you came here for? In '91.'

'Teaching. Primary school. In those days you went wherever they sent you.'

'My mum was a teacher. Mostly kindergarten and year one.'

Mum loved her job. She loved kids. She was her most animated, her most performative, when she was teaching. To watch her front a captive audience of five- and six-year-olds was pure magic, her doing the voices of the characters in books, them hanging off her every word. Her cheeks actually turned rosy with joy, it radiated from her.

'Wonderful. Is she retired?'

'No, she passed away.'

My right hand plunges back into the abyss, determined.

'Oh, hon. I'm sorry. Is that why you showed up here looking so sad? God, listen to Miss Busybody here.'

'It's fine. I don't mind talking about it. No, that's not why. Well, it's part of it, I guess, but she died ten years ago.'

My hand clasps another small cylinder.

Success!

'Geez, you must have been young.'

'Twenty-four. Youngish, but an adult.'

'Barely. Were you close?'

'Very.'

I apply lip balm.

'So you never went back to Tamworth?'

'I used to go visit my folks while they were still here. The missus and I talk about moving back sometimes, but it'd be hard to leave this.'

She gestures at the ocean.

'What's your partner's name?'

'Liz. Been together over twenty years now.'

'That's awesome. Does she come here much?'

'Sometimes. Rarely in summer, she hates the crowds. But we both love this place.'

'It's pretty magical.'

'We want to get married here.'

'I want to be buried here.'

She snort-laughs.

'Not sure the committee would go for that.'

'They wouldn't have to know.'

'Fair enough. But you're too young to be thinking about that.'

She stands up.

'Alright, I'm choofin' off. I have a date with a very neglected garden. Nice chatting to ya.'

'You too. Are you here tomorrow?'

'We're closed, remember?'

'Oh yeah, the renos.'

'See you next month.'

*

Several years ago, I worked at a glorified fashion magazine masquerading as a serious tome for the fabulous feminist. Read about the women escaping war in South Sudan then learn how to take a $3000 dress from boardroom to bar.

Just what the first wave wanted.

I actually loved the job, but I was having a rough time trying to work and look after my Nanna. And my boss was being a stone-cold bitch.

My boss *was* a stone-cold bitch.

'You're letting the team down, Yael,' she'd say. 'You can't keep running off every time Nanna stubs her toe.'

Nanna was a Holocaust survivor with bipolar disorder and early-stage dementia who spent much of her last year of life reliving her horrific childhood. A stubbed toe wouldn't even have registered.

When I had interviewed for the job two years earlier and told my would-be first boss that I had an unwell grandmother for whom I was responsible and I might sometimes need to run off to care for her, she was unfazed.

'Oh lord, that's fine!' She smiled. 'I have kids. Sometimes I have to run off, too. And you can write from anywhere.'

It was such a relief.

Unfortunately (for me), she got promoted about a year into my tenure and one of my colleagues became my editor. A colleague I didn't like. A colleague nobody liked. A nightmare in heels who belittled other women to prop herself up and ride on their shoulders all the way to the top. A woman who would sell her own mother to become editor-in-chief one day. She had less empathy than a Liberal prime minister and she made my life a living hell.

Nanna had been in the hospice for a while and wasn't expected to hang on for much longer. But if I'd learned anything from watching my loved ones die, it was that even filled with disease and bereft of nourishment, the human body, the human spirit, could grip life so tight it defied even doctors' expectations.

Nanna could have died any minute, or not for weeks.

On the way home from the baths, I have a sudden urge to eat udon noodles and agedashi tofu. I order Japanese takeaway when I get home, but by the time it's delivered, the craving has passed.

I force some down anyway and think about how, for some unknown reason, Mum couldn't say tofu. She pronounced it 'torfu'. Tor-fu. Like the Greek island, with a *t*. It made no sense. She could say toe. She could say total. She could say Tony Danza. But throw in an *f* and a *u* and she was f-u-cked.

Back then, I found it really annoying. Now, I'd give anything to hear her repeatedly mispronounce soy-based protein sources.

I don't think she was particularly fond of tofu but she endured it occasionally in solidarity with my life choices, mostly when we made what we came to call Pad Dannii after the younger Minogue implied 'Asian' was a language in an interview.

The dish was an ever-changing, bastardised potpourri of flavours and ingredients from various Asian countries, thrown together with as much respect for authenticity as a cavoodle breeder. Hokkien noodles with 'Japanese-style' tofu, Chinese vegetables in a sweet chilli sauce, soba noodles with fish sauce.

It was the early 2000s. We didn't know any better.

*

Liora and I think Zeida had another family before the Holocaust. He was almost thirty when the war broke out, and thirty-year-old men in the 1930s had wives and children. We've talked about looking for them, for proof of their existence, but we don't even know what happened to him during the war, let alone his imagined kin.

Zeida's story lived and died with him. I don't think even Mum knew much about it. Liora and I have discussed trying to find out, but I don't think he wanted us to know and I feel we should honour that.

Nanna was more open about her Holocaust experiences. I feel like I've always known the outline of her story, if not the specific details, and she recorded her oral history with the Sydney Jewish Museum.

Liora and I have the tapes and transcripts.

They're as harrowing as you'd imagine, but sometimes I relisten to the tapes just to hear her voice.

I was at my desk, transcribing an interview, when Liora rang.

'You need to come right now!'

'What? Where are you?' I said.

It's important to note that at this time Liora was six months pregnant with Hannah, and panicked phone calls came with multiple possibilities.

'I'm at Sacred Heart. Are you at work?'

'Yup,' I whispered, observing open-plan office etiquette. 'What's happening?'

'Nanna's gone.'

'Fuck!'

Half the office turned around.

Quieter: 'When?'

'I've only been here an hour. I gave her a kiss when I came in and she looked at me and gurgled a bit. I was reading a magazine and when I looked up, she was gone. I called the nurses and they pronounced it. Can you come quick? I'm stuck here with her until the Chevra picks her up. It's creepy.'

The Chevra is the Chevra Kadisha, a kind of Jewish morgue and funeral venue. By Jewish law, a dead body shouldn't be alone for even a second before burial. Something about guarding it from desecration and the soul not being able to rest until the body is returned to the earth. There are people – called shomrim – who sit with corpses in shifts until their funerals. It's considered an honour and the purest act of kindness, as the deceased can never return the favour.

Liora couldn't leave Nanna's room unless someone else stayed.

'Okay.' The tears started. 'I'll get there as soon as I can.'

Trying to be discreet, I got up to go to the bathroom and compose myself but somehow ended up in the stationery cupboard in an inelegant yoga child's pose, all knees and forehead.

A knock.

'Yael, it's Romy. Can I come in?'

I sat up against the shelves, crammed with pens, notepads and all manner of branded office supplies, hugging my knees and wiping tears with my fingers.

'Yup.'

Romy came in and sat on the floor in front of me. 'Is it your grandmother?'

I nodded.

'She's gone.'

'I'm so sorry.' She put a hand on my knee. 'Where do you need to go?'

'To the hospice. Darlinghurst.'

'Alright. Let's go. I'll drive you.'

'My car's here.'

'No way I'm letting you drive, mate.'

I looked at Twitter this morning. Instagram too. Even Facebook.

I hadn't been on any social media since the thing.

Everything was new. New gossip, new memes, new false idols.

Do we like Justin Bieber now?

As someone used to being in touch with the zeitgeist, someone paid to do so, it was super weird to suddenly have no idea what people were talking about.

It felt like I'd awoken from a very long coma.

People had noticed my disappearance.

Hey, just wanted to check in. Noticed you've been offline for a while.

People had enquired.

Have you been kidnapped? Blink twice for help.

People I know.

You okay, mate? I worry when you don't post.

People I don't know.

Loving it here without you. Please never come back.

People I immediately blocked.

It was nice to feel missed until I started to feel anxious and inadequate, social media's signature cocktail.

166

I reminded myself that nothing is real and deleted all the apps again.

No more social media.

It's not safe there.

When I got to the hospice, I kissed Nanna on the forehead and told her I loved her. Her eyes were closed and she looked peaceful.

But all the Nanna was gone.

Tears.

Liora was sitting on the room's lone chair, busy on the phone. Organising.

'So we'll need those urns for coffee and tea, soft drinks, juices, disposable cups, the usual. But not as many as for Mum's and Dad's. There won't be as many people. I'd say maybe fifty. Yep. Hey, Yael's just got here, can I call you back? Okay, thanks so much. Bye.'

Jewish funerals are held as quickly as possible after someone dies, ideally the next day. Zeida died in the morning and was buried in the afternoon. We're a very efficient people.

'Hi.' Liora stood.

'Hi.'

We awkward-hugged.

We're not huggers.

'She's gone,' she said, sitting back down.

'Evidently.' I sat on the floor. 'Was that Anita on the phone?'

'Yeah. She was checking on Nanna and offered to organise the drinks when I told her.'

Morphine and Dexamethasone sauntered in looking for pats. Morph and Dex, as they were most often called, were giant tabbies with beautiful temperaments who wandered around the hospice demanding attention and spreading peace and love to patients, loved ones and staff alike.

That the hospice had cats made me very happy, that they were named after palliative drugs even more so. I love a death hotel with a sense of humour.

'I take it we'll do it at your house?' I said, as the furry painkillers presented their bellies to me.

'I think so. I'm waiting for a call back from the synagogue to confirm when the rabbi can do the funeral, but they said probably Thursday.'

It was Tuesday.

The last time I had seen the rabbi was at the cemetery for Mum's headstone consecration. At the end, when the dementia had completely taken over, Dad would sometimes only speak Arabic or French, his first languages. Liora, Mum and I spoke neither, but the rabbi spoke both. Every few days he would come and chat to Dad, playing along with whatever reality he believed he was in.

'How did you get here?' Liora asked.

'Romy.'

'One of us can take you to get your car later or tomorrow. Did you speak to your bitch boss about when you'd be back?'

'Nope. I set an out-of-office and said "I'll be back in two weeks" as I walked past her desk.'

'Well played. I don't think you should ever go back.'

'I'll go back, even just to give proper notice. I've got two weeks to ruminate, anyway.'

'Maybe you should ruminate somewhere else. Maybe we all should.'

'Ooh, what about Spain? Or Italy?'

'What about both?'

'That's why you're in charge.'

Without warning, Morph jumped onto the bed and Liora screamed, leaping out of her chair to shoo her off. The hospice was a quiet, tranquil place, but I imagined the occasional scream was par for the course.

I grabbed Dex so he wouldn't follow as two nurses ran into the room.

'What happened?' Mary was a lovely Irish nurse I'd grown quite fond of.

'I'm so sorry,' Liora said. 'One of the cats jumped onto the bed and I panicked.'

'Oh, they're cheeky buggers, those two. They know they're not allowed on the beds unless invited.'

'Maybe Nanna invited her,' I offered.

Liora laugh-snorted.

'You never know,' Mary said as she left the room.

'See?' I said to Liora. 'You never know.'

'I hate you.'

Hours later, I was still at Sacred Heart.

Liora had gone to get food and coffee and I was alone with Nanna.

It's impossible to convey the utter weirdness of spending several hours in a sterile room with your dead grandmother. It is a surreal and humbling experience, perhaps also farcical only to those of us au fait enough with death to mock it.

Morph and Dex wandered in and out of the room, as if to check whether Nanna was still dead. They meowed insistently at me, perhaps demanding that we hit the road, so the room could be readied for a new expiring human and their weary entourage.

'Sorry guys, I want us to leave too,' I said, amid pats and nose boops. 'But we can't until the Hebrew hearse comes and gets her.'

Mary stuck her head in and asked if I needed anything, which was very kind and not at all in her job description. She agreed to stay with Nanna while I went to the bathroom, though I told her to leave if actual living patients needed her.

When I got back to the room, she was still there.

'Thanks so much,' I said. 'Any change?'

She laughed.

'You'd hear me screaming from the street if there was. Now, love, shall I put the sheet over her? Would that be better for you?'

'Um, maybe? Actually, no, I think that would be worse.'

'As you want.'

When she left, I stood next to the bed, looking at Nanna and trying to process her departure from this world, from her pain, from my life.

'I hope you're at peace now, wherever you are, which I'm ninety-nine per cent sure is nowhere, but in case it's not and you can hear me, I love you and I'll miss you. I hope Zeida and Mum and Dad are with you. And your parents and your brother and sister. Thank you for being my nanna and looking after me and loving me and trying your best. I hope you knew how much I loved you.'

I didn't know what I was going to do now. There was no one left to care for.

With the baths closed, I soon discover just how much yoga a person with no job, children or social life can do.

*

I was glued to the floor next to Nanna – crying, watching.

Feeling a hand on my back, I swung around to find Sean behind me.

'Jesus Christ, you gave me a heart attack!'

'Sorry,' he said, giving me a quick squeeze. 'You okay, mate?'

'Yeah.' I wiped tears from my cheeks. 'Just having a chat.'

'I wish you long life. May her memory be a blessing.'

'Thanks. I can't believe she's gone.'

'Well, it's only been a few hours.'

He looked at the bed.

'Bye, Nanna. You were pretty cool.'

'Touching,' I said.

'Hey, you're the wordsmith.'

When Liora returned, we ate sandwiches and raised our coffees to Nanna.

'So sad she didn't get to meet baby three,' Liora said. 'It was so close.'

'At least she got a decent run with babies one and two,' Sean said.

And there we stayed until the men from the Chevra came to take away the body, our last link to the past.

I only found out about her because Margot mentioned 'his new girlfriend'.

'Oh?' I said as nonchalantly as I could. 'I didn't know he was seeing someone.'

'Some woman from his work. She seems nice. Puts up with his bullshit.'

She didn't know about us then. She knew we'd hooked up at that party but thought it had stopped there. My desire to keep it quiet, driven by his chronic dickishness, worked extremely well for him.

Things between us were still casual around the time they started dating and if he'd told me then, it would have been a relatively clean ending. But by the time I found out, there were feelings involved.

It was like a sliding doors moment, except in my case the doors got jammed, caught fire and the whole train blew up.

A text.

Sean.

Hey, I'll be there in five. Can you wait out front?

It's Ethan's birthday tomorrow, so tonight we're going to a teppanyaki restaurant to blow his little mind. But I thought Liora was picking me up.

I bid Julia Louis-Dreyfus adieu and go out to wait for him.

'Hi,' I say, getting into his hatchback. 'I thought Liora was getting me?'

'Yeah,' he says. 'She's held up at work, so you get me instead.'

'Where are the squids?' I ask, double-checking the back seat. 'Are we celebrating Ethan's birthday without him?'

'Ha, no. They're coming with Kerrie,' he says. 'She took them bowling.'

Kerrie is Sean's aunt. The kids spend a lot of time with her.

'Oh god,' I say. 'I hope it goes better than last time.'

Last time, Ethan broke his wrist and Hannah had a massive tantrum because Lexi used the ball she had deemed hers.

'There haven't been any calls from the emergency department, so I'm quietly confident.'

I take a makeup bag out of my handbag.

'How are you?' I ask, applying dots of liquid foundation to my face. 'Do you mind if I roll my window down?'

'I'm good and sure, go for it.'

I add concealer under my eyes and pat it all in with a beauty blender.

'How's the job hunt?' I ask. 'Oh, oops, am I allowed to know about it now?'

My bad.

'Yeah, she told me you know. And it's soul destroying.'

'I'm sorry. Have you had interviews?'

'Yeah,' he says. 'A couple. But they were for shitty jobs and I kind of threw them on purpose. Don't tell Liora.'

'Vault.'

I can't be bothered contouring – quelle horreur – so I take out bronzer and cream blush and slap them on my face with the precision of Hannah's fingerpainting.

'Have you seen anything good?' I ask.

'Nope, but if it takes much longer, I'll go for something subpar until a better gig comes along. We can't survive on one paycheque unless we stop feeding the kids.'

Highlighter, brow liner, brow gel.

'You should make them get jobs,' I say. 'It's about time those lazy little freeloaders started pulling their weight.'

'That's an idea.'

'Or teach them to pick-pocket and turn them into a gang.'

'Who's gonna teach them to pick-pocket?' he asks.

'There's probably someone on Airtasker.'

He laughs.

Damn, I forgot to bring eyeliner. Cancel the dinner!

'How are *you* doing?' he says. 'Sorry I haven't checked in in a while.'

'Dude, I practically live at your house. I'm sorry about *that*.'

'I know, but I haven't checked in properly.' He looks over at me. 'What the hell are you doing?'

'Curling my eyelashes,' I say. 'Doesn't Liora do this?'

'Not that I've seen. Looks painful.'

'It's not.'

I finish curling and add mascara. Lots of it.

'You haven't told me how you're doing,' he says.

'Every day's a blessing.'

'And your real answer?'

'Every twelfth to fifteenth day could possibly be a blessing.'

He was the first man to call me beautiful.

He's the only man who's ever called me beautiful.

The things I tolerated, ignored, excused just to hear that word again.

Sometimes I even believed him.

'I want to know more about your husband.'

I'm at Costco with Shirley. She didn't believe me when I told her they sell coffins and engagement rings, so we're in the food court sharing a mega slice of doughy cheese pizza and churros with caramel sauce.

I'd rather be at home watching TV and crying, but today is my Everest.

'What do you want to know?'

'How did you and Peter meet?'

'He worked for my father. We had a small chain of mixed business stores. Peter stocked the shelves and did the books.'

'My grandparents had mixed business stores.'

'Really? Where were their stores?'

'One in Bronte and one in Bondi. Where were yours?'

'All on the north side. We only moved to the east after we sold the business.'

She picks up a churro and dips it in the sauce.

'How old were you when you met Peter? You said he was much older?'

'I was sixteen. He told me he was going to marry me one day, but he didn't ask me on a date until I was nineteen. He was thirty-five. I know that would be frowned upon today, but it was a different time.'

'Nanna and Zeida had a similar age gap.'

'Seems like your nanna and I have a lot in common.'

'Same.'

She bites into the churro and looks at me like I've provided her first orgasm.

'Wow.'

'I told you.'

'You're not even eating any. And you hardly touched your pizza.'

'I had a big breakfast.'

No I didn't.

Change the subject, Yael.

'So, what was Peter like?'

'He was quiet but not in a shy way, he'd just get lost in his thoughts. He was very smart, he wanted to be an aerospace engineer but his family didn't have money so he left school at sixteen to work.'

'At least he ended up getting you in that deal.'

'Such a prize! After we married, I encouraged him to follow his dream, but he felt too old to start again. "I'd be over forty when I finished, Shirl," he'd say. "Who's going to hire a middle-aged rookie?" It broke my heart.'

She consoles herself with another bite of the churro.

'Did you have career dreams you didn't follow?' I ask.

'I suppose I did, yes. Gosh, I haven't thought about it in a long time. I wanted to be a fashion designer. I loved clothes and I thought it would be a great adventure. I started as a seamstress for a fashion brand and I hoped to work my way up into the design team and one day have my own company.'

'What did you want to make?'

'I was drawn to tailoring. I loved the idea of making smart suits for women. Skirt suits and pantsuits. Like Chanel and Yves Saint Laurent, but probably not quite as fancy.'

'Oh god. I love a good suit. If I ever get married, I'm wearing a YSL tux.'

'I'm sure you'd make a stunning bride.'

Shirley finishes the last churro and dabs her mouth with a napkin.

'Oh dear, that was too much,' she says. 'For someone who barely eats, you're a very bad influence.'

'Maybe I've become a feeder.'

'What's a feeder?'

176

'Someone who gets off on making someone gain excessive amounts of weight. It's actually gross and all about control and power, and I shouldn't joke about it.'

'Ah yes, I saw a program on it once. Shall we walk off the carbs with a turn around the shop?'

'Let's.'

Two weeks after Nanna died, I went back to work and immediately gave my notice.

As luck would have it, my boss had just started a month of leave, so I got to resign to her boss instead, and I never had to see the bitch again.

I stayed for three weeks, finishing a couple of long-form stories I'd worked really hard on and wanted to see through. Whether they'd be published or not was another thing.

It was a fraught time. I loved that job. I had a great team and a licence to work on stories that I actually cared about. Plus, I got to see Romy every day. It felt incredibly unfair to be leaving because of one awful person, but I was processing Nanna's death and grieving for my whole family.

Liora and I were now officially the oldest generation in our lineage.

During my exit interview, the HR woman asked if there was any feedback I wanted to give the company.

'Well, I was pretty disappointed you only agreed to three days when I asked to take unpaid leave while my grandmother was dying.'

She looked confused.

She looked at my file.

She looked at me.

'Who told you that?'

'My boss. She said that's all you could give me.'

She looked at her notes.

She typed something into her computer.

She looked at me.

'I'm so sorry, Yael,' she said, as if she was about to tell me she'd run over my cat. 'I probably shouldn't tell you this, but she never asked.'

'My word, they really do sell coffins,' Shirley says.

'Told you.'

I manoeuvre a giant trolley around the store.

'So what happened to your fashion career?'

'Well, I left my seamstress job when I had Andy, then I was a full-time mum until he went to school. After that, I helped Peter with the shops. And that's how it was until we retired.'

I put five gigantic packs of toilet paper in my trolley. Shirley looks at me, troubled.

'My bowels are fine,' I say. 'They're for Liora. She gave me a list.'

'I love that you're going to a bulk retailer,' Liora had said when I'd told her I was coming here. 'You can barely get through one pack of anything.'

'Giant bags of chips are an investment in my future,' I'd replied.

She couldn't argue with that.

As Shirley and I continue moving through the oversized aisles, I ask, 'Andy didn't want to take over the family business?'

'Not at all. And that was fine with us. What happened to your grandparents' shops?'

'I actually don't know, but Mum definitely wouldn't have wanted them. She loved teaching, and Dad had his real estate agency, though I'm not sure they would have passed it on to him anyway. There was a lot of tension there.'

I spot the bulk croissants and grab a bag for Liora and the squids.

'I love a croissant,' Shirley says.

'Well, you're human.'

I stop.

'And here are the engagement rings.'

Shirley peers over the glass-top cabinet full of diamond rings, almost pressing her face into the glass. Then she bolts upright and turns to me.

'They're so expensive!' she says. 'There's one for $89,000! What is this place?'

'Heaven.'

He'd show up at my apartment at all hours of the night, demanding a bath. Then he'd sit in the tub, naked and wasted, and try to get me and Julia Louis-Dreyfus to join him, oblivious to the fact that we were both fully sober and tired of his shit.

The first few times, I got in the tub with him, maybe with a glass of wine. But after a while I'd just get annoyed and I'd go back to bed while he splashed around like a toddler, hoping he wouldn't drown, but also that he would, and he'd eventually come in, soaking wet, too high to remember how towels work.

He'd try to have sex with me, unable to comprehend what a boner-killer the whole situation was and unable to do it anyway.

Finally, he'd give up and spoon me so tight I'd make peace with dying.

'I love you,' he'd breathe into my ear, his alcohol breath making it to my nose intact. 'I usually only love skinny girls.'

But a few times he called me beautiful.

'So your mum's parents and your dad didn't get along?' Shirley asks.

We're crossing the Anzac Bridge on our way home from Costco. I love driving across this bridge, especially at sunset, but tonight I just want to get home.

'I mean, nobody ever told me that outright, but it was pretty obvious. I don't know if it was always the way or if something happened. I have so many questions about my family, but Mum and Dad were both only children, and there's no one left to ask.'

'That must be frustrating.'

We drive in silence, my sad girl playlist serving chill vibes.

Chill, sad vibes.

'One funny thing did happen with Nanna,' I say. 'Funny to me at least. On the way to Dad's burial.'

'Oh no.'

'So, we're in the car with her – me, mum and Liora – en route to put our husband and father in the ground, extremely prematurely, and Nanna says to me in all seriousness, "Now that it's finally over, can you come fix my television?"'

Shirley claps a hand to her mouth.

'Oh lord, she didn't.'

'Yup. That was classic Nanna.'

'I'm glad you can laugh about these things.'

I miss her so much.

'It wasn't her fault. She had a horrible start to life and got through the rest however she could. Part of that was putting up emotional walls. She was so stoic when Mum, her only child, died. Occasionally I'd get exasperated with her and want her to comfort me, but then I'd remember she was just a kid when she lost her own parents, in unimaginable circumstances. It wasn't her fault, she never had a chance.'

'I understand.'

Soon Shirley falls asleep and I drive the rest of the way in silence.

I think about Nanna, about how smart she was despite only getting to year three in Poland, and what a good grandmother she was, even learning to drive so she could help Mum with us. I think about her often fraught relationship with Mum, who, like all children of survivors, grew up with irrevocably damaged parents and six million ghosts.

When I pull up outside Shirley's house, a rambling old terrace on a beautiful leafy street, she's still asleep.

'Shirley.' I put a hand on her shoulder. 'We're home.'

She stirs, opening her eyes and adjusting to reality.

'Oh no, did I fall asleep on you? I'm sorry.'

'It's okay. I didn't feel much like talking anymore.'

She rubs her temples.

'I'd make you dinner,' she says, 'but I can feel a headache coming on.'

'Don't be silly, you're exhausted. And Julia Louis-Dreyfus needs food.'

'We mustn't keep the queen waiting.'

She picks up her handbag and opens the car door.

'Don't forget your Costco haul,' I remind her.

'Oh yes.' She walks around to the boot.

'Alright, I've got everything. Thank you for taking me to that marvellous shop.'

'Thanks for letting me take you.'

As I drive off, a sad girl sings a sad song about sadness.

A phone call.

Margot.

'I'm having withdrawals. Send help.'

She finished the *Fifty Shades* books.

'Hello to you too.'

'Yes, yes, hi blah blah,' she says. 'I'm considering reading all three books again.'

'Please don't do that.'

'Then how will I fill the gaping void left in their wake?'

'I don't know. Spend time with your children?'

'Ew.'

I laugh.

'Have you watched the movie?' I ask.

'No! Have you?'

'Yup. Absolute nonsense. Do it.'

'Sold. How are you?'

Terrible.

'Not great? But not as bad as I was. Sometimes I feel like I'm heaps better but then one thing sets me back a bunch. I'm really over it.'

'I'm sorry, hon. I wish I was there. Should I be there? Would it help?'

Maybe?

'Nah. I mean, I'd love to see you but I don't think it would speed up my recovery or anything.'

'I feel like an arsehole for not being there.'

'You shouldn't. I don't think you're an arsehole for not being here.'

It had never occurred to me that she could or should be here.

'How are you?' I ask. 'How's Josh? And the kids?'

'I'm good. Josh is good. Kids are good. Tokyo is insane. I insist you visit as soon as you're up to it, or we can go somewhere quieter in this beautiful country.'

'That would be nice,' I say. 'How's work?'

'Work's fine. I remain an ever-humble member of the proletariat, exchanging my labour for yen and a dream.'

'I need to do that. For dollars and a roof.'

'Ooh, she's ready to work?'

Not even a little.

'She's not, but she's almost broke and that yen don't earn itself.'

'You could be a live camgirl. Get those glorious tits out.'

'I will if you will.'

'You go first.'

'Okay. Gonna call myself Anastasia Schpiel.'

She laughs.

'I have to sleep now,' she says. 'Goodnight Anastasia.'

'Night. Love you.'

'Love you.'

I dreamed about my grandparents. And cake.

I used to wake from dreams about my parents and grandparents feeling cheated. I'd close my eyes and try desperately to go back to sleep. Fuck flying, if I had one superpower, that would be it. But I've come to enjoy their cameos in my subconscious, grateful to have spent time with them, in any dimension.

My phone starts ringing while I'm eating muesli on the couch.

I don't feel like talking.

'Hi, Shirley.'

'Hello, my dear. Just checking in after our big excursion. You seemed a bit low at the end. How are you today?'

Julia Louis-Dreyfus is staring out the window like she's waiting for her husband to return from war.

'I'm okay,' I say. 'I had nice dreams.'

'I rarely remember my dreams.'

'My meds make mine all trippy and vivid, like Wes Anderson movies.'

'You know I never get your references.'

Julia Louis-Dreyfus jumps off the windowsill and sits on the floor by my discarded muesli, waiting for her moment.

'How are you feeling? Has your headache gone?'

'For now. But I'm happy because Andy says he's coming to visit.'

'That's great.'

The cat starts eating my breakfast. I don't stop her. She probably needs the fibre.

'I'd love for you two to meet if you're up to it.'

'I'll try and fit it into my packed social calendar.'

'Wonderful.'

Done with rolled oats, Julia Louis-Dreyfus commences grooming, because she's a lady, then sprawls across a ray of morning sun, and I wish, I wish, I wish I was a cat.

Dad would have turned seventy-five today.

Happy birthday, Dad.

184

As is tradition, tonight we're getting takeaway from Nada's, his favourite Lebanese restaurant, our favourite Lebanese restaurant. Falafel, hummus, tabouli, baba ganoush, selek beloubie, kibbeh, kafta, the lot.

They still remember him at Nada's.

'Ah Aleks, the Egyptian Jew. Good man.'

He'd speak Arabic and drink Lebanese coffee with them, truly in his element.

Liora and I always come to the cemetery together on Mum and Dad's yahrzeit, but I usually come on their birthdays alone. I like to sit by their graves and tell them about my life and about Liora and the squids. Sometimes I do the same with Nanna and Zeida, and even Grandma Ruth.

It's not that I believe their souls or spirits are buried here with their bones six feet down. But it's a place of respect and ritual, where nobody looks at you weird for crying openly or talking to nobody.

It's a two-hour round trip, or more, depending on how lost you get trying to find all the graves.

Rookwood Cemetery is colossal, the size of a suburb or a small town. A sleepy, creepy town.

Death Town.

It doesn't help that the five graves are in two different sections and Jewish headstones all look almost identical.

Judaic law – Halacha – mandates that in death, everyone is equal, so all headstones in a cemetery (and coffins and everything) should be as similar as possible.

Anyway, we get lost every time.

Today I found Mum and Dad in record time and I'm sitting on the path in front of their double plot, drinking hot chocolate and having a chat. Monologuing, really.

'Shalom Imma and Abba, how are you doing?'

It's the first time I've been here since their yahrzeit last year.

'I miss you both so much. I wish I had good news to report, but it's been a pretty rough year. For me, anyway. For Liora too, I suppose. But that's mostly my fault. She's generally good, I think, though Sean lost his job so that's been stressful for them.

'The kids are good, more than good. You would have loved them so much.

'Ethan is a little big man and looks like a mini-Sean, with hints of Dad. He's super smart, funny, and obsessed with sports. I'm scared I won't have anything to talk to him about soon. You know how much I care for sport.

'Lexi is so beautiful. There's so much of you in her, Mum. She's already desperate to grow up, always wanting to know what adults are talking about and bossing Hannah around. She's somehow a total maths genius which, like her blue eyes, makes me question her lineage.

'And Hannah is just pure joy. She's messy and hilarious and constantly hurting herself, and she worships the ground her big siblings walk on. I can already tell she's going to give Liora and Sean hell as a teenager. Remind you of anyone?

'And I'm terrible. Getting better, I think, but I, I did a thing.

'I fucked up.'

Very hot, very slow tears. I wipe my face with the back of my sleeve.

'I just didn't want to do it anymore. Anything.

'I didn't want to be sad anymore. I didn't want to miss you or love him or hate me.

186

'I didn't want to be a thorn for Liora – which has proved ironic in the aftermath.'

I imagine them laughing at that. They would have laughed at that.

'Basically, I just didn't want to be me. I'm still not fully on board with it. I felt like such a loser. Like I've failed life. Everyone has partners and kids and futures. And I have drunken international phone calls and a cat.

'She's a good cat, though.

'I'm trying to get better and be positive and not be this boring, sad white lady with boring, sad white lady problems. I'm trying to stop wallowing in self-pity. To live with my bad choices and try to make better ones.'

A young family gets out of a car right near me and I watch in silence as they all look on the ground for stones to put on the graves. When they have them, they walk towards me, the parents tilting their heads at me as if to wish me long life.

I hope they aren't visiting someone close to me and the folks but, of course, their person is only two graves up from us.

'Okay, I'm gonna go now,' I say to Mum and Dad. 'I'll be back for your yahrzeit with Liora. I love you forever. Bye.'

If Triple M plays when I turn the car on, I swear I'm going to murder someone.

A text.

Him.

Past tense.

London.

Can you talk tonight? I have to tell you something.

I'm busy tonight, tell me now.

I really want to do this over the phone.
I really want to sleep with Dev Patel. Tell me.
I'm getting married.
Mic drop.

AUGUST

A text.

Liora.

Do you want to invite Shirley for Shabbat?

Bless her, she's trying.

Bill's off his game today.

No compliments.

No complaining.

No talking at all.

He acknowledged my presence with a solemn nod and went back to his work or group chat or Tripadvisor reviews. You just know he'd write the bitchiest, most incredible reviews.

Priya is a vision in head-to-toe, print-clashing Dries Van Noten spring/summer 2013, my favourite ever collection.

'You're killing me with this outfit,' I say.

'I knew you were coming.'

We spend the session talking about something Liora said around the time of the thing. I don't remember most of that

189

conversation, as with much of that time, but I said something about having a baby on my own and she said I shouldn't, that it would be foolish, selfish even. It hit me hard and I've been thinking about it a lot.

'Have you talked to her about it?' Priya asks.

'No, I know she wasn't being deliberately insensitive. She just hadn't fully grasped the severity of the situation. And she had a point, it would have been foolish and selfish to have a baby on my own.'

'You could argue that having children is often foolish and always selfish.'

I've always said that if I didn't meet someone by my mid-thirties, I'd do it alone. I've always pictured that would be the case, perhaps a self-fulfilling prophecy. And here I am, in my mid-thirties, without a someone, but in no state to look after a child.

'How would I look after a baby?' I ask. 'How would I afford a baby?'

I can barely look after myself.

'Right now, you couldn't,' she says. 'But you're going to get past this. You're already much better.'

'But this could happen again, and worse, when I have a child. I'm a prime candidate for postpartum sads and what happens then? Or what if I actually kill myself next time? Either way, that's a lot on Liora.'

'Firstly, let's not assume there will be a "next time". There's every chance this was a one-off and that you'll never have an episode anywhere near this acute again. So let's quit it with the doom and gloom, okay?'

'I'll try.'

'Good. And secondly, this would all still be true with a partner.'

'Yeah, but at least then if anything happened it wouldn't all be on Liora.'

'I don't think you should base your life decisions on the possibility of inconveniencing your sister.'

'I do.'

Despite her pathological aversion to baking, Mum was a decent cook.

A tad reliant on ready-made sauces, but the woman worked full-time, ran my school's aftercare centre, drove me to and from my 10,000 extracurricular activities and cleaned our house. If she needed to throw a jar of Dolmio on some penne and call it arrabbiata, more power to her.

Dinner in the Silver household was a mix of European and traditional Ashkenazi dishes, with some generic Australian fare like overcooked roasts, nationally ambiguous canned curries and burgers with pommes noisettes thrown in. I loved pommes noisettes. Liora and I always begged Mum to make them.

We also ate Middle Eastern food, but most of it came from the shops or a few of Dad's Lebanese clients who were horrified his Polish wife didn't make falafel and kibbeh from scratch.

It took Mum a while to accept my vegetarianism, declared at age fifteen, which she and Nanna took as a personal affront. When I told Nanna, she threw me a look that said, 'Bitch, I stole meat to survive the Holocaust, eat the fucking cow,' and pretended she didn't know I meant no lamb and chicken, too.

Mum did cook lots of good vegetarian food for me, especially her veggie lasagne, which Liora says I'm remembering through rose-tinted tastebuds.

'It was good, but maybe not the three-Michelin-star extravaganza you've canonised it into.'

Either way, I'd sell my left boob to eat it again, but neither of us thought to record the recipe.

I found frozen pommes noisettes at the supermarket.

They're still a thing, apparently.

I'm making them for the squids when they sleep over tomorrow so Liora and Sean can have a night to themselves. It means a lot that they're entrusting me with them again.

'You're gonna cook?' Liora asked, incredulously.

'I'm buying frozen food and putting it in the oven. So, no.'

'Does Andy have a partner?' I ask Shirley when I call to invite her for Shabbat.

'No. Well, I don't know for certain. He's pretty cagey about these things. He was married, he moved to Melbourne for her, but it didn't work out.'

'And he stayed in Melbourne anyway?'

'He loves his job. He says he'll come back one day.'

'No grandchildren?'

'No. I do hope one day, he'd be a wonderful father. But I don't push, it's his life.'

'That's good of you. Whenever I talk to some of my relatives, all they want to know is when I'm going to get married and spawn young.'

'Ha! Spawn.'

'"A career isn't everything, Yael," they say. "Don't end up like Great-Aunt Rose."'

I'm never going to end up like Great-Aunt Rose. She was clearly a raging lesbian and I'm frustratingly heterosexual.

I do want spawn though.

For her last birthday, Liora asked for a DNA test.

When she sent the kit off we hypothesised about exotic countries, illicit affairs and ties to royalty to spice up the little we knew about our Polish-Russian-Jewish lineage.

Then I had a nervous breakdown and we both forgot about it.

When she called me this morning, it had been over seven months since she swabbed some saliva and sent it off for science.

'Are you sitting down?'

'I'm lying down.'

'Baths?'

'Couch.'

'I got the DNA test results back.'

'Oooh. Are we a quarter Mongolian?'

'Nope.'

'A sixteenth Tanzanian?'

'Afraid not. It's extremely boring.'

'What does it say?'

She attempts suspenseful noises. I don't know why, she knows she's bad at sound effects.

'Just tell me!'

'We're 99.6 per cent Ashkenazi Jews.'

'Oh god.'

'Yep.'

'What about the other 0.4 per cent? Or 0.04 per cent? Ugh. Fuck this breakdown brain.'

'Your inability to do maths predates your breakdown.'

'True. But what about whatever tiny percentage is left?'

'It says inconclusive, but possibly Central Asian.'

'So we're not definitely *not* Mongolian?'

'I mean, we can't rule it out entirely.'

'We'd be fools.'

'Good talk.'

'Bye.'

'Ugh, yucky!' Hannah says, spitting the contents of her mouth on her dinner plate. 'I don't like them.'

'I don't like them either,' Lexi says.

'They're not very good, Yaya,' Ethan opines.

Turns out pommes noisettes are rubbish. They taste like cardboard and disappointment.

So, the '80s lied to us, but it's so good to have the squids here again.

Julia Louis-Dreyfus does not share my sentiments. She's hiding in her anxiety nook, a corner of my wardrobe with a blanket on the floor where she hides from thunder, cleaners and five-year-olds.

'It's okay, guys, you don't have to eat them,' I say. 'I'm sorry, they're not like I remember. Just eat your schnitzel and cucumber.'

'Can we play the shoe game after dinner?' Lexi asks.

The shoe game is a memory card game where you find matching pairs of iconic shoes from fashion greats like

Christian Louboutin and Robert Clergerie. The squids gave it to me for my birthday one year and it's tradition to play it whenever they're here.

'I already got it out.'

'Yay!' shout the girls.

'Is there dessert?' Ethan asks, unmoved by news of the footwear-centric game.

'Is there always dessert at my apartment?' I ask.

He makes one of my favourite faces, his thinking face.

'Yes.'

'What is it? What is it?' Hannah asks.

'Brussels sprouts!'

'Yuck!'

Hannah.

'Noooooooooo!'

Lexi.

'Der, she's obviously lying.'

The big ten-year-old.

'Don't der your sisters, der brain,' I say to Ethan. 'And it's chocolate cake from the bakery up the road.'

Another round of yay.

'But you have to finish all schnitzel and cucumber first.'

I watch them eat: Ethan and Lexi with their clumsy grasps of cutlery, and Hannah just shovelling pieces of schnitzel into her mouth, tomato sauce covering her chin and hands. Occasionally someone stops for a sip of water or to tell me breaking news.

'Jess's mum let her get her ears pierced,' announces a jealous Lexi, who has been begging for holes in her lobes since birth.

'I scored two goals at soccer yesterday,' Ethan states proudly.

'I found my fingernail!' Hannah says, food in her mouth, raising more questions than answers.

We play the shoe game and Hannah emerges victorious two out of three times, causing minor sulking and less minor accusations of cheating.

'She's too young to win twice,' claims Ethan, and we all have a talk about being gracious losers and kind winners.

Squid oral hygiene time is always a treat, the three at their most congenial, chattering away with mouths full of toothpaste, so much little people's business too important to wait for later. Then spit and rinse, spit and rinse, spit and rinse and they return to light combat.

'Who's sleeping in my bed tonight?' I ask.

'Me!'

Lexi.

'Me!'

Hannah.

'Not me, I'm too big now!'

Ethan, breaking my heart into eighty-three pieces, a new development since last sleepover.

Hannah and Lexi both fall asleep in my bed during a few Dr Seuss books, and I take Ethan to the spare room and tuck him into bed.

'Thanks for having us, Aunty,' he says, his almost British tendency for over-politeness a trait observed since preschool.

'You're welcome, munchkin. This is always your home too. Goodnight.'

I grab bedding and turn off the light, setting up a couch bed and washing the dishes in lemongrass-scented detergent and complicated tears.

*

I never asked him to leave her.

I told him he should, for her sake, not for me.

He kept saying he was going to.

'It's practically over,' he'd say. 'I just need to get some things in order.'

I never believed him, but I do think he believed himself. At least in that moment.

I'd tell him it was over and date other men, trying to move on. But he always hooked me back in.

I loved him, despite myself. Despite himself.

But I knew I could never trust him.

I'm not even sure it was just me and her.

Shirley has invited me to dinner with her and Andy at Una's, which is apparently Andy's favourite Sydney restaurant.

I'm not mad about it.

Mum and Dad loved Una's. Liora and Sean love Una's. Ethan, Lexi and Hannah love Una's. Most people love Una's.

What's not to love?

Schnitzels the size of the Austro-Hungarian empire, beers the size of very big beers, goulash to bring any Hungarian to tears. Sure, there's, like, three vegetarian things on the menu, but one of them is apfelstrudel, and I love eating and saying apfelstrudel. It's like stepping into 1940s Germany, which doesn't sound very appealing now that I think about it.

The dinner isn't for a few weeks, but my life is so small right now that I'm already thinking about what to wear to meet my much older new friend's adult son.

This isn't something that's covered in the fashion etiquette books.

Ooh, maybe I should wear the blackout dress and sandals?

Una's is super casual, so I don't want to wear anything too formal, but having worn little but activewear and swimmers for what feels like a lifetime, the thought of putting on nice clothes gives me a hit of sartorial dopamine.

The thought of doing my hair and putting on makeup, however, is terrifying. Do I even remember how?

I go to the bathroom and look at myself in the mirror.

Like, *really* look at myself.

My skin is radiant thanks to going for so long without makeup, but oh god my eyebrows. My many, many eyebrows, but somehow also just one eyebrow.

I call Liora.

'Why didn't you tell me about my eyebrows?'

'I assumed you knew.'

'I didn't.'

'Have you not looked in a mirror since January?'

'Not properly.'

'Okay, well, you should get your eyebrows done.'

'Thanks.'

One of Liora's friends had Mum's veggie lasagne recipe.

Liora remembered her asking Mum for it, and she's going to make it for Shirley's Shabbat.

I'm actually excited about food.

I don't think Dad ever knew who I was in his last months, but I could tell he sensed that he was supposed to know me, and so he feigned familiarity, a consummate gentleman to the end.

I still struggle to reconcile the thought that no matter how much time I spent by his side at the end, nor how many times I told him I loved him, he never saw or heard me. Our relationship had been so strained for so long, and I wanted so badly for him to know how sorry I was for my part in that and how much it hurt that we'd never get to repair it.

People often said 'he knew', as if his subconscious, his id, could comprehend my love, my guilt and regret, on a level somehow beyond the reach of the Lewy bodies that ate his brain. Some said it lackadaisically, consoling without conviction, others actually believed it. And sometimes I believed it too.

But I don't know if he did 'know'.

What comforts me is that between him going into hospital with pneumonia and coming out dead, he was in a happy – or at least calm – place for the majority of the time.

Watching someone you love suffer physically is excruciating; watching someone you love lose their mind, their inhibitions, their intellect, their very self, is worse.

This can take myriad forms, and while the cancer in Mum's brain externalised in an exigent, exhausting mania, and Nanna's dementia was a time machine of terror, at least Dad occasionally seemed to be having a good time.

'I went for a walk with Danny Rose this morning,' he told me one afternoon.

Danny Rose had been dead for a decade.

'I'm taking Sara on a Mediterranean cruise.'

Safe travels!

He never had to pretend to know Mum. He never forgot her. She was his world, his everything, his number one shayna maidel. He also thought every female nurse was her. He'd tell them he loved them and that they were beautiful and they'd tell him they loved him back. Those wonderful, patient, tender-hearted women.

We'd smile and nod and humour his delusions, sometimes able to pinpoint their stimulus, other times none the wiser. When he spoke of boats, we'd look to the painting of a ship hanging opposite his bed. When he mentioned penguins, we realised I'd been wearing a jumper with a small penguin on it days earlier.

One thing we couldn't explain, however, was a recurring fixation with helicopters.

'And then I was on a helicopter …'

'Did you see the helicopter?'

'We're going to take a helicopter …'

We chalked it up to randomness and went back to our magazines, until one day, very close to the end, as Liora and I were trying to feed him – all thirty-five kilos that was left of him – the window started rattling and a super loud engine noise threatened to deafen us all.

'What the fuck?'

Then, like a scene in a movie, we watched a real-life helicopter ascend past the window and take to the sky.

'My helicopter!' Dad beamed.

Turned out the hospital helipad had been right by his window the whole time.

Still, his few moments of something resembling lucidity, when he somewhat understood where he was and what was happening, were abject torture.

*

We're having morning tea on Shirley's back deck, overlooking her garden. She's made scones because I told her that Mum loved Devonshire tea.

Mum would also have loved Shirley's garden, especially the African violets, of which she was particularly fond. She contemplated divorce when Dad, who was colourblind, pulled out all her African violets thinking they were weeds.

'Is there much mental illness in your family history?' Shirley asks.

'Yeah, on both sides, the little we know at least. Dad had an uncle with bipolar and agoraphobia, who was basically a shut-in from his early twenties. Nanna had a lot of mental health issues, and I think Dad might have had depression. But it's hard to know, because we don't know when the dementia set in.'

My eyes start to fill as a lone sparrow flits about the garden.

'The dementia possibly explains a lot,' I continue. 'Like, that's why he lost his business and couldn't hold down a job. Every time he got a new one, he'd be so excited, and then it would go bad and he was so sad and confused.'

Shirley passes me a napkin.

'Let's talk about something else.'

'I'm fine.'

Shirley's brewing proper leaf tea in an ornate teapot with matching teacups and saucers, and the scones sit on matching plates. It's classic waspy elegance, like the rest of her house. Like Shirley. Good quality, but not showy or gauche.

As she pours the tea, her hands shake and some tea spills onto the saucer and tablecloth.

'Oh gosh, I'm so clumsy.'

'Don't worry.' I grab more napkins and soak up the spill. 'You didn't get any on the scones.'

I pour the tea in my saucer onto the ground and use the tiny silver tongs to put a sugar cube into my tea just so I can use the tiny silver tongs. It's deeply satisfying. Then I apply jam and cream to both halves of a scone.

Jam first, of course. I'm not a monster.

'Yum. These are delicious.'

I made scones once with a friend. We called them Ron Swanscones, which is not a reference Shirley would get.

'I'm glad you like them.'

The sparrow inches closer towards us, becoming more brazen.

'Such a beautiful set.' I motion to the teapot and various accoutrements.

'It was my mother's.'

'Are there any mental health issues in your family?'

'Not my immediate family, but my mother's cousin went to an asylum in the fifties or sixties, I can't recall exactly. It was a huge scandal. They said she had hysteria, but my mother suspected she was trying to leave her husband and he had her committed.'

'God, men are trash.'

She laughs.

Mia Sparrow gets a fright and seeks refuge behind a pot.

'Do you think you were born with the depression?' Shirley asks.

'I think so? I have vivid memories as a kid of feeling what I now call existential angst, like all the pain and fear in the whole world was suddenly inside me. Are normal kids existential?'

'Did you tell your parents?'

Shirley throws scone crumbs to our flying friend.

'No,' I say. 'Something told me to keep it to myself and it's not like it was happening every day.'

'I imagine you wouldn't have had the words to describe it so young.'

She looks at her watch.

'Forgive me, Yael, I must start cleaning up. I completely forgot I have a meeting this afternoon.'

'Oh, no problem,' I say.

'I'm very sorry, it's unlike me to forget.'

She's flustered.

'I'm totally fine,' I say. 'I told Liora I'd meet her and the squids at the park soon anyway.'

'Take scones for your family,' she says.

'Thanks, I'm sure they'd love that.'

Nanna was only diagnosed with bipolar a few years before she died, but it explained so much. She was never formally diagnosed with PTSD and it's impossible to know what was because of the war and what was genetic or inherent.

She had her first breakdown as a child, and several more spanning three countries, but I have few details about them. I only know the little she said in her oral history testimony with the Sydney Jewish Museum, because the topic was off limits growing up.

I'm desperate to know more. I want to know how the breakdowns manifested, what the catalysts were and how she was treated. I want to know how Zeida handled it all, if he was supportive, and if Mum was. I keep imagining how scared Nanna must have been, how ashamed. The oral history mentions a stay in a psych hospital in Sydney, but why was she there? And what did they do to her?

I'm so aware of how good I have it. Like, I'm sick, but I'm sick in the now, and when I broke I already had a good psychiatrist and the means to stop working temporarily to recover. It's a far cry from being a Jewish child in World War Two Poland or a poor migrant woman in mid-twentieth-century Australia.

I want to know if she ever contemplated suicide or attempted it.

I feel like I *need* to know.

But I never will.

The energy at Casa Squid is pure chaos.

Shirley's coming to Shabbat dinner and Liora's making Mum's veggie lasagne and doing an almost believable impersonation of a woman happy to be cooking for her damaged younger sister's new old friend.

Sean is setting the table, I'm making a salad and the children are watching *The Little Mermaid* and butchering 'Under the Sea' for the seventy-eighth time.

'I'm Dory.' Hannah runs into the kitchen making a fish face and pretending to swim.

'Hola, Dory.' I make a fish face back at her.

'Wrong movie, dum dum,' Ethan yells from the couch.

'Don't call your sister dum dum, dum dum,' Sean says.

'Sean!' Liora snaps.

'SHOOSH!' Lexi shouts. 'I CAN'T HEAR THE MOVIE!'

'Oh fuck, I left the challahs in the car,' I say.

'Language!' Liora snaps again.

'What challahs did you get?' Sean asks.

He's really asking if I got the challahs with the sesame seeds on top from Grandma Moses Bakery, his favourite.

'You'll just have to wait and see,' I say, grabbing my keys and heading outside to fetch the Grandma Moses sesame seed challahs sitting in my car.

Almost as soon as I return, the doorbell heralds Shirley's arrival and Ethan runs to the front door screaming 'I'LL GET IT!' at the top of his lungs.

I follow behind him.

'Who are you?' Ethan demands, opening the door.

'I'm Shirley. I'm a friend of Yael's.'

'Who's Yael?'

Shirley looks puzzled.

'She means me, munchkin,' I say as I reach the door. 'Sorry, Shirley. The kids call me Yaya.'

'Mum, a Shirley lady is here!'

Ethan runs back to the television.

I lead Shirley into the living room and introduce her to Sean and the squids.

'And this is Pumpkin and Kumera,' Ethan says, pointing to the two ginger balls curled around each other on the couch.

'Nice to meet you, Pumpkin and Kumera. Both excellent vegetables.'

Shirley has come laden with gifts. Flowers and wine for the grown-ups, pre-approved chocolates and lollies for the kids.

'Can we eat them now?' Lexi asks. A chorus of 'please' follows from all three.

'Hi, Shirley,' Liora says, coming into view.

And to the squids: 'You can have sweets tomorrow if you're good. Aunty Yaya brought ice cream for dessert. But first, you have to eat all your dinner.'

The last bit is just for Lexi, a sugar fiend in kids clothing and the world's most painful eater. She refuses to eat all but five foods, all either white or yellow in colour. Two food therapists have said she'll grow out of it. We live in hope.

'Can I get you a drink, Shirley?' Sean asks. 'Wine? Sparkling water?'

'I'll have a wine if others are having some, but otherwise tap water is fine. You have a lovely home.'

'We like it,' he says. 'I'll have a beer so you're not drinking alone.'

'Such a giver.' Liora turns off the television and threatens to withhold the aforementioned ice cream when the squids whinge. 'Alright, Shabbat time.'

'Have you ever been to a Shabbat?' Sean asks Shirley as he guides her to the table.

'I have a very long time ago. My husband and I were very close to a Jewish couple and we joined them for Shabbat on many occasions.'

We all stand while the candles are lit, the wine drunk and the challah blessed. Then it's dinner time.

Sean gestures to Shirley. 'Please, have a seat.'

Liora places the veggie lasagne on the table beside a bowl of plain pasta and cheese and starts slicing pieces.

'Who's having Grandma Sara's lasagne?'

'Me!' Ethan shouts.

'Not me,' Lexi says, shocking nobody.

'Not me!' Hannah parrots.

'But you love lasagne,' Liora says to her youngest.

'I want what Lexi's having.'

It's weird to see history repeating itself in your sister's dining room.

'Okay, but you both have to have cucumber.'

Thankfully they love cucumber. Weirdos.

Liora hands Shirley the first serving of lasagne.

'Thank you, it looks lovely. It's your mother's recipe?'

'It is,' Liora says. 'A friend of mine found it in one of her cookbooks recently. Yael and I stupidly never wrote it down and it was probably her best dish. She started making it when the tree hugger went vegetarian.'

Liora looks at me pointedly.

'Well, I'm honoured to try it. And to see you all have it after so long.'

'What's a tree hugger?' Lexi asks.

'Der, it's someone who hugs trees,' Ethan says.

'Don't "der" your sister,' Liora chides. 'Lexi, a tree hugger is somebody who cares about animals and the environment.'

'Doesn't everybody care about animals and the environment?' she counters.

'Unfortunately not,' I respond.

'That's sad.'

'Very.'

'Okay, indoctrination over,' Sean declares. 'Shirley, Yael tells me your son works in this field?'

'Oh yes, he's an academic. Actually, I don't think I know what it is you do, Sean.'

'I run sports programs for kids. I don't have enough children ignoring me at home.'

'Oh, that must be fun. Better than being stuck in an office all day, I imagine.'

'Depends who you're asking,' Liora says.

Liora would rather do her taxes daily than ever touch a ball.

Shirley laughs.

'Actually,' Liora says. 'Sean has some news.'

'Ooh, I love news.'

'Go on,' Liora says to Sean, a twinkle in her eye. 'Tell her.'

'Well,' he says, 'I bought the business!'

'*We* bought the business,' Liora says.

'Sorry,' he says. 'We bought the business.'

'Wait,' I say. 'What business?'

'My boss's business.'

'Oh wow,' I say. 'I didn't realise that was an option.'

'Nor did we until last week. But it's done now.'

'That's awesome,' I say. 'Mazel tov!'

'Thanks. Maybe you should come work for me.'

'I think we can all agree that's a terrible idea,' I say.

'I'll second that,' Liora says.

'You might be surprised, but I played on the girls soccer team at my high school,' Shirley says. 'But there were only three teams in the league, because it wasn't proper for ladies back then.'

'I play soccer and I'm a lady!' Hannah says.

'You're not a lady, you're a girl,' Lexi snaps.

'I am so and I scored a goal last week.'

'How wonderful,' Shirley says. 'You must be very talented.'

'I am!'

Laughter.

'I play soccer too,' Ethan jumps in.

'I bet you taught your sister everything she knows,' Shirley says.

'Dad taught her too,' he says, suddenly humble.

My first bite of lasagne is visceral. With one mouthful, I'm transported back in time. I don't think it's exactly what Mum's used to taste like – Liora's a far better cook – but it doesn't matter. It's a hug with cheese.

'It's so good to taste it again,' I say to Liora. 'Thank you so much.'

'It's delicious,' Shirley says. 'And it's good to see you eating proper food.'

'I'll second that,' Liora concurs.

The kids tire of eating and ask to be excused because 'adults are BO-RING'.

'It must be lovely watching siblings bond and grow,' Shirley says.

'Some days,' Liora says.

'Odds are only two will make it out alive, though.'

'Yael!'

'What? I don't make the rules.'

'I've missed this Yael,' Sean grins. 'Welcome back.'

It's weird to think that if Mum and Dad hadn't died prematurely, I probably wouldn't be close to Liora's kids, because in this alternate, parent-filled reality, I definitely wouldn't be close to Liora.

Liora was determined for Mum to meet a grandchild, so she and Sean tried hard to get pregnant in that last year. I think it was her way of coping as much as it was her wanting to bring some joy into our lives.

Ethan was born three months before Mum died. The poor kid might as well have been born in a Bethlehem manger with the weight he had on his tiny shoulders.

He had come to save us.

Watching Mum and Ethan together in that final season of her life was heartbreaking, exquisite. She doted on him with whatever strength she had left, and he was always calm in her presence. In the very last days, we would lay him on or next to her and they would nap together. He wouldn't cry, she wouldn't whimper.

They knew.

I can't imagine how any of us would have got through that time without this tiny perfect boy.

Lexi and Hannah didn't arrive in quite such dramatic circumstances, but I can't imagine a world in which I'm just a distant birthdays-and-Jewish-holidays aunt.

These children are the reason I couldn't go through with the thing. Them and the thought of Julia Louis-Dreyfus eating my face.

Growing up, I spent an inordinate amount of time in the Centennial Park rose gardens. Every weekend for years, decades even, Nanna and Zeida would sit in portable fold-out chairs, at portable fold-out tables, playing rummy with half of Sydney's Polish-Jewish community. Mum would bring Liora and me here to see them and we'd climb trees, catch tadpoles and cause mischief with the other kids.

This whole park blooms with memories. It was here, I learned to ride a bike; here, I hid with friends in high school, smoking in the bushes; here, I fed ducks stale bread with the baby squids, before we knew not to feed ducks stale bread.

'I like your beanie.'

Shirley and I are sitting on a bench in the rose gardens, drinking hot chocolates from the silver food van opposite the duck pond. I'm all rugged up in a giant woollen coat, scarf and beanie. I love winter clothing. I can hide underneath it.

'Want to try it?' I say, taking it off.

'Oh no, I'm too old.'

'You can't be too old for head warmth. Try it.'

She takes the beanie from me and stretches it over her hair.

'I love this for you.'

'It is very cosy, isn't it?'

'I'm getting you one.'

'Don't get me a beanie. You're not working. Save your money.'

I consider giving her this one, but it has too much history.

He gave it to me for my birthday one year, remembering I'd said I liked it in a shop on one of our rare outings. I thought it was really sweet until I learned he'd given her the matching scarf.

I kept it anyway. Fuck him.

'Andy's taking me up to Seal Rocks when he visits.'

'Oh nice. I've never been to Seal Rocks.'

'It's a lovely place. We went almost every year when he was growing up. My uncle had a beach house there. It's long gone, as is my uncle, so Andy's booked one of those air houses for us.'

'Ooh, what's an air house?'

'The ones you book on the internet. There's a website with houses all over the world.'

'Oh, Airbnb!'

'That's it.'

'Anyway, I have to have surgery,' she mentions ever so casually. 'Then he's taking me to Seal Rocks to recuperate.'

'What kind of surgery?'

'Oh, it's minor. Nothing to worry about.'

Hmm.

'It sounds like something to worry about.'

The word 'surgery' doesn't exactly inspire serenity.

'Is it about the migraines?'

'It's about being an old woman. You just think about your own health.'

'Okay. But if you're lying to me, I'm never taking you to Costco again.'

'Understood.'

A call.

Liora.

'There's a Jewish speed-dating event at the Sheaf next month.'

Ugh.

'And?'

'And there's a Jewish speed-dating event at the Sheaf next month.'

'I'm an emotional mess, I don't date, and I hate the Sheaf.'

And if there's one thing straight men love, it's emotions.

'But you're doing well,' she says.

'No, thank you.'

I'd rather forgo a limb.

'What if your dream man is there?' she persists.

'My dream man is a silent benefactor.'

'He could totally be there.'

Two limbs.

'Hard pass.'

'Coward.'

'Goodnight.'

SEPTEMBER

Eighteen months after Mum died, I left the red-brick house I'd called home – my halfway house, the grief hotel, et cetera – and pitched my wagon a few suburbs over at Liora and Sean's two-bedroom, one-bathroom apartment, which already housed a couple, a baby and two cats.

It was crowded, but our mother hadn't died there.

If you'd told me in the early 2000s I'd be living happily with Liora before the decade was out, I would have laughed in your face. Then I would have apologised for laughing in your face.

We stuck a proper mattress on a sofa bed in the doorless sunroom and called it my bedroom for a year. I had no idea I'd stay as long as I did.

I had many feelings about leaving Liora and Sean's. I was sad to leave my family, particularly a certain adorable toddler, and pretty damn scared, but I was also excited, and ready. I was working full-time in my first grown-up job and finally able to afford my own place. I couldn't fourth-wheel forever.

It was time to put down roots, to sleep in my own bed, in my own place, surrounded by my own stuff – okay, largely Mum's, Dad's and Nanna's stuff.

'Please tell me you're not keeping that.' Liora pointed at Dad's recliner chair.

We were marking items in our storage cage bound for my new home.

The chair was a truly hideous grey-and-brown striped velour abomination. But it was his.

'I'm afraid I can't do that.'

'Ya-elllll, it's so ugly. I've always hated it.'

'Lucky it's not going to your house then.'

None of my lipstick shades suit me anymore. Either breakdowns alter skin pigment or the colours never suited me in the first place.

I'm in the car on the way to dinner with Shirley and Andy. I'm pretty anxious, and not just because of lipstick.

I wonder what she's told him about me. Does he know how old I am? Does he know I'm sick? Is he wondering why the hell I'm spending so much time with a woman twice my age?

Oh god, does he think I'm trying to scam her?

Panic starts percolating in my belly and I dig around in my bag for Valium. I cannot show up in a state. I desperately want to cancel, but I don't want to let Shirley down or give Andy reason to doubt my character. I locate the sweet, sweet pills, wash one down and put on a guided relaxation podcast.

I find a parking spot in Darlinghurst suspiciously quickly. A free, untimed parking spot in Darlinghurst. It's such an impossible feat that I check the sign eleven times to make sure I'm reading it right.

As I walk up to Una's, I start to regret my outfit. After seven hundred changes, I settled on the dress and sandals I don't remember buying, but now I feel too bougie. Andy's an academic. An environmental academic. I should have worn a hessian sack and Birkenstocks. At least the sandals are Simone Rocha. Irish neo-romantic fashion is healing.

Shirley and Andy are already seated when I arrive and I couldn't feel more awkward as I walk over to them.

'Hi,' I say, about thirty decibels too loud.

'Welcome,' Shirley says. 'Yael, this is Andy. Andy, Yael.'

He's a good-looking guy. Low-key handsome. Attainable hot.

'Great to meet you,' he says, making eye contact and holding out his hand. 'Mum's told me so much about you.'

He's definitely suss I'm a scammer.

'Likewise.' I shake his hand.

Does this outfit say 'I don't need to swindle old ladies for cash' or 'I've already swindled old ladies for cash'?

A waitress comes over and Shirley and Andy order booze. I really want wine but I've seen too much to mix alcohol with benzos.

'So, Mum tells me you're a writer.'

'Sadly, yes.'

'Why sadly?'

'Because my dreams of dancing backup for Madonna never eventuated. No, I love it. It's just increasingly hard to earn a living.'

I talk too much when I'm nervous.

'Ah, that's a song I know well.'

'Yeah, my academic friends aren't exactly swimming in riches. How fun is late-stage capitalism?'

He laughs and I see Shirley in him. It's nice.

The waitress brings their drinks.

'Cheers, everyone,' Shirley says, raising her glass.

'Cheers,' Andy says, clinking Shirley's wine and my water.

'L'chaim,' I say. 'It means "to life".'

'Lovely,' Shirley says, opening her menu.

'So, what do you write?' Andy asks me.

'Um, a bit of everything. Advertising, media, TV. Whatever needs writing.'

'I should confess I did google you.'

'As I did you. How long were you in police custody for?'

Shirley looks at him, aghast.

'Excuse me?'

Andy sips his beer.

'I'm kidding,' I assure Shirley. 'Just keeping everyone on their toes. Should we look at the menus?'

In 2004, Andy was arrested with several fellow environmental activists for chaining themselves to trees on privately held land.

Shut up, Yael.

I really did dream of dancing backup for Madonna.

And for Paula Abdul and Janet Jackson and Michael Jackson (that one hurts).

I was going to be a huge star, believing back then that backup dancers could be stars. My poor mother schlepped me around from rehearsal to rehearsal like I was a rich Southern lady in a racist movie.

Liora wasn't big on extracurriculars and around our late teens, she lost it because Mum spent so much time driving me to and from dance activities.

When my curfew was extended to 2 am in year eleven, she lost her mind.

'2 AM! ARE YOU SERIOUS?' she yelled at our mother. 'You never let me stay out that late in high school!'

'Liora, honey. You never wanted to.'

Sick burn, Mum.

Anyway, I loved dancing. I *love* dancing. I still dance.

Well, not right now. But in recent history.

Dance classes helped keep me going when Mum was sick. Once or twice a week I could block out everything that was going on and be happy for ninety consecutive minutes.

I really should go back.

As far as Ethan Joshua Blum, eighteen months old, was concerned, I was a constant; the third big human charged with his care. I played with him, fed him, put him to sleep. We'd go for walks together to the park, for coffee, and he had a permanent seat in my car.

We were bonded.

I was there for damn near every day of his little life.

And then suddenly, I wasn't.

At first, my absence seemed not to affect him at all and when I would see him, it was as if nothing had changed. His big brown eyes that so resemble my father's would light up when he saw me and our bond felt unbroken.

But the cracks soon emerged.

Like a fully grown heterosexual man, Ethan's ability to process and express his feelings was greatly lacking, so his abandonment response manifested physically. Whenever he'd see me, he'd hit me. Sometimes once, sometimes more. And hard.

It was awful.

They took him to a child psychologist who deemed it separation anxiety and I'd never felt more guilty about anything in my life. To know I'd caused pain to this tiny, perfect boy, who came into existence bearing the burden of our happiness, was devastating.

Also, my arms hurt from being hit repeatedly.

The therapist said it would fade with time and shouldn't affect his long-term mental health, and I believe we have The Wiggles to thank for that, at least in part.

It's my birthday.

Woo, et cetera.

I wanted to spend the day at the baths, but Liora insists on celebrating my existence so we're crammed into her beast, en route to an indoor trampoline park, which is what happens when you let three squids plan your birthday. I'd just as well skip the whole ordeal, but I've vowed to be a pillar of joy and pep for the squids.

'Have you heard from your friends? Or do they all think you're dead?'

'Interesting choice of words.'

'Too soon?'

'Never. And yup, had some messages.'

'Are you still off social media?'

'I check it occasionally, but have yet to actively participate. I may never go back.'

'You so will.'

'Aunty Yaya,' the middle squid says from behind me.

'Yup, Lex?'

'How old are you?'

'How old do you think I am?'

'Umm ... sixty?'

'Ooh, brutal,' Liora says.

'If I'm sixty and your mum is older than me, how old is she?'

'Umm ... eighty-seven?'

'One hundred and twelve!'

The youngest has joined the age auction.

'Very close,' I say. 'I'm thirty-four and your mum is thirty-seven.'

'How old is Daddy?' Ethan asks.

'One hundred and twelve.'

Liora doesn't correct me.

'Did Shirley message you?'

'She doesn't know it's my birthday.'

'Of course. Oh shit, how was dinner with her son?'

'Mum said "shit"!' Ethan says excitedly.

'Mum's naughty,' Lexi says.

'Yeah, you're naughty, Mummy,' Hannah chirps.

'Sorry, everyone. What's my punishment?'

'You have to participate in the trampolining,' I say.

'Yay!' all three squids shout.

'Not in a billion years.'

'But you're gonna make me do it, aren't you?'

'Happy birthday!' She grins at me.

For some unspoken reason, no matter the activity, Liora always gets to sit out and I'm the schmuck who feels beholden to participate.

'I hate you.'

'You love me more than life.'

'I literally just had a nervous breakdown. I love most things more than life.'

'What's a nervous bakedown?' Hannah asks.

Liora and I laugh.

'It's when you're scared of baking,' I say. 'But you try anyway.'

Miraculously, there are no further questions.

Liora pulls into the car park.

'We're here!'

Inside, I'm forced to purchase a $17 pair of regulation socks because it's the bouncy company's world and I'm just a visitor.

Once my feet are appropriately dressed, I follow the squids into battle.

Trampolining is intense.

Who knew jumping up and down could be a core workout *and* a fun way to fast-track your breasts' inevitable surrender to gravity? I really should have worn a sports bra.

I spend a good third of my trampoline time doubled over, yelling at the squids to go on without me like a wounded soldier. After my eleventh dizzy spell, I tell Ethan to look after his sisters and find Liora sitting near the snack bar, her core unworked, her boobs unshaken.

I know that dizziness is a potential side effect of my meds, but until today I hadn't exerted myself enough to experience that particular pharmaceutical quirk.

This doesn't happen in yoga.

'Where are my children?'

'They're fine. Ethan's keeping an eye on the girls.'

'Well, that's reassuring.'

'I've had a hundred dizzy spells. I'm done.'

She drops it. Another birthday miracle.

'So, what's Andy like?'

'He's nice. Smart. Very protective of Shirley – he was fussing over her a lot.'

'Is he hot? Single?'

I knew this would happen.

'Don't.'

'What?'

She knows exactly what.

'I'm simply enquiring as to the nice, smart man's marital status.'

'I'm not ready to date, he lives in another city and his mother is my friend.'

'And yet it would still be better than most of your relationships.'

I laugh.

'True.'

'But I'll be quiet.'

'I highly doubt that.'

'MUMMMMMMMMMMMMMMMMMMY!'

We turn around to see Hannah running over, trailed by her siblings. She throws herself at Liora and howls.

'What happened, chicken?' Liora asks.

'THEY' – sob – 'SAID' – sob – 'I'M' – sob – 'AN' – sob – 'ALIEN.'

Big sob.

'Oh, not this again.'

Ethan and Lexi both look guilty yet defiant, a difficult look to pull off.

'She was being annoying!' Lexi says.

'She wouldn't let us go to the basketball trampoline!' Ethan echoes.

'Arrest her!' I say.

'Not helping,' Liora says to me. Then to the defendants: 'What happened last time you convinced your sister she was an alien? Huh? What?'

'We got punished,' Ethan whispers.

'And what was your punishment?'

'Being Hannah's slaves for a day.'

'Harsh.' I'm genuinely impressed.

'If you two aren't on your best behaviour for the rest of Aunty Yaya's birthday, there'll be no cake and you'll work for Hannah tomorrow. Now say sorry.'

'Sorry, Mummy,' they say in unison.

'Not to me! To your little sister who loves and worships both of you.'

'Sorry, Hannah.'

'And?'

'And you're not really an alien.'

'That we know of.'

'ETHAN!'

Hannah starts crying again.

'So, birthday lady, where are we going for lunch?'

A series of texts.

Him.

Past tense.

I promise I'll make everything up to you.

He never made anything up to me.

I love you.
I never said it back.
Not once.

As a toddler, Ethan was obsessed with The Wiggles. I mean, really obsessed. A full-blown stan.

If he wasn't listening to or watching The Wiggles, he was talking about them or singing their disgustingly catchy tunes.

I became so used to all things Wiggles I'd go whole drives on my own, oblivious to a Wiggles record blasting through my car stereo. A sort of skivvy-based capture-bonding oblivion.

One time, a good friend was working on the children's show *Hi-5* and she invited me and Ethan to one of their live concerts. I can't remember if he'd ever seen *Hi-5* before, but I didn't think that would matter.

How wrong I was.

At his first ever concert, he broke the first rule of concerts: don't mention other bands.

My three-year-old nephew spent the whole show asking me when The Wiggles were coming on and screaming 'I WANT WIGGLES!' every time a song ended. It was like going to a Beatles concert and yelling out for The Rolling Stones.

I doubt the performers heard him, but the parents thought it was hilarious.

I can't wait to give him shit for it when he's older.

Lexi didn't care much for The Wiggles per se, but she did have a strong Dorothy the Dinosaur phase, which culminated in a Dorothy-themed fourth birthday party.

Unfortunately – mostly for me – the party took place in the middle of a forty-plus-degree heatwave; that is, the worst

223

possible time to have agreed/been bullied into putting on a giant dinosaur costume with zero ventilation and dancing around the house to surprise your niece.

It was so hot in that god-awful suit. Every few minutes I'd dance away into my sister's bedroom, take off the huge, airless dinosaur head and chug half a beer.

At one point, I was followed into the room by one of Ethan's little friends and his mum. I left the head on, not wanting to ruin the illusion for him.

'Would you mind doing me a favour?' she asked, as I sweltered to death inside the suit.

'Of course.'

'Zacky's scared and doesn't believe you're really Aunty Yael in a costume. Can you take the head off to show him?'

'Oh god, yes! I'm dying in here.' I removed the head. 'See, Zacky? It's me. It's Aunty Yael.'

Zacky looked like he'd seen a ghost and not a grown woman close to suffocating in a dinosaur costume. But he relaxed.

'Are you Dorothy all the time?' he asked quietly.

'I am. But it's a secret so you can't tell anyone. Ethan and Lexi don't even know. Can you promise me you won't tell anyone?'

'I promise.'

'Pinky swear?'

He curled his tiny pinky around mine.

'Pinky swear.'

For a while, whenever I saw Zacky, he'd assure me my secret was still safe with him.

I'm still waiting for my medal.

*

'You seem really present today,' Priya says. 'Much closer to your old self.'

'That's what Bill said.'

'Really?'

'Well, he said I should change my name to Stella, because my groove is back.'

'That sounds more like him.'

'You should keep him.'

'We'll see.'

Priya has outdone herself today. She's in a yellow midi dress with black and silver flowers. The woman loves a chic floral.

'Erdem?' I guess.

'Right as always.'

When I first started seeing her, she would always tell me that her clothes had been bought on sale, like we all tell our partners when we've splurged. I never believed her.

'Adidas,' I say, motioning to my sweatshirt as I take a seat. I have most certainly not outdone myself today.

She laughs.

'I'm so glad to see your playfulness coming back.'

'But not my dress sense.'

She feigns offence. 'Nothing wrong with Adidas. I have quite the collection.'

'The thought of you in streetwear just greatly sped up my recovery,' I say.

'Hey, I can be street. I can be street, to quote you, "as fuck".'

It just gets better.

'And,' she continues, 'you'll start dressing more like your old self when you feel more like your old self. No need to rush it. Though I do miss all your fabulous shoes.'

'Someone should.'

'So, how was your birthday?'

'Liora and I took the kids trampolining and we had lunch at a Jewish cafe in Double Bay my parents and grandparents loved.'

'Monty's?'

'Yup.'

'An institution.'

'Terrible coffee, excellent cakes. Mum was obsessed with their sour cherry pancakes.'

'I haven't tried those. I love the matzo ball soup.'

'Romy and I love people-watching and eavesdropping on old Jews there.'

'There are definitely some characters there. Tell me, I keep forgetting to ask, is the women's baths open again?'

'Yeah. I've been a couple of times.'

'How does it feel to be back?'

'It's really nice, even though it's not that warm yet. I just like being there. It feels like home.'

'I love that. What's the water temperature like?'

'I don't know. I haven't been in.'

She looks concerned. I mean, she has resting concerned face, generally. This is more puzzled, I guess.

'Why not? I thought you didn't mind swimming in the cooler weather.'

'I don't, I'm just a bit scared. The last time I went before it closed, it was really choppy and I got slammed against the rocks, and I seem to have regressed a bit.'

'I see.'

'I didn't realise it had spooked me until I went back and tried to go for a swim.'

'Is there anything else going on? Anything else scaring you?'

'Everything scares me!'

She laughs.

'But has anything happened that I don't know about?'

'Did you know Kourtney Kardashian dumped Scott Disick?'

'I don't know what those words mean.'

'That must be nice.'

'Okay, well, you've overcome your water fears before and I'm sure you will again. But let's talk about it more next session.'

'Okay.'

'Have you given any thought to what we talked about last time?'

'As in what to do when I'm well enough to be a contributing member of society again?'

'Yes.'

'Every day.'

I never got to the bottom of why Mum was so vehemently anti-therapy. I never got to the bottom of a lot of things about Mum. She was a deeply private person and there were a lot of unspoken no-go zones.

One time she alluded to therapists 'making you remember things you don't want to', which kind of answers my question while generating a thousand more.

'Happy birthday!' Romy says, handing me the rather large gift-wrapped box she arrived with.

We're eating grapes on a rock under the sun by the sea. It's not exactly balmy yet, but the sun's good for an hour or two of warmth on clear days.

'You didn't have to get me a gift!' I say. 'We never do gifts.'

'Shut up and open it.'

I carefully take off the wrapping.

'Oh wow, Rom, you didn't have to do this!' I say, admiring my fancy new blender.

'I know, I didn't. But now you can make your own smoothies.'

'Thanks so much, it's wonderful.'

She takes off her bandeau bikini top and lies on her side, facing me.

'So, what's this plan you alluded to the other day?' she asks. 'And why isn't it writing?'

'It's writing,' I say. 'At least, I think it's writing. What else would I even do?'

She sits up.

'What do I tell you every time you go off on a weird professional tangent?'

'That I'm a writer and I should just write.'

'Amen.'

She lies back down.

'Then again,' she says, 'you're different now. Maybe you're a painter.'

'I wish. I always wanted to be an artist.'

I reapply sunscreen everywhere, because I'm nothing if not sun smart.

'I'd hire you myself,' she says, 'but I like you too much to subject you to that infernal hellscape.'

'When are you going to quit? You'd easily get another job, a better one.'

'Just waiting for my moment.'

I take off my bikini top, now clad only in black high-waisted bikini bottoms and big, round '70s-style sunglasses.

'Hey,' Romy says, sitting up. 'When did this happen?'
She points at my bare chest.
'Um, just then?'
'What, for the first time?'
'Yup.'
'Oh my god, I can't believe I got to be here for this milestone.
What a moment. What a triumph.'
I laugh, but it is amazing how liberating it feels.
'Seriously though,' she says, 'you are different.'
'Different how,' I say, topless in public for the first time.
'It's everything – your expression, your posture, your
demeanour. You even talk differently. Slower, softer, but not in
a sad, monosyllabic way like you were at first.'
'That's probably the Valium.'
'How much are you taking?'
'Not a lot. Barely any, recently.'
It's impossible to convincingly deny a drug problem when
someone asks if you have a drug problem, even if you don't
have a drug problem.
'Well, that sounds mega suss, but I'm not one to talk.'
For the record, I don't have a drug problem.
'Am I being weird?'
'No, just different.'
'And people can tell?'
'Only people who knew you before this year.'
'Maybe they'd think I was high.'
'And what a crazy assumption that would be.'
'I haven't taken drugs in years!'
'Says the girl who almost overdosed.'

*

I couldn't bring myself to swim with Romy today.

I walked to the pool with her, determined to go in, but I couldn't do more than dangle my legs in and reconnect with the crabs.

I wish I could stop cock-blocking myself, but I'm still back at square one.

At least square one is a safe space.

A text.

To him.

Past tense.

I really hate you, you know.

I'm pretty hateable. I hate myself too, if it makes you feel any better.

It doesn't.

I'm in Centennial Park, waiting for Shirley on our usual bench, watching toddlers taunt ducks.

I'm studying *Vogue China* in the downright glorious spring sun and thanking my faulty mental health for getting me off social media and back onto fashion magazines, my first love.

I'm nose deep in editorial when a man's voice breaks my sartorial reverie.

'Hey, Yael.'

'Hi?' I look up, trying to block the glare to see properly.

'It's Andy, Shirley's son.'

What? Why?

'Oh, sorry. I was expecting your mum.'

Flustered, I close the mag and shuffle along the bench to make room for him.

'Yeah.' He doesn't sit down. 'She's got a migraine. I tried calling, but you didn't pick up.'

'Oh, I forgot my phone at home.'

He's still standing. It's unnerving.

'Thanks for coming,' I say. 'You didn't have to.'

'She was worried you'd think she ghosted you and I was worried she knew what ghosted meant.'

Is he ever going to sit down?

'Have you had a coffee?' he asks. 'I'm dying for one.'

'Let me get you one. You bought me dinner the other night.'

'All good. Do you want anything?'

'A hot chocolate?'

God, this is awkward. Does he hate me? He must hate me.

I watch him in the coffee line, my first chance to look at him properly without looking like a creep. He's dressed pretty well, understated but not without style. Dark jeans, vintage Adidas sweatshirt, excellent kicks.

He greets all the dogs in the vicinity, pats a geriatric golden retriever, then a beagle.

He looks over at me and I quickly look down at the magazine, not raising my gaze until he returns with the beverages and finally sits down.

Success.

'Thanks so much,' I say.

Awkward silence.

Weird half-smiles.

Someone say something.

'So, did you always want to be a writer?'

Oh, thank god.

'Um, no. At school I was good at writing, but I wanted to be an activist, work for the UN or Amnesty, because they were the only human rights organisations I knew. I kind of fell into writing.'

'Did you ever work for the UN?'

'Sadly, no.'

'There's still time. I hear they're hiring.'

Ha.

Now you ask him a question, idiot.

'Did you always want to be an academic?'

'Hell no. I did two years of law at uni and then realised I hate lawyers and money, so I switched to political science and environmental policy and here I am. I also had dreams of crusading, but it was Greenpeace and Sea Shepherd for me, the full greenie cliché.'

'Are we still saying greenie?' I ask.

'Probably not. I'm deeply uncool. Anyway, I fell in love with teaching and have never left university.'

'I've always wanted to go back to uni and study writing.'

'Why don't you?'

Yeah, why don't I?

'I don't know. I only just finished paying off my undergrad. It would be very me to go straight back into debt, though. I'm not bursting with financial literacy.'

'Me either. I'm an academic who just went through a divorce. And I like guitars.'

'Shoes are my guitars and I haven't worked since January, but I've never been through a divorce.'

'I wouldn't recommend it.'

We sip our drinks and watch a staffy seduce a dachschund.

'Would you ever move back to Sydney? Closer to your mum?'

'I do consider it. I know she'd love it but I really like my job and it would be hard to leave for something subpar. Is that awful?'

'I don't think it's awful. I think most people would struggle with that decision.'

He miscalculates a sip and coffee spills onto his jumper.

'Oh fuck, good one, Andy,' he says. 'Clearly I've never used a cup before.'

I laugh, grateful – shocked – that it wasn't me for once.

'Mum's seemed so much happier lately,' he says. 'Like since she met you. She used to be so full of life, but when Dad died she withdrew, stopped enjoying things. I can't tell you how nice it is to have her back, even briefly.'

'Why briefly?'

'Oh, just 'cause I don't live here.'

We sit in silence and premature overfamiliarity.

'I know it's probably super weird seeing your mum hanging out with some random chick half her age.'

'I'll admit, I've been wary since she told me about you.'

'As you should be. My sister's been wary of Shirley.'

'I feel like I have to say something threatening. So … um … if you hurt my mum, I'll come after you.'

'As you should.'

'I'd better get back and see if she's okay.'

Driving home, I think about our conversation.

I also think about Ozzy Osbourne, because my car still hates me.

I have always wanted to study writing, but would I be up to it?

I really feel like the breakdown changed my brain, made it slower, stupider. Priya says that's not how brains work, but what does she know?

I'd just hate to enrol in a degree I'm incapable of doing.

What would Liora do (WWLD)?

OCTOBER

I called Lifeline the other night.

I've never done that before.

A very kind and patient Scottish man named Mark listened to me ugly-cry and repeatedly told me, with remarkable conviction, that everything was going to be alright.

I didn't always fully understand what he was saying, but it didn't matter. Just the sound of his voice soothed me, wrapping around me like a velvety tartan blanket.

He should be a yoga teacher or host a bedtime story podcast. Maybe he is. Maybe he does. I don't know his life.

Mark.

Scottish Mark.

I cried and cried and every so often he'd ask me a question, not seeming to mind if I answered or not.

Except for one.

'Yael, do you think you're in danger right now?'

'I … I don't think so?'

I don't know why I called. I don't think I was feeling especially life-endy. And yet there I was, crying hysterically while a Scottish man asked if I was in danger. It was like someone else had dialled the number; like someone else was sobbing on the phone.

'Did something bad happen today, Yael?' Scottish Mark asked.

'No.'

'Have you felt like this before?'

'Yup.'

'I understand. What happened then?'

I chickened out.

'I took some pills but spat most of them out.'

'Are you thinking of taking pills again, Yael?'

Was I?

'No. I don't think so.'

'I'm glad to hear that.'

'I just wanna talk to her.'

Wait, who?

'Who is she, Yael?'

I was about to say 'Mum', but someone else spoke for me.

'Eva.'

I remember the exact moment I decided to do the thing.

I was at the park near my apartment, watching the dogs play. I'd go down most days, hoping they'd venture my way in search of pats.

It's impossible to be sad when patting a dog.

On this particular day, as I climbed the park hill back towards home, the sun was putting on a performance, lighting the sky all pink and orange. When I reached the top and turned around to catch the last of the sun show, a voice in my head made a suggestion.

It wasn't the first time the idea had been floated. It wasn't the second or even third. But all the other times, I'd immediately shrugged it off.

'Don't be an idiot,' I'd say to me and then forget about it.

But this time, something shifted.

This time, I thought it was a great idea.

'Is Eva a friend of yours?' Scottish Mark asked.

'Yes. She was. She died.'

Well, this came out of nowhere.

'I'm sorry to hear that.'

I sobbed harder.

'I'm sorry,' I stammered.

'What are you sorry for, Yael?'

I could listen to Scottish Mark gently say my name for hours.

'For wasting your time.'

'You're not wasting my time. This is precisely what I'm here for.'

'Thank you.'

'Is there something you'd like to say to Eva?'

I thought of Whoopi Goldberg in *Ghost* because I'm a terrible person.

'I just miss her.'

'I understand.'

'And I wish she hadn't done it. I should have checked in more, I should have known and I'm sorry.'

Julia Louis-Dreyfus walked into my room, clocked the state I was in and walked straight back out. I didn't blame her.

'I feel like I shouldn't be here if she's not.'

'Feeling guilty is natural when you've lost someone and when you've attempted to take your own life. You've got a double whammy there.'

'What do I win?'

We stayed on the phone a while longer, him trying to assuage my guilt, me shocked to learn I had any. Then I felt bad for tying up his phone line when other people might need it more and he tried to assuage my guilt about that.

Thank you, Scottish Mark. Excellent crisis counselling.

Would recommend.

Five stars.

At the end of *Clueless*, fashion icon Cher Horowitz is walking aimlessly around Beverly Hills in a cropped silver tank over a sheer white ruffle shirt with a monochrome, diamond-print mini, sheer white knee-high socks and silver Mary-Janes – an outfit I will never pull off. An outfit nobody but Alicia Silverstone will ever pull off.

Her internal monologue, told through voiceover, sees her grappling with why she's bugging (sic) about her friend dating her stepbrother.

As night falls, she suddenly stops.

'Oh my god,' she says to nobody, as neon lights flash and a fountain erupts behind her. 'I love Josh!'

It's kosher to date your stepbrother if your stepbrother is Paul Rudd.

This is how *I* think about that moment on the hill.

I am Cher Horowitz, minus the mini and knee-highs, walking around having thoughts and feelings, but clueless about what they actually mean.

Until one afternoon in a park painted neon by the sun.

'Oh my god,' I said to nobody.

There's a yoga school above the cafe near the baths where I get my smoothies. Somehow, I didn't realise this until I saw a group of women with yoga mats emerging from the side gate the other day.

This morning I woke up anxious and decided to try a hatha class there, only to find that Mei, one of my all-time favourite yoga teachers, was leading the class.

'Yael!' she said, when I crouched down in front of her to pay. 'What a lovely surprise. I didn't know you came here.'

'It's so nice to see you,' I said. 'This is my first time here – I've still been going to the Bondi place.'

'You're gonna love it – same practice, better view.'

She was right. The yoga room overlooks Coogee Beach, so you can look at the ocean while saluting the sun and doing all the standing postures. It may be the closest I've ever come to a spiritual experience. Namaste.

After class, I got a smoothie (of course) and came to the women's baths, where I've spent much of the day trying to will myself into the water. It didn't work, but I've been content enough lying in the sun, listening to an audiobook of *The Magic Faraway Tree*, one of my favourite books when I was a kid.

I'm slowly getting back into proper adult literature but I had an urge to check in with Moon-Face, Silky and, especially, the Saucepan Man, who may have had a hand in my sexual awakening. A small but deeply troubling hand.

As I'm packing up to leave, the leather couch lady appears before me, as fluoro as always. Susan, I think her name is. Or maybe Janet? Either way, I haven't seen her in months.

She takes headphones out of her ears and taps her phone.

'I finally got into podcasts,' she says, and though I'm genuinely happy for her, I have no idea why she's telling me this.

She can see my confusion.

'Remember? You told me about that bad-movie one you like. Must have been six months ago now, maybe more.'

'Oh yes,' I say. 'I'm sorry, my memory of this year is vague at best. That's great. Are you liking them?'

'Some yes, some not so much.'

'What are you listening to now?'

'That *Serial* one, about the high school girl that was killed in America.'

'Oh, that's so intense. I found it hard to listen to at times. But it's very well done.'

'Yes, I'm finding the same. That poor girl.'

I pick up my bag and get out my keys, ready to go home.

'You off then?' she asks, eyeing my spot.

'Yup, it's all yours.'

'Thanks, love.'

What a goldmine this place is.

As far as plans go, it was rubbish. By definition, it can't even be called a plan.

I had no idea what the random combination of pills would do to me nor how many I would need for the desired result. I was just gonna take as many as possible and hope for the best.*

*worst.

240

I'm not sure what I'm more embarrassed about – the terrible not-plan or the fact I didn't go through with it.

Eva and I met on Twitter.

Oi, smarty, she wrote, sliding into my DMs after months of tweeting jokes at each other. *Seems we're both sad orphans. Let's have a fucking drink.*

She was fifteen years older than me, a ridiculously beautiful, cashed-up, raging hot mess, and the most generous person I've ever met.

On our first friend date, she insisted on paying for dinner and brought along a nineteen-year-old she'd met that day at the gym because he'd just moved to Sydney and didn't know anybody.

That was Eva. I'd call her and she'd be driving her hairdresser to the airport or walking her neighbour's cousin's dog. During one of her episodes, she gave a hospital cleaner her favourite pair of sunglasses because he said he liked them.

She collected strays. We had that in common. We collected each other.

On our second friend date, I went to her fancy apartment and she threw multiple pairs of expensive shoes at me, insisting I keep them because we were the same size and she was drunk. I kept a pair of black patent Balenciaga stilettos because she wouldn't let me leave unless I agreed to take something. And also, because they're Balenciaga stilettos.

On our third friend date, we sat courtside at a basketball game between a Gangnam-style PSY impersonator and Irene from *Home and Away* because Eva was dating the coach. This isn't an example of her generosity, it's just very funny.

I didn't see Eva regularly, but we were always in contact. The last time we spoke we were both at Sydney Airport by total coincidence.

I was going to Vietnam and Thailand with friends when Eva suddenly popped into my head.

I'm on a plane about to go to Vietnam, I texted. *Can we dine when I'm back?*

She responded immediately.

I'm on a plane about to go to Bali! Get off yours and run across the tarmac onto mine. Let's pretend we're in a rom-com.

And she meant it.

Nah, I've done my one Australian citizen compulsory trip to Bali. You're gonna have to Eat Pray Love without me.

FINE. We'll hang when we're home.

A text.

8 am.

A number I don't recognise.

Hey, it's Andy. Mum has to go to an appointment this morning and can't meet you for a walk but wants to know if you're free to come for dinner instead?

It's a welcome cancellation. I don't feel like getting out of bed.

Thanks for letting me know. I hope everything's okay. I'd love to come for dinner but you guys have a lot going on and she doesn't have to cook for me.

The covers on my bed start to move and Julia Louis-Dreyfus's tiny head suddenly pokes out from beneath. She looks hungover.

Don't worry, she won't be cooking for you. I'll try my best not to poison you. Is there anything other than God's creatures you don't eat?

I hate people feeling obliged to do things for me. Or being forced to by their mothers.

You really don't have to do that.

I wish the cat could make me coffee.

She insists and therefore I must insist.

I guess I'm going to dinner.

Okay. May I underwhelm you both with my amateur baking?

Sounds good/average.

Any allergies for dessert purposes?

No. But I hate sultanas.

Extra sultanas it is!

On a stifling morning, soon after I'd returned from South-East Asia, I'd just got home from a spin class when Gen, Eva's best friend, called. I thought she wanted to talk about Eva's upcoming birthday.

'Hey lady,' I answered, grabbing a yoghurt from the fridge.

'Hi, Yael. I, I have some news.'

She didn't sound like herself.

'Okay?'

'It's Eva,' she said, her voice breaking.

Why the hell did I say I'd bake?

*

I didn't go to Eva's funeral. Her sisters kept it strictly to family and Eva's very closest friends. Fewer than ten people were there.

There was a memorial a few days later at a bougie pub in Surry Hills. I didn't want to go, predicting – correctly – the circle jerk of faux mourning it would no doubt be.

But I knew I had to.

I dressed for Eva: a leopard-print pencil skirt she'd convinced me I needed that I'd never worn because it was a leopard-print pencil skirt, the black blazer we both owned before we'd met, and the black Balenciaga stilettos she'd given me on our second friend date.

I got my hair blow-dried and my nails manicured and made a few hair and beauty professionals very uncomfortable in the process.

'So, what's the occasion?'

'My dead friend's memorial party.'

'...'

The memorial was horrible. At least, for me.

Others seemed to be having a great time. And Eva would have wanted that. The woman was hedonism on a stick figure. It just felt less like a celebration of her and more like a celebration, period.

There was performance-grieving, social-climbing and hashtags. At one point, a wannabe influencer asked if I'd mind taking a photo of her and some famous models. I said I'd mind a lot, actually.

I spent most of the evening with Gen and when I couldn't take the sycophancy any longer, I looked for Eva's sisters to say goodbye. I found them sitting at the bar, staring out at the sea of people who may or may not have actually ever spoken to their little sister.

'We're leaving soon, too.'

'Do you think it's okay if we do?'

'I think you can do whatever the fuck you want,' I said. 'You don't owe anyone here anything. Get out of here.'

'I have to pee first.'

'Me too!'

They stood and thrust a large rectangular shopping bag from Eva's favourite fancy shoe store at me.

'Can you hold Eva?'

'Huh?'

'Eva's ashes. We thought she should be here.'

I looked into the bag and, yup, there was an urn in there.

'Oh wow, of course.'

And so there I stood, in a bar full of D-list celebrities and tabloid flogs, holding my dead friend.

'Goodbye, legend,' I said into the bag. 'I love you.'

In a world of dessert-based pain, I call Margot, the best baker I know. She once got a standing ovation for a carrot cake at a dinner party.

'Hello, loverrrrr,' she answers.

'I'm having an emergency.'

There's no time for pleasantries.

'What's wrong?' she says. 'Where are you?'

'Oh sorry, it's not an emergency emergency.'

'Okay …'

'I need to bake a cake.'

'Seriously?' she says. 'You almost gave me a heart attack.'

I see how that could have worried her.

'Sorry, I've forgotten how to be a person.'

'Clearly. Why do you need to bake a cake?'
Because I'm an idiot.
'I volunteered to for some stupid reason.'
'Just buy one and say you made it.'
Who does she think I am? My mother?
'You know how I feel about lying.'
'I also know how you feel about baking.'
I laugh.
'For some reason I need to do this.'
'Okay then, how can I help?'
'What should I make? Something easy without sultanas.'
'You could do a lemon drizzle or there's this vegan chocolate cake that's better than any dairy chocolate cake. Oh, or the Russian honey cake from that *Monday Morning Cooking Club* cookbook you gave me.'
'I love it when you make the food of my people.'
'It's really good. And super easy.'
'Okay, I'll do that one.'
'Mazel tov!'
'That doesn't make sense.'
'I'll send you pics of the recipe.'
'My saviour – Dessert Jesus.'
'I thought your people didn't believe in Jesus.'
'We don't. Well, technically we believe he existed, just not that he was magic.'
'Ah.'
'I mean, I don't believe in any of it, but that's the generally accepted gist. Okay, I have to go fuck up a cake.'
'Godspeed.'

*

Eva was beautiful and clever and funny and amazing.

She was a huge vibe and everybody loved her.

But it didn't matter. It wasn't enough.

As I slumped on my kitchen floor, crying with Gen on the phone, I didn't hear the voice inside me start to whisper.

A year later, it had grown too loud to ignore and I almost did the thing on the first anniversary of Eva's suicide.

It felt poignant at the time.

Now I feel bad for almost stealing her spotlight.

She would have been so angry.

'What the FUCK, Yael? Get your own day.'

She could have also gone the other way.

'TWINSIES! What did you wear?'

I'd lie and say luxury. And her Balenciaga stilettos.

I have almost none of the ingredients needed for the cake because I haven't baked at home since Margot and I threw a dress-up viewing party for the *Gilmore Girls* reboot.

I refuse to be ashamed of that sentence.

I have six hours to go to the supermarket, bake an edible cake and get ready for dinner, which is not enough time.

First, I'll screw up some essential part of the recipe and have to start over again. Twice.

Then I'll try on all my clothes, hate everything and ugly-cry, before having to do my makeup in the car because I spent too long trying on all my clothes, hating everything and ugly-crying.

'Who cares what you wear?' says my brain. 'It's just Shirley.'

It's not though, is it, brain?

*

I was wearing leggings and a stained old hoodie.

No bra.

No makeup.

Dirty hair.

If I'd actually gone through with it, Eva would have killed me all over again.

By the power of Nigella, I appear to have successfully baked a cake.

As expected, I'm frantically contouring, highlighting and lash-curling at every red traffic light on the way to Shirley's. Gonna have to skip the eyeliner. I learned that lesson the smudged way.

My easy, breezy, just-threw-this-on outfit – a slip dress, oversized jumper, socks and sandals – belies the hours of turmoil that went into its creation, but I'm feeling good about it. Perhaps my anxiety about the cake has eclipsed all my other nerves.

Andy answers the door with pure chaos energy and I give thanks to sweet Beyoncé I'm carrying a cake so there's no awkward hug-slash-handshake situation.

'That looks amazing,' he says, 'What is it?'

'Just a sultana cake with extra sultanas.'

'Perfect.'

He takes it and leaves me in the living room while he deals with a 'minor culinary crisis'.

I've been to Shirley's a few times now, but I've never really looked around. Family photos on the mantel reveal Andy as an adorable dork of a teen and Peter as a solid ten. I make a mental note to congratulate Shirley, whose youthful beauty comes as no surprise.

'I really should have hidden those,' Andy says, joining me.

'You don't like people knowing about your *Lord of the Rings* phase?'

'Not especially. But at least she hasn't framed evidence of my cybergoth phase.'

'Ooh, where are those pics?'

'I think in a storage cage somewhere in Melbourne.'

'I'll show you my bat mitzvah photos.'

'As an ignorant gentile, I have no cultural reference point for that. You could have looked amazing for all I know.'

I touch a photo of Shirley and Peter on a boat.

'Your parents are such babes. And they look so in love.'

'I know. Disgusting, isn't it?'

'Sickening.'

Silence.

Don't do it. Don't do it. Don't—

'How old were you when your dad passed?'

Dammit.

'Twenty-nine. You were younger, right?'

'Yeah. But twenty-nine is still pretty young.'

'I guess so. I was more concerned about Mum. Classic male avoidance. But she loved him so much and I hated seeing her cry.'

'It should be illegal for parents to cry in front of their kids, at any age.'

'Ah, my two favourite people.'

I turn to see Shirley standing in the archway, smiling. She's pale. I think the migraines have taken a toll.

'Well, hello. I'm fawning over you and your insanely attractive husband. Had I known you back then, I would have made all manner of inappropriate propositions.'

'Wow.' Andy is still not yet accustomed to my mouth.

'I'm sure Peter would have been delighted,' Shirley says.

'You've totally corrupted my mother,' Andy says, playfully. I think.

'Sorry.'

Not sorry.

'Andy,' Shirley says, in a tone I imagine she used a lot when he was little. 'Have you not offered our guest a drink? Who raised you?'

'I honestly don't know anymore.'

Eva lived twice a life in half the time.

If I'm really going to live, I have to up my game.

'Your mother didn't tell me you cook so well,' I say to Andy, several bites into dinner.

He's made an entire Ottolenghi cookbook, no wonder he was stressed.

'That's because he never cooks for me,' Shirley says.

'I'd cook for you more if I lived here.'

'Exactly.'

'Well,' I say. 'Thank you for cooking for me.'

'I realised far too late that I was making Israeli food for a Jewish person and had no choice but to keep going.'

'Everything is delicious,' I say. 'This Jewish person is impressed.'

'Thank you.'

'Bevakasha – it's "you're welcome" in Hebrew.'

Why am I teaching them Hebrew now?

'So,' I say. 'Are you all packed for Seal Rocks?'

'Not even a little,' Shirley says.

'Are you going straight after the operation,' I ask, 'or do you have to stay in the hospital overnight?'

'The surgery's been postponed,' Andy says. 'But we're gonna go anyway, tomorrow morning.'

'Oh cool.'

After dinner, I offer to help wash up, but Andy won't let me.

'Go talk to Mum. I'll bring the cake out when I'm done.'

Shirley and I move to the living room. She's clearly fading. I won't stay long.

'I got you something.'

I retrieve a gift bag from my bag.

'No, you didn't.'

She takes the bag from me and pulls out the contents.

'Oh, you wicked child. I told you not to waste your money.'

'I didn't waste my money. I bought you a beanie.'

'Thank you, sweet girl.'

She puts it on.

'I love it,' she says.

'It suits you,' I say.

She leaves it on.

'Andy told me he tried to coerce you into studying again.'

'He did. Damn academics, they're worse than missionaries.'

'Well, I think it's a marvellous idea. I didn't get to go to university and it's one of my only grievances.'

'You could go now. We could be study buddies!'

'Oh no, that ship has well and truly sailed. You can study enough for the both of us.'

Andy appears with the cake.

'Sultana cake for everyone,' he announces. 'Wait, is my mother wearing a beanie?'

'I really think we should have turned left at that last intersection. None of this looks familiar.'

'It looks familiar to me and I was here more recently.'

It was Mum and Dad's yahrzeit yesterday, and Liora and I were driving around Death Town. Like *Thelma and Louise* but without the gun. Or Brad Pitt's abs.

Thelma and Jewise.

'Why don't we ever write the numbers down?' Liora asked, as one of us does every time we're there.

''Cause we thrive on chaos.'

'We should take photos of the section numbers when we find them.'

'We should.'

We didn't.

'Okay, I'm turning around. This section is ancient.'

I gave up and attended to our soundtrack, which was not easy considering that the Venn diagram of our musical appreciation has a crossover so slim it could walk a runway.

'Taylor Swift or Whitney Houston?' I asked.

'Both highly appropriate cemetery choices.'

'If you make me listen to the *Rent* soundtrack again, you'll be burying me here with the rest of them.'

'You love *Rent*!'

A huge stretch.

'I've never even seen it,' I said.

'Well, that's on you.'

As we passed a Chinese temple for the twenty-third time, I couldn't help but wonder if our loved ones' graves had been moved.

The Chinese sections there are beautiful, all gold and red with statues. The Russian sections are also a treat, ostentatious and aggressive, many with photos on the headstones.

'How was dinner at Shirley's, by the way?' Liora asked.

'It was nice. She wasn't feeling great – she gets bad headaches – so Andy cooked and I made a cake.'

'You made a cake?'

'I did.'

'With your hands?'

'Both of them.'

'And people ate it? And they're still alive?'

'Yup, and I believe so.'

'Wow.'

Meanwhile, Whitney was saving all her love for a loser who treats her like dirt.

We've all been there.

'Do you think Mum and Dad would be happy if they were alive?' I asked, while we drove around a cemetery looking for their graves. 'Like, if they hadn't got sick and they'd gotten out of debt and everything?'

'Sheesh, I don't know,' she said. 'That's an impossible question, really. Obviously, I'd like to think they'd be happy. That they'd be enjoying retirement and being grandparents. That they'd travel like they wanted.'

'Yeah, same.'

'But I try not to idealise because, realistically, they'd have problems. Because everyone does. And maybe they wouldn't be good grandparents. Or some big drama would happen and we'd be estranged. Or lots of things. All my friends complain about their parents and have fights with their parents.'

'Yeah, mine too,' I said. 'But at least they can.'

'I Wanna Dance with Somebody' picked an amazing time to start.

'Remember that we both fought with Dad constantly. His temper could have become even worse.'

'Or his worldview.'

'Both.'

Whitney wants to feel the heat with somebody.

'But we never fought with Mum,' I said.

She guffawed. You don't see people guffaw enough these days.

'Yael! You fought with her all the time.'

'No, I didn't. Maybe you did.'

'No, you did. All the time. About money and housework and your drinking and lots of things. We rarely fought. I didn't want to upset her 'cause she had enough on her plate with Dad and you.'

'Well, weren't you the perfect child?'

'Yes! I was. I had to be.'

'Why? Nobody made you do that.'

'She did. She leaned on me. It was totally unfair.'

'That was your choice. She didn't force you.'

Liora stopped the car. Oh no.

'Can I be brutally honest?' she asked.

'History has shown you can.'

'Don't joke! I'm trying to have a fight with you.'

'Sorry. You're a stupid bitch.'

She laughed despite herself.

'Look,' she said, facing me. 'I know how much you miss Mum. I do, too. But you have her on a pedestal so high you've forgotten that she wasn't perfect.'

'What's wrong with that?' I asked.

It was a genuine question.

'Nothing, in a way. But I think you believe that if Mum hadn't died, your life would be magically better, and it's just not true.'

'My life would definitely be better if Mum was alive.'

'In some ways yes, but you had depression long before she died and you'd still have it now even if she'd lived.'

Ouch.

'True, but what does this have to do with Shirley?'

'Whether you're conscious of it or not,' she said, 'you keep trying to replace Mum with these older maternal figures. And when they inevitably fail to live up to your expectations, I'm left to pick up the pieces.'

I stared down at my hands, trying not to cry.

'So the note was right,' I said, barely audible. 'I am a burden.'

I had to get out of the car.

'No, sorry,' she said, grabbing the steering wheel with both hands before swivelling to fully face me. 'I didn't mean it like that.'

Her voice was shaky.

'Yes, you did.'

Steeling myself, I took a deep breath and very calmly undid my seatbelt, got out of the car and closed the door behind me. Then I took off running across the Lawn of Remembrance. It was a bit dramatic but I committed.

Liora started the car and drove the perimeter of the military garden, cutting me off as I was about to cross into a different section of the cemetery.

She got out of the car.

I was doubled over, trying to catch my breath, but instead I threw up.

I was super unfit, having done zero cardio for almost a year, but at least I could finally cross 'cry-spewing in a cemetery' off my bucket list.

'Oh god, Yael, I'm so sorry,' Liora said, bending down next to me and pulling my hair back. 'I shouldn't have said all that. Not today.'

A few people walked by in funeral blacks and gave me pitying looks. I guess if you're going to cry so hard you vomit, a cemetery is a pretty choice location.

'I don't want to be this person,' I said, still crying. 'You shouldn't have to pick up my pieces forever because you promised Mum.'

'That's not—'

I cut her off. 'You have your own shit. And children to look after and Sean and a life to lead. And I just ruin everything.'

'You don't ruin everything. And you do look after yourself most of the time.'

'I keep trying to unburden you and you keep telling me not to, but deep down you clearly want me to.'

She took a deep, loud breath, in and out.

'Okay, yes. It's been a rough time and I could have done with one less thing to worry about. And yes, you make things hard sometimes. But you also make things fun and weird and interesting. And you help so much with the kids and they worship you and it would have destroyed them if you'd gone through with … It would have destroyed all of us.'

She cried. She never cries.

I leaned against her car.

'We can't lose you too,' she said.

She leaned next to me.

'I just miss her so much,' I said.

'I know you do.'

'When will it stop?'

'I don't know. Maybe never.'

More mourners passed us by and we exchanged mutual condolence nods.

'I don't want to take her off the pedestal,' I said.

'You don't have to.'

'I know she had faults, but I don't care. They were far outweighed by her good points.'

'They were.'

We stayed there for god knows how long, leaning against her car.

'I'm really sorry,' she said in a voice I'd never heard before. Maybe because I'm always the one apologising.

'You should be.'

She whacked my arm.

'Sour cherry pancakes?' she asked.

'Sure.'

As I walked around to the passenger side of the car, I saw it.

'Liora, look!'

We were parked right next to Mum and Dad.

*

'I called Lifeline the other night.'

I'm having coffee with Priya in her office.

Well, I'm having chai, but it's giving coffee vibes.

'Okay,' she says. 'What happened?'

'I just had a really bad day. It was Mum and Dad's yahrzeit – death anniversary – and Liora and I had a big fight and apparently I was subconsciously thinking about Eva, and I just needed to talk to somebody.'

Even though it's a rogue thirty-degree October day, Priya's wrapped in a thick woollen shawl like it's the middle of July. In Antarctica.

'You know you can always call my emergency number in these times,' she says. 'It's why I gave it to you.'

'I know, but I didn't want to bother you. I wasn't in danger, I don't think. I just needed someone to listen and aurally stroke my hair.'

I'm seriously schvitzing over here.

'And is that what happened?' she asks.

'Actually, yes. The Lifeline guy was really good. He mostly just listened to me cry. He didn't try to counsel me or anything.'

'I'm glad you called.'

I kind of feel like I cheated on her.

NOVEMBER

Some time after Dad died, we found a piece of paper in the bad house with ripped punched holes along the left side, from one of those spiral-bound notebooks with yellow covers that everyone used to have.

'My Dreams List' is scrawled across the top in Dad's unmistakable handwriting, which always takes at least two read-throughs to comprehend. I like to imagine he bribed some poor Egyptian primary school teacher for his pen licence.

It's basically a bucket-list-meets-letter-to-Santa of things he never got to do or have. We don't know if he wrote it before or after he was diagnosed, but either way it's fucking heartbreaking and I cry every time I think about it.

'In the criminal justice system ...'

Liora and I are bingeing *Law & Order: SVU* in my living room because we're trash and we'll always be trash. Also because Sean threatens divorce if we watch it at their house.

Julia Louis-Dreyfus, who was very nearly named Detective Olivia Benson, is curled in a ball between us on the couch, snoring. It's one of my favourite ever sounds and, upon the occasion of my death, my one request is that I be entombed in whatever vessel is handy with a recording of her snores playing on loop, forever.

'Do you think in the future, people are going to look back at us and think we were cruel to keep pets?' I ask. 'Or will they be too busy choking on carbon and burning alive to care?'

Liora pauses.

'Is that what it's like in your head all the time?' she asks.

'Yup.'

'No wonder you broke.'

Dun dun.

A text.

Andy.

A photo of what takes me a minute to work out is him, in full cybergoth mode.

OMG.

A few weeks before Mum died, Liora and I met with the hospital palliative care team. It was time to start end-of-life care but they were happy for us to keep her at home if we hired a hospital bed and private nurses. The team would check in daily with us by phone, the doctor would come to the house, and someone would be available at all hours to take our calls.

As we wandered around the hospital car park, neither of us having noted where we parked, I recalled the month or so immediately after Dad died. The constant visitors, the endless phone calls, the kitchen overflowing with food none of us felt like eating. I was grateful so many people cared about us and Dad, but I just wanted them all to leave.

On level 3B, I stopped in front of a silver Audi, my everything-deprived brain mistaking it for our Toyota. Liora kept walking, eventually noting my absence and turning around.

'You wish,' she said.

'Hey.'

'What?'

'I don't think I can do it again.'

'Do what?'

'Shiva.'

'Yael.' Stern voice. 'We have to do shiva. At least for one day.'

'No, I mean after that. Endless people and questions and pity. The pity will be so much worse this time.'

'I'm not sure how we can avoid it. People will want to pay their respects. We can't tell them not to come, Mum and Dad would be horrified.'

'I'll be horrified if we do.'

'You'll live.'

'At least someone will.'

'Okay, so I've been thinking about my future.'

I'm with Priya.

'Music to my ears,' she says.

She's wearing a puffer vest. Inside. In November.

'You need to get out more.'

'Hey, it's a big step. At the beginning of the year, you couldn't even contemplate the next day.'

'I love that the bar is now so low, thinking is an achievement.'

'Just take the win, woman,' she says. 'So tell me, where has all this thinking led you?'

Rarely anywhere good.

'A few places.'

'Do tell.'

'I love writing,' I say, 'and it's pretty much my only skill, so I'm not starting a new career or anything. I'll keep writing for dollars. But I'm gonna find a steady part-time job or line up some contract gigs, 'cause it's dismal out there.'

'Good plan.'

'Next thing, I'm going to get back into volunteer work. Probably something to do with refugees. I want to find an organisation actually helping them. There are so many useless charities out there.'

'Don't get me started.'

'I kind of want to, though.'

She laughs.

'So,' she says. 'Writing and volunteering. I'm on board so far.'

'And studying. I'm gonna apply to do a master's.'

'A master's in what?'

'Creative writing,' I say. 'I never studied writing and I've always wanted to.'

She contemplates.

'I'm worried about you taking on too much at once, but I'm not going to discourage you. I know you love learning.'

'Here lies Yael, she loved learning.'

'Nothing wrong with that.'

'Oh,' I say, remembering more fuel to add to the psychiatric fire. 'And I want to go on a trip.'

'Okay,' she says hesitantly. 'A trip where?'

'I haven't got that far yet. Somewhere overseas?'

'Let's talk about it next session.'

Her poker face needs work.

'Are we gonna talk about this situation?' I say, pointing at the puffer vest. 'And the fact it's twenty-eight degrees outside?'

'Would you look at that?' she says, looking at her watch. 'Time's up.'

MY DREAMS LIST

If I had unlimited time, talent, money, knowledge, self-confidence and support from my family, here is a list of everything I would like to do with my life.

- *Bachelor of Arts, Bachelor of Commerce or Bachelor of Business*
- *Memorials: Maman y Papa, Grand-mère, Zeida*
- *Travels: Seattle, New York, Boston, LA, Switzerland, France, Israel, Mexico, South America, Sweden*
- *Open new office (strata and property management)*
- *Aim for financial security: own family, Géraud y Camille, Tante Joseline*
- *Acquire Saab*
- *Acquire small cabin cruiser*
- *Learn Greek, Spanish, Hebrew*
- *Learn computer (rapid learning, better memory)*

I'm in a gym for the first time since the thing and hoo boy, I'm unfit.

What kind of smoothie-filled idiot does a spin class after living cardio-free for almost a year?

I thought maybe months of yoga would make up for my near-total sedentary lifestyle, but alas, how wrong I was.

I've been lying on my back in the stretching area for what feels like hours and I'm not entirely sure I'll ever move again.

Send help.

Unlike half of Instagram, I've never thought of the universe as sentient or godlike.

I don't believe it's some sort of benevolent force with the power to shape our destinies. I've never 'put something out' to it.

However, after telling Priya I wanted to find a part-time job when I get back from Europe, one of my old editors reached out to see if I wanted to do a part-time contract in-house next year. It's fashion writing, which I haven't done in a long time, but I can write some practice stories before I start.

I accepted the gig and reluctantly thanked the universe for making it happen.

Now, what else can I manifest?

'Hi fellas,' I say to my favourite crustaceans as I reach the bottom of the stairs leading to the baths pool. 'And ladies and enbies and all crabs across the gender spectrum.'

Wait, should man crabs even be here? Seems wrong.

It's a cool, overcast Wednesday and I came here knowing the place would be relatively quiet and hoping the water would be relatively calm. Thankfully, the goddess has provided.

It's time.

I want to dive in, literally and symbolically, but there's no diving allowed here – the pool is too shallow and the vibe too serene.

I sit on the pool ledge with my legs in the water and take a deep breath. The ocean twitches and hums and I try not to think about anything.

And with neither pomp nor anything remotely resembling grace, I plop into the water.

*

Liora's taco nights are about twenty-seven per cent more authentic than Mum's were, with soft tortillas and no Old El Paso kit box in sight.

How I laughed when I went to Mexico and discovered no pre-2010s Australian 'taco' resembled anything even vaguely close to the real thing. Despite what Old El Paso had us believing, there were no corn chips, no mince, no cheese and no sour cream. And the biggest betrayal of all? No nachos.

'I'm going on a trip,' I announce one taco night.

'Can I come?' Lexi asks.

'I haven't even said where I'm going.' I dollop guacamole on a mini tortilla.

'I don't care,' she says. 'I wanna go on an aeroplane.'

'Me too!' Ethan says.

'Me too!' Hannah's face is a Pro Hart masterpiece of various ingredients.

'Where to?' Liora looks panicked. 'Do you think you're well enough?'

'Is Aunty Yaya sick?' Lexi asks. 'Are you sick? You said you weren't sick.'

'Just a teensy little bit, munchkin,' I tell her. 'I'll be better tomorrow.'

'Is this an overseas trip?' Liora asks. 'I'm not thrilled about you travelling alone.'

'I want to visit Margot.'

'I'd love you to be with Margot. But don't you think Tokyo might be a bit much right now?'

'She said we'd only stay in Tokyo for a few days and then go to Kyoto.'

'Okay,' she says. 'That's a good idea.'

'Then I want to go to Iceland,' I say. 'Like Eva and I always talked about.'

'Alone?' she asks.

'Probably. But not for long.'

'Oh, Yael, no.'

I knew she wouldn't like that.

'I know you've been wanting to go there forever and I get that you want to honour Eva,' she says, 'but can you wait a bit longer? It's like the most isolated place on earth.'

'I'll only go for three or four days,' I say. 'What's the worst that can happen?'

She makes quite the face.

'Pity you sent back those thermals you blackout-bought,' says Sean.

'Not. Helping. Sean.'

Death stare.

He holds up his hands in surrender.

'And then Italy and Spain with Romy.'

I slather two tacos in hot sauce, as God intended.

'When would you go?' Liora asks. 'And how long for?'

She's freaking out.

'Soon-ish?' I say. 'Mid- to late December, I think. And I don't know how long. Maybe a month?'

'Look,' she says. 'I don't want to be a total downer. I know you're getting better, I'm just scared about you relapsing halfway across the world.'

'I know. Me too.'

'Then again,' she says, her tone changed. 'If you relapsed I'd have to come get you and I've never been to Spain.'

'You're welcome to meet me there even if I don't relapse,' I say, thinking out loud. 'Or anywhere. We could go somewhere in Japan together before I meet Margot.'

'I can't go on a trip!' she practically yells, like I've suggested she cut off her legs.

'Why?'

'Because I have children.'

'And,' I say, 'a perfectly capable, very handsome husband.'

'Thanks, mate.'

'Any time.'

'I'll buy your tickets,' I offer, showing off that famed financial literacy again.

'Okay,' Liora says. 'I'm coming around to the idea.'

'See?' I say. 'Everybody wins.'

'Except me,' Sean says.

A phone call.

Andy.

Weird – who calls?

'You're right, that is the ugliest dress I've ever seen.'

I sent him a photo of me in my bat mitzvah dress, a hideous purple abomination with a sweetheart neckline, puffy sleeves and a sash. A SASH.

'Liora's dress for hers was equally awful,' I say. 'I think our mother might have hated us?'

'It certainly looks like it. I thought only boys have bar mitzvahs?'

But seriously, who calls?

'Boys have to have them to be considered real Jewish men but they're not mandated for girls. I think bat mitzvahs were eventually introduced for non-Orthodox Jews because girls felt left out.'

'Jewish feminism, hey?'

'I'd wager it was less about liberation and more about parties and gifts.'

So many gifts.

'Wait, can I have a bar mitzvah?'

'I don't see why not.'

Awkward silence.

'How's your mum?' I ask.

'She's good. Loving it up here. It's a really nice part of the world.'

More silence.

Again, who calls?

'Did you get your master's application in?'

'Yup. Thanks.'

'Congrats. No, wait, mazel tov.'

I laugh.

'Thanks. It wasn't particularly hard, though.'

'It's a big step. Some people talk about studying for years and never apply. You've overachieved already.'

'Finally.'

*

268

I've started reading the news again and after a quick debrief on the Prime Minister's latest nonsense, I tell Priya I'm going overseas in December.

'I want to put this period behind me, literally and figuratively.'

'Okay, I think that's great.'

Wait, where's her mug?

'I know it's not as simple as going away and coming back and everything's fixed, but it feels right.'

'I understand.'

'And maybe I'll meet Björk.'

I scan her desk, then the room. No mug in sight.

'Who's Björk?' she asks.

'Seriously?'

'You know I'm not hip.'

I laugh.

'Not if you say hip,' I say. 'Björk's an Icelandic singer.'

'Wow, so Iceland?'

'Yup.'

'Wait,' she says. 'Won't Iceland be dark and freezing?'

'Yes, but apparently there are still awesome things to do, less tourists and a high chance of seeing the northern lights.'

'Okay then. Iceland it is.'

'And Japan and Italy and Spain.'

'What a trip. Please tell me you're not going alone.'

Do she and Liora have secret meetings?

'I'll be alone in Iceland, unless I meet Björk. Margot's in Japan and Romy's coming to Spain and Italy. I also told Liora we could go somewhere together before Japan, and she's contemplating it. I offered to pay for her flights.'

'Yael, you haven't been working and the trip already sounds expensive. I hope she doesn't let you do that.'

But back to her mug …

'I've just put her through so much. I want to say thank you.'

'Buy her a pot plant. Not tickets to Europe.'

'I'm starting that new job when I come back. Anyway, I doubt she'll let me pay. Or come at all.'

There's a light knock on the door and Bill comes in with a mug for Priya. He wasn't in reception when I got here.

'Killer shoes, toots,' he says to me as he scurries out, and balance is restored.

'Yes,' says Priya. 'I noticed the shoes. She's back.'

'She's wearing jeans and an ancient t-shirt,' says she.

'Baby steps. And we both know it's all about the footwear.'

Amen.

'Okay,' she says. 'Back to your trip. While I'd prefer to get a little more distance between you and what happened before you traverse the globe, I know you're going to do it no matter what I say, so let's just make sure we have a plan.'

'Can we schedule a couple of calls or video chats?'

'Yes, we can.'

'Gracias.'

I didn't know Liora was morbidly scared of birds.

Somehow it had never come up in the thirty-plus years of our close acquaintance.

But one day, when Hannah was a toddler, the three of us were having breakfast in a cafe near my apartment when a pigeon flew in through the open bay windows, a not altogether uncommon occurrence in Sydney establishments.

I noted it as it flew by our table, turning back to my granola in time to see Liora scream, jump up, shove Hannah into the bird's path, and dive under the table.

When the bird had cut and run, and I determined Hannah was okay, I bent down to Liora's eye level.

'Did you just use your child as a human shield?' I asked.

'You know I'm terrified of birds!'

'I absolutely did not know that.'

She crawled out from under the table and reclaimed her daughter and her seat.

'Well, I am,' she said.

'Noted. But again, did you just use your child as a human shield?'

'Please don't tell Sean.'

Sunrise at the baths.

There's barely anyone here. Just me, Lynne and a woman I don't recognise sitting on the grassy knoll near me. She's wearing a headscarf and big sunglasses, but I can tell she's crying.

I want to reach out to her, but I don't. I didn't want strangers bothering me when I cried here. Though she did choose to sit very close to the only person here today.

I get my book out of my bag, *The Year of Magical Thinking*. One of my faves. Yes, I know. A female writer who loves Joan Didion, how novel. But it's still my favourite text on grief and it came out the year Mum died, so it holds an extra special place in my heart.

I found small comfort at the time in knowing that Joan Didion and I were grieving in symmetry. That someone so glamorous and hallowed was feeling the same pain – or similar pain – I was.

As I read, I'm aware that the woman keeps stealing glances at me. I look up and meet her gaze.

'Do you want some hot chocolate?' I motion to my thermos.

Why yes, I did bring a thermos full of hot chocolate for a daybreak swim in November.

'Oh, thank you. No, I'm fine,' she says quietly. 'You have it.'

'It's alright. I can't drink half a litre of liquid Cadbury.'

I can absolutely drink half a litre of liquid Cadbury.

'Okay, thank you.'

'I'm Yael, by the way.'

'I'm Bushra.'

I pour Bushra a cup and pass it to her.

'Do you come here a lot?' I ask.

'Not as much as I'd like. I just needed somewhere to think, somewhere safe.'

'Same.'

We sit in safe silence.

'It's funny,' I say. 'Every woman who comes here describes it as safe and every woman understands what that means. But men just can't wrap their heads around it. They say, "Are you scared of men hurting you at normal beaches?" and I try to explain that safety is multifaceted for us, but they just can't conceptualise it. Sorry, I must sound like a first-year gender studies student.'

'No, you're right. I've had the same conversation with my husband. He also thinks me being able to wear a bikini here without men seeing is a win for him, not me.'

'I don't know if they're clueless because nobody tells them or because they don't listen when somebody does.'

'Both, I think.'

She sips the hot chocolate.

'This is so good. Thanks so much.'

272

'You're very welcome.'

I return to my Didion, but I soon hear sharp, rhythmic inhales.

'Hey, just so you know, I'm a very good listener.'

'Thank you, that's very kind. I just need to think.'

She resumes staring at the ocean and I go back to my book.

An hour or so later, I get hungry.

'I hope everything works out okay,' I say to Bushra as I gather my things. She thanks me and gives me back my cup.

On my way out, I ask Lynne to keep an eye on her.

'She's been crying since she got here,' I say. 'Doesn't want to talk.'

'Now, who does that remind me of?' Lynne says.

'I know, I know. It appears I've passed the baton.'

'Believe me, love, you weren't the first and she won't be the last.'

I get halfway to the gate when she shouts out to me.

'Oh, wait, Yael!'

I walk back down to her.

'Sorry,' she says. 'But have you spoken to Shirley recently?'

'Not for a while. She's in Seal Rocks with her son and not much of a texter.'

'Do you know if she got the results from her tests?'

What?

'What tests?'

'The ones from after the seizure.'

'Sorry, what?'

'She didn't tell you? Well, maybe it's not my place but last time she was here, she had a seizure in the pool. We had to get an ambulance.'

What the hell?

'I had no idea. She didn't say anything.'

'She probably didn't want to worry you, love. I called her the next day and she was still in hospital. Said they were doing tests.'

'When was that?'

'Must be two or three weeks ago.'

Fuck.

'Okay,' I say, my stomach starting a rinse cycle. 'Thanks Lynne.'

'Please pass on my regards if you speak to her.'

I sit in the car for a very long time, paralysed, and eventually I drive home in silence.

When I get there, I feed Julia Louis-Dreyfus and take to my bed.

I don't watch anything, I don't read anything, I just lie there.

Should I tell them I know? Or should I play along and pretend I don't know?

Am I allowed to be mad? Am I mad?

Not knowing what to do or feel, I do and feel nothing.

The phone wakes me up a few hours later and I'm annoyed to find it's still daytime.

Liora.

'Nope,' I say to Julia Louis-Dreyfus, asleep at my feet.

Liora calls again several times over the next few hours and eventually I turn my phone off and go back to sleep, hoping not to wake again until morning.

I'm startled awake by someone inside my apartment screaming my name.

Am I being robbed?

Why would a robber know my name?

Liora bursts into my bedroom.

'YAEL!'

'What? Why are you screaming?'

It's pitch-black. I sit up and turn on the lamp. Julia Louis-Dreyfus is not amused, rising from her slumber and blinking her eyes to adjust to the light.

'Oh my god,' she says. 'Where have you been?'

'Here. What's wrong? What time is it?'

'It's nine. I've been trying to call you all day, but you weren't picking up and then your phone was off and phones only get turned off on planes and after murders.'

Now who's being melodramatic?

'And then you didn't show up for dinner.'

Oops.

'Sorry, I was asleep.'

'Since 3 pm?'

'I didn't want to be awake.'

'Why, what's going on? This is why I'm worried about you going overseas.'

That sentence is gonna come out a lot.

'I think Shirley's dying.'

'What?'

'I think Shirley's dying.'

'No, I heard you. Why do you think that? Isn't she on holiday with her son?'

'I think it's a goodbye holiday. Like when we took Mum to Jervis Bay.'

If a holiday before a kid arrives is a babymoon, what's a holiday before a parent leaves?

'Has she been sick?'

275

'She's been having really bad migraines and Lynne told me she had a seizure at the baths. Remember when Mum had migraines and seizures?'

She sits on my bed.

'Okay, but you don't know for sure?'

'No.'

'And you haven't asked?'

'I found out and then went to sleep. But she clearly doesn't want me to know.'

'Maybe because there's nothing to know.'

There's definitely something to know.

'You don't think that maybe you're catastrophising?'

'I'm not catastrophising!'

I'm totally catastrophising.

'I told you to be careful with her from the start.'

WTF?

'Woah! You can't "I told you so" me because she's *dying*.'

'I just knew something like this would happen.'

'You knew she was going to contract a terminal illness and not tell me about it? Are you psychic now?'

'Firstly, we don't know that she has a terminal illness. But I just knew something wasn't right.'

'She's sick! You're being incredibly unfair.'

'Maybe, but I knew you were going to end up hurt and you've ended up hurt.'

'Well then, congratulations. You won. Are you happy now?'

Too far?

'Now you're being unfair. Of course I'm not happy. Is that how you see me? Do you really think I'm that petty?'

Too far.

'No.'

'Do you think I look out for you just so I can laud it over you or win some game?'

'No.'

'Why do you think I do?'

Ooh, I know that one.

''Cause Mum asked you to.'

'Yes, partly. But also because I love you.'

'Are you gonna try and kiss me now?'

She slaps my arm.

'But you can't do this to me,' she says. 'You can't just go into hiding without telling me. I was so scared about what I was going to find here. You can't do that to me. You're the only one left.'

Oh man.

'I'm sorry. I love you, too. I won't do it again.'

We both know I probably will.

'You know you have to call her, right?'

A phone call.

Me.

'Hey, Yael,' Andy says.

I was expecting Shirley.

'Oh, hi,' I say, thrown. 'Um, is your mum around?'

'She's still asleep, actually.'

8.30 am is still early, I guess.

'We're back in town, though. Do you wanna come over for a cuppa later?'

'Sure.'

That Dad never got to tick off any items on his dreams list breaks my heart.

But I'm glad he died before Saab stopped manufacturing. I'm not sure he would have coped.

Andy answers the door and immediately it's a disaster. He goes in for the cheek kiss, I think he's going in for a hug, and the next few seconds are a mortifying blur.

I should have brought another cake.

He leads me into the living room.

'Do you want a coffee or tea?'

'I'd love a tea, thanks.'

'How do you have it?'

'White, please.'

'Done.'

I sit in a giant armchair and doomscroll social media. I'm still not posting, but I've started to miss covert advertising and dogs who love ducks.

'Here you go,' Andy says, startling me. He puts a coaster, mug and little bowl on a side table next to the armchair. 'I didn't know how strong you like it, so I left the teabag in.'

'I'll take it any way.'

Damn.

'Well, that came out wrong.'

He laughs.

Where's Shirley?

'How was Seal Rocks?' I ask.

'It was really nice. Nostalgic. Made me realise just how good I had it as a kid.'

'I have that realisation all the time.'

Maybe she's in the kitchen?

'How have you been?'

'I've been good. Just swimming and reading and planning some travelling.'

This is so awkward.

'Oh, cool. Where to?'

'Japan, Iceland, Italy and Spain.'

'Fuck, that's quite the trip. Jealous. When are you off?'

'Christmas Day.'

'Santa Claus won't be happy.'

'And that's just something I'm going to have to learn to live with.'

Seriously, where's Shirley?

'Well, I hope you have some serious thermals.'

What's with men and thermals?

Nobody says anything for several uncomfortable moments as the elephant in the room shakes its head.

'Where's Shirley?' I blurt out when I can't take it anymore.

Andy shifts uncomfortably on the couch, clearly desperate to be anywhere but here.

'I wanted to tell you in person,' he says.

'Tell me what?'

More silence.

'I'm sorry, Yael. I really don't know how to say this.'

He's really struggling.

'It's okay,' I say, cutting the guy some slack. 'Take your time.'

He takes a deep breath.

'Okay, so, Mum's had headaches since I can remember. Generally mild ones, fairly easily fixed. But not long after she met you, the headaches gradually became stronger and more frequent. When they became unbearable, she started having tests.'

I feel sick.

'Is she gone?'

Such tact.

'Sorry, I didn't mean to be so blunt.'

'That's okay.'

He looks relieved.

'She's not gone. She's in the hospice.'

And with that word, with that big little word, it's real.

'She deteriorated really quickly up north. The doctors said they've rarely seen it happen so fast.'

I'm trying hard not to cry.

'So, you came up from Melbourne because she was sick?'

'Yeah.'

'And the surgery she was supposed to have got cancelled because it was too far advanced?'

'Yeah. I'm really sorry for not telling you sooner. I wanted to, but she swore me to secrecy.'

'Why?'

'She said you've watched enough people die.'

I let that sink in.

'I get it. It's terrible logic, but I get it. And she's only known me for five minutes.'

'No, she adores you.'

I'm suddenly very aware that it's his mother who's dying, not mine, and try to pull myself together.

'I'm sorry, this is wrong, I should be comforting you. How are you doing?'

'I have no idea.'

'Is she still conscious?'

'In and out. She's still pretty lucid, just a bit confused sometimes.'

'Can I see her?'

'I can take you tomorrow.'

DECEMBER

'What if we went away somewhere?' Liora asked from somewhere far left field.

We'd stopped for lunch on the way back from our meeting with Mum's palliative care team at the hospital. Sean was with Mum and Ethan, and we felt like pretending life was fine and normal for an hour.

'What? While our mother is dying?'

'No, I mean after. All of us. You, me, Sean and Ethan. I've been thinking about what you said about having to sit in that horrible house for a month being pitied by the entire Eastern Suburbs Jewry.'

'And some from the north.'

A flustered waitress brought our coffees over and I asked for sugar.

Why didn't cafes keep sugar on the tables anymore? Was it a single-origin, filter-only 'real coffee drinkers don't use sugar' snobby thing? Exhaustion and misery were turning this into a whole thing in my head.

'I know it sounds crazy, but what if we did that for a week or two and then went somewhere else?'

'Like where?'

'Anywhere. Preferably somewhere warm. Definitely somewhere beautiful.'

The waitress returned with two chicken salads, one without chicken, and a surplus of sugar packets.

'And here's your sugar,' she said deliberately, basically calling me trash.

'So,' I said once my nemesis was gone. 'You want to go on a tropical holiday a week after Mum dies?'

'Basically.'

'Okay, wow. I'm gonna need a minute with this.'

I ate my chicken-less chicken salad and mulled a potential National Lampoon's Grief Island Vacation, perhaps to a destination where there was sugar found on every cafe table.

'People will think we're arseholes,' I said, picking tomatoes out of my salad.

'You don't care what people think, remember?'

'Oh yeah.'

'I'll talk to my travel agent friend to see where's good this time of year. And possibly on very short notice. I'm sure she'll happily book everything for us. What do you think?'

I ate and mulled some more.

'This is a very weird idea, but sure, I'm in.'

'Hey, we've been sad in Sydney for two years. Let's be sad somewhere else. Ideally with a pool bar.'

Three weeks later, we were sad all over Hawaii.

*

I wait for Andy outside the hospice first thing.

Being back at Sacred Heart for the first time since Nanna died is mildly triggering, but I'm hoping Morph and Dex are still here.

Andy arrives bearing beverages.

'I got you a hot chocolate,' he says a smidge too loud, thrusting a keep cup at me. 'Sorry, hi. How are you? I got you this. You don't have to have it if you don't want to. I probably should have asked.'

'Thanks.' I take the cup from him. 'You didn't have to do that.'

'Do you wanna go up?'

We take the stairs.

Andy leads me into Shirley's room and it could be Nanna asleep in the hospital bed – grey hair, ashen face, little gasps. It might even be the same room. North facing, pale blue walls, single chair.

Andy kisses Shirley on the forehead, whispers 'Hi, Mum,' and goes to find another chair. I stand glued to the spot.

She's really dying.

It's all happened so quickly that a not insignificant part of me didn't believe it was real.

But I know dying when I see dying.

I take her hand in mine. I've never noticed how beautiful her hands are. Tiny palms supporting long, delicate fingers with perfect almond fingernails.

'Thank you for being my friend,' I whisper.

Then I sing a bit of the *Golden Girls* theme song because I have no boundaries.

'I don't know how I would have got through this year without you.'

Tears are imminent.

'And I can't believe you tried to literally ghost me.'

My mother's last words to me were perfect.

She'd barely been conscious for days and I was in the spare room talking to Sheila. Mum had lost so much weight she was almost skeletal, and her face was so drained of colour she was almost unrecognisable. It took years after her death for me to conjure a happier, healthier image of her whenever she came to mind. Dad looked even worse at the end. That took even longer.

Sheila and I were chatting on either side of Mum's bed and I made a joke about her baking skills.

And with full volume and clarity, my beautiful dying mother opened her eyes, looked straight at me, said 'I can still hit you!' and lay back down, never to speak to me again.

Like I said, perfect.

'Is there anything I can help you with?' I ask Andy.

I'm still in Shirley's hospice room.

'I honestly have no idea. Mum did everything for Dad's fu—'

'Actually, let's not discuss it here.' I nod towards Shirley. 'Do you wanna go to the visitors' lounge?'

'I'm not sure there is a visitors' lounge.'

'I am.'

'Lounge' is a bit of a misnomer. It's a bleak, pale blue room with a couple of old couches and a small table and chairs. Two mottled moggies are stretched out in a sunny patch.

'I was hoping they'd still be here,' I say, running over and giving them both belly rubs. 'Do you want tea?'

'Nah, I'm good, thanks.'

I head into the mini kitchenette attached to the lounge.

'Okay, I'm going to make you a to-do list,' I say, getting a mug. 'I mean, if you want me to. I want to help, not take over.'

Sometimes I take over.

'You don't have to do that.'

'I know. I've never done this for a non-Jewish funeral, but I'll work it out.'

'Thank you. I don't know what I'm doing.'

I locate teabags and milk.

'Is there anyone you need to call?'

'Mum's cousin Joyce is on her way with her daughter from the UK. They're very close. She's scared they might not make it. Mum didn't tell her she was sick and it all happened so fast, I didn't think to tell her earlier.'

'Oh no! I hope they make it. Anyone else?'

He leans back against the sink and covers his face with his hands, breathing deeply.

'I'll call a few more relatives tonight. I meant to bring Mum's address book today, but my brain isn't functioning properly.'

'It'd be weird if it was.'

'I have to call her friends, too.'

'Do the lunch ladies know?'

'Who?'

'The group she has lunch with every week.'

The kettle boils.

'Ah yes, that's who I mean. They know she's sick, but not that we're here. She asked that nobody but Joyce be allowed in here.'

'Joyce and me?'

He makes a strange face.

'Just Joyce.'

Oh.

'I don't want to be here if it will upset her.'

'It won't. I'm pretty sure it was more about protecting you than her actual wishes, so I'm okay with defying her.'

'One last childish rebellion.'

'Totally. Oh wow, I'm not going to have parents. That's weird. I mean I know it happens to everyone, I just didn't think about it until now.'

'Yeah, as an old rabbi said to me literal moments after my mother died, welcome to the orphans club.'

'Yikes, that's rough. And thanks, I guess?'

'I'll teach you the secret handshake after the funeral.'

He laughs.

'We should get back,' he says.

I make the tea and we head back to Shirley's room.

She's awake.

'Andy?'

Her voice is soft, strained.

'I'm here, Mum.'

He takes her hand.

'Is someone else here?'

She's barely audible.

'Yael's come to visit,' Andy says. 'I know you said she shouldn't come, but I made an executive decision.'

I walk around the bed and take her other hand.

'Well, hi,' I say, trying to brave-face it. 'Not sure I like your new living arrangements.'

'Beautiful Yael.'

I have to lean in to hear her.

'I didn't want you to see me like this,' she says.

'I'd rather see you like this than not at all.'

'I'm sorry.'

She looks on the verge of tears.

I'm trying not to cry.

'Hey, I understand.' I stroke her hair. 'I'm just happy I get to see you now.'

She nods.

'I'm glad you're here.'

'I'm not glad you're here. But I'm glad we met.'

'At the lovely baths. I wanted to go one more time.'

'I'm sorry.'

'You're a good girl.'

'Hold on.' I look at Andy. 'Can your phone FaceTime?'

'Yeah, course.'

I have an idea.

Post-death paperwork can really challenge my ingrained love of admin.

There's all the obvious financial and legal stuff like reading wills, closing bank accounts, and clearing or selling living spaces, but there's also a seemingly endless list of small tasks that can differ from one deceased person to another.

One of the least fun of these is cancelling telecommunications and utility contracts. Phone contracts, home internet, gas, water, electricity – each phone call a new fresh hell of keypad menus, hold music and forced verve; of informing bored strangers on minimum wage of your loss.

Usually a phone call, final payment and death certificate ensure the closure of such accounts and the cessation of communications from the relevant companies.

But where human error is possible, human error is probable on occasion.

Maybe six months after Mum had died, I found a forwarded letter addressed to her in Liora's mailbox. This will generally happen for years with decreasing frequency. Voiding a life isn't easy.

As I let myself into the apartment, I tore open the envelope and examined what looked like a sympathy card from Mum's former mobile phone service provider. When I reached the living room, I stopped and let out an involuntary 'oh my god'.

'What?' Liora was breastfeeding Ethan on the couch.

'What happened?' Sean came in from the kitchen, holding a spatula.

'Um, Mum got a card from Optus.'

'Why?' Liora said. 'Didn't you cancel her account?'

She loves it when I forget to do things.

'I did.' I passed her the card. 'I swear to Cher.'

She examined the card.

'Wow,' she said. 'Like, really, just wow.'

She gave Sean the card.

'This is fucking hilarious.'

The front of the card showed a flock of birds flying towards the top right corner, as if away from the cardholder.

'We're sorry to see you go' was printed beneath them.

On the inside of the card, the flock was flying towards the bottom left corner, as if flying back towards you, and it said, 'We'd love to have you back.'

Either Optus believed the dead could rise or someone didn't tick the 'deceased' box in Mum's profile on the database.

Lucky for them we have a sense of humour.

*

Thank god, Lynne's here.

I hope she's in a good mood.

'Miss Yael! A sight for sore eyes if I ever knew one.'

It seems she is.

She's wearing a Santa hat and candy cane earrings, and the volunteers area is covered in so many Christmas decorations that you'd think an elf threw up on it. There's also a token menorah, bless.

'Hey, Lynne. Do you mind if we have a quick chat?' I ask.

'Sure, love.'

She stands and passes the donation bucket to the other volunteer on duty.

'Remember, Sharon, it's either a gold coin donation or a membership fob. No excuses.'

Sharon doesn't look like a woman who thrives under pressure.

'Step into my office.'

I follow her into a cramped kitchenette.

More Christmas. And a sign about washing one's own mugs 'cause the maid's on holiday.

'What's up, hon?'

'Well, I have bad news and a big favour to ask.'

'I'm not good with bad news. Favours I can do.'

'So, Shirley's in the hospice. Those migraines turned out to be symptoms of a bigger issue, but by the time she was diagnosed, it was too late.'

Lynne lifts one hand to cup her mouth and chin, the other finds her stomach.

'Oh love, that's awful. Such a nice lady. I'm so sorry, the two of you have such a lovely friendship.'

'Yeah, it's horrible. I only found out two days ago.'

'Have you seen her?'

'I went this morning. She's mostly sleeping, but she woke up and said she wishes she could have come to the baths one last time. I wish I could have brought her, but that window has closed.'

'That's a shame.'

'Which brings me to the favour. Is there any chance you can ever so slightly bend the rules just this once, in these extraordinary circumstances, and let me FaceTime her and take her on a tour of the place?'

After a moment's pause, Lynne goes to a cupboard and retrieves a loudspeaker.

'Follow me.'

'ATTENTION,' she booms through the speaker to the women present. 'In highly unusual circumstances, we're permitting a video call to a dying woman so she can see this joint one more time. If you don't want to appear on screen, duck for cover or come stand at the vollies station till it's over.'

'Thanks so much,' I say, giving her a quick hug.

'Also,' she bellows, holding the speaker up again. 'If anyone asks, this never happened and I wasn't here.'

Over the years, Liora and I got really good at hospitals.

Practice makes perfect.

We spent most of our time at Prince of Wales and St Vincent's because they were the closest and most of our doctors were there, but RPA, Royal North Shore and a few small private hospitals all hosted us over the years.

We even thought about writing a guidebook.

We knew where the best coffee and vending machines were located.

We knew to take jumpers to emergency visits, even in summer, because emergency departments run cold.

We knew discmans, and later iPods, were good for calming or distracting patients.

And we knew where all the untimed street parking was so we wouldn't go bankrupt in hospital car parks.

We also got settling patients in for a long stay down to a fine, depressing art.

During one of Mum's hospital visits, she was sharing a room with a lovely Greek lady named Helen. She was about the same age as Mum, maybe a little older, and bore the telltale signs of cancer: a soft head turban, a silk scarf tied around her neck to hide a scar, and a variety of ginger-based products on her bedside table to help soothe the nausea.

Helen had already been there a few days when we arrived, and after we introduced ourselves, she watched as Liora and I unpacked Mum's clothes and toiletries, talked to nurses about her medications and – our favourite – filled out the meals order form for the following few days.

'I wish I had daughters,' she said with a sigh.

'They're a well-oiled machine,' Mum said.

'I have sons. They're good boys, but they wouldn't know how I have my coffee let alone all this.' She gestured towards us.

'We can train them,' Liora said.

'Would you?'

*

'If I had one wish,' Mum used to say, 'it would be for you and Liora to get along.'

I wish she could have seen it come true.

I text Andy.

Is she awake?

Yes!

I go outside the gates and video-call him.

'Hey,' he says.

He looks so tired.

'Hi, I'm at the baths. Is she up to it?'

'I think so. Hold on, I'll ask.'

I lose sight of him as he moves the phone away from his face but I can hear him talking to Shirley.

'Mum, Yael's at the women's baths. She thought you'd like to see the water again.'

Shirley says something I can't hear and then Andy's face comes back into frame.

'She's keen.'

'Awesome. The only thing is, you're not allowed to see anything beyond this point. They're breaking the rules allowing me to FaceTime at all.'

'No prob. I'll just hold the phone up for her.'

'Thanks.'

'Okay, give me a sec to wind the bed so she's sitting up. If I can work out how to do that.'

'Sure.'

He puts the phone on the bed and all I see is white.

'Alright, done,' he says, returning to view. 'I'll put you on with Mum now.'

Shirley comes into view. Her sunken face is a shock, even though I saw her only a few hours ago.

'Well, hi there. Welcome to your personal tour of your favourite place. I'll be your host, that damaged girl you met here who won't go away.'

'You're not damaged,' she says so softly I almost miss it. 'You're wonderful.'

'You're a liar. Anyway, let's go in and have a look around. Lucky it's a beautiful day.'

I walk through the gates and down the concrete path towards the volunteers stand, holding the camera phone away from me so Shirley can feel like she's here. I stop in front of Lynne and turn the camera phone to me again.

'In another stroke of fortune, our old fave Lynne is here. Can I put her on? Only if you're comfortable with it.'

'Yes.'

I hand the phone to Lynne.

'Hi, Shirley,' she says, waving.

'Hello, my friend.'

'She said hello my friend,' Andy says, in case Lynne didn't hear her.

'I miss your bright smile, love. I'm so sorry you're in a bad way, but I'm glad Miss Yael has brought you with her now.'

I let them chat and get undressed. I stopped at home on the way here to get my swimmers. It would be wrong not to take her right into the pool for the full baths experience.

'Okay,' I say when I reclaim the phone. 'Let's keep going.'

Trying not to catch any strangers in the crossfire, I walk her past the grassy areas and down the concrete steps towards the giant rocks, taking my time so she can see every detail.

'This is the exact spot where we met.' I turn the camera on me again. 'When you heard me laughing at bad porn.'

I hear Andy snort in the background.

'I remember.'

She's clearly tired so I hustle down onto the rocks, pointing her out to sea, then over to the pool, entering slowly via the steps on the shallow side. The water's icy, but I'm too distracted to care.

'I hope you know I wouldn't risk water damage to my phone for just anyone.'

She smiles and I make my way over to the rock wall, hoping the crabs will cooperate. I spot a few scurrying around and get as close as I can to them.

'Crab friends, you remember Shirley. Shirley, wave to my crab friends.'

'YAEL! YAEL, LOOK!'

I look up to find Lynne bolting down the steps towards the pool.

'What?'

'Quick! Turn around.'

I almost forget I'm holding a phone as I swivel around.

'Oh my god! Shirley, look!'

I swim over to the pool ledge and hold the phone up. There is a lone dolphin about fifty metres away.

'Can you see it, Shirley?'

I turn the phone to me and see she's nodding.

'Isn't that something?' Lynne says, standing on the ledge. 'Haven't seen any in months. They knew you needed it.'

'Okay, I'm gonna let you rest now.'

Shirley's barely awake but manages a soft thank you.

'Sorry you didn't get to see me half-naked one last time, you big perv.'

And in the worst timing ever, my phone dies.

What if 'you big perv' is the last thing I ever say to her?

Actually, that's kind of perfect.

A call.

To Andy.

'How is she today?'

I haven't seen Shirley since the women's baths FaceTime. He's only letting Joyce and her daughter in now.

'Worse. Every time I think she can't deteriorate more, bam, she unlocks a whole new level.'

'Yeah, I remember that feeling. Is it cool enough in there? For both of you? Do you want me to drop off a fan?'

It's thirty-five degrees outside.

'It's great here. Well, it's fucking miserable here, but the temperature's good.'

'Okay, can I bring you anything else? Food? An iPad? MDMA?'

'I'm good. Though that last one is tempting.'

We hang up and I go back to my busy afternoon of lying in front of a fan and watching a documentary about these amazing Japanese women who free-dive for abalone.

*

At the minyan for Mum's friend Tova, her daughter, Nessie, gave a speech.

It was a beautiful, funny, devastating tribute and I'm amazed she had the strength and composure to deliver it. It's not really the done thing, but they're not really the kind of people to care.

One thing she said in particular stuck with us, especially with Mum. A friend had told Nessie that sometimes the dying need permission to die; that some people need their partner or children or those closest to them to tell them that they'll be okay, that it's okay to go; that they can stop fighting.

Nessie gave Tova permission to die. A few hours later, she was gone.

Another phone call.

To Andy again.

I thought of something urgent I wanted to tell him in spin class, so I'm sitting on a bike in the spin room running my legs.

'Hey, sorry to bug you again,' I say. 'But I just thought of something.'

'You're not bugging me. Call anytime. What's the thought?'

'Someone once told me that sometimes the dying need permission to die. Like, you need to tell them that it's okay to stop fighting, and that you'll be okay, because they might be holding on for your sake.'

'Did you do it?'

'Yeah. Dad died a few hours after Mum told him we loved him and we'd be alright, and Mum passed a few hours after Liora and I told her the same.'

'I'll give it a go.'

*

Mum gave Dad permission to die.

Liora and I gave Mum permission to die.

Nanna didn't need permission to die.

Apparently I did.

Bill's gone.

Bill's gone and Priya's new receptionist forgot to tell me my appointment had been pushed back an hour, so I'm sitting in reception, in an uncomfortable chair, reading about how celebrities are just like me.

'They drink coffee!'

'They stop for petrol!'

Truly fascinating stuff.

'Yael?'

I look up to see a vision in a simple black sheath dress and the emerald-green version of the Manolo Blahnik heels Carrie wore to marry Mr Big.

I wish I didn't know that.

I follow Priya into her office and take a seat.

'You've got to be kidding me with those shoes,' I say.

'You've got to be kidding me with those pants. And mine were on sale,' she says.

'No they weren't.'

She holds her index finger to her lips.

'So, how are you doing? How was the funeral?'

'I'm okay. It was okay. Small. Andy gave a beautiful eulogy and I learned a lot about Shirley's life. I love that about funerals.'

'I love that you love things about funerals.'

'Mafia widow cosplay, valid public crying, other people's dramas – what's not to love?'

'I think maybe you just love *The Sopranos*.'

'I also love *The Sopranos*.'

'I must say, you seem to be coping with Shirley's passing extremely well. I was worried. I imagine your sister was, too.'

'I'm super sad, but I'm trying to be measured. I may still crash, but I just don't think I have another all-encompassing grief in me. Is that awful?'

'No, it's survival.'

'I also want to go on my holiday and if I crumble, that might not happen. That's definitely awful.'

'It's not awful at all. You're allowed to enjoy yourself, Yael. It doesn't mean you don't miss Shirley or love your parents or care about the suffering of others. You're allowed to be happy, to have fun.'

'I'm not sure I know how anymore.'

'You don't have to, it will just happen. Just don't fight it when it does.'

'I'll try.'

'Now, about your trip. Do you have enough of your medications?'

'Not yet.'

'Remember, you need to take at least a week extra, just in case. The last thing we want is you going through a withdrawal in the middle of Iceland.'

'Okay.'

'And carry half in your hand luggage and the other half in your suitcase.'

'They're gonna think I'm a drug mule.'

'Well, that will make for a great story.'
I laugh.
'I'm really proud of you, you know.'
Tears.
I didn't know how much I needed to hear that.

A phone call.
    Him.
    Present tense.
    What if I just don't answer? What if I never answer again?
The ultimate ghosting.
    It rings out.
    He calls again.
    Fine.
    'Hey.'
    'Hi, Bard.'
    I cringe a bit.
    'What time is it there?' I ask.
    'Midday.'
    'Where are you?'
    'Work. You?'
    'Home.'
    'Wanna FaceTime?' he asks, maybe sensing what's coming.
Maybe horny. Probably both.
    'Not really.'
    'I miss your face.'
    'Good.'
    'I miss you. I'm coming home in February to see the folks.
We can spend some time together.'
    'I don't think we can.'

'Are you going somewhere?'

I can tell in his voice that he's catching on.

'Nope. I'm just done.'

'What do you mean done?'

'I mean done. I don't want this anymore.'

That felt good.

'Wait, Yael. Why? Please don't do this.'

'You did this. You did everything.'

I wish I wasn't crying. I'd feel more badass if I wasn't crying.

'Is there someone else? Have you met someone?'

'You don't get to ask me that.'

'So there is then. Do I know him?'

Oh for fuck's sake.

'Can I still see you when I'm back?' he pleads when I don't answer. 'Just one last time?'

I consider it for a millisecond.

'No.'

'But I love you.'

'You don't treat me like you love me.'

'I'll be better.'

Too late, mate.

'You're incapable of being better.'

'I'll change.'

I laugh.

'You live in another country with another woman.'

'But I really do love you.'

'It's not enough anymore.'

*

'It was a beautiful service,' Lynne says when Andy and I meet her outside the women's baths about a week after Shirley's funeral. 'You spoke so well.'

'Thanks,' Andy says. 'And thank you for this.'

'No need to thank me. It's an honour. Alright, Miss Yael, let's do this.'

She unlocks the gate.

It's 5 am.

'Are you sure this is what you want?' I quintuple-check with him.

'It's what she wanted, so it's what I want.'

He hands me a small mauve urn.

'Do you wanna say goodbye?'

'I already did.'

'Okay, we'll be back soon.'

'Take your time.'

'Sorry you can't come in, Andy,' Lynne says.

'Wouldn't dream of it.'

I put on the torch light on my phone and follow her onto sacred ground.

Lynne bounds down the path, past the change rooms and the grass mounds, and stops at the top of the main steps.

'Where should we do this?' she asks.

'I don't know,' I say. 'I haven't thought this through.'

'Yeah, me either.'

'I'm just glad it's not windy.'

'Yes,' she says. 'I was worried about that. Hmm. It feels kind of wrong to pour her into the pool.'

'I agree. Should we go out onto the rocks and let her fly out over the ocean?'

'Perfect.'

I follow Lynne's lead until we reach the rock jutting out the furthest into the water.

'Do you want to say something?' she asks me.

'One of us should.'

'You're the writer, love! All I can offer is goodbye.'

'Five o'clock in the morning isn't my most eloquent hour, but I'll try.'

I hold the urn out in front of me.

'Okay. Shirley, I still can't believe you're gone. I only knew you for a hot minute, but I'll never forget you. You were a mum when I needed a mum and a wonderful friend, and I hope I gave you whatever you needed, too. Maybe you just needed mango smoothies and a trip to Costco, in which case, you're welcome.'

Lynne laughs.

'Anyway, I hope Peter and your parents are showing you the ropes out there, wherever you are. Goodbye, lovely lady, beautiful ghost. I'll miss you.'

'Bye Shirl. We'll miss you around here.'

We look at each other.

'Should we do it?'

'I reckon.'

The sun sticks its head up out of the ocean as the new day dawns. I hold out the urn on its side and lift the lid. Lynne puts an arm around my waist and we stay that way for a while, watching Shirley scatter and fade.

Eventually we hear voices behind us and turn to find a few early birds heading down to the pool.

'I should get back to Andy,' I say. 'I hope these ladies weren't freaked out by the lone man lurking outside the women's baths at sunrise.'

'Oh god, I didn't think about that.'

'Thanks so much for this, Lynne.'

'Pleasure, treasure.'

'I hope you get your wedding here one day.'

'Me too, love.'

'When are you going back to Melbourne?' I ask.

Andy and I have been sitting on the beach since Shirley's scattering.

'I dunno. I have to work out what I'm doing with the house and all the legal stuff first.'

He closes his eyes, inhales.

'I just feel so guilty. I should have moved back years ago. I shouldn't have left her alone for so long.'

'Maybe not. But children aren't supposed to live their lives for their parents. She wouldn't have wanted you to give up a job you love for her. And you showed up when it mattered.'

He sits with that for a while.

'You're going on Christmas Day, yeah?'

'Yup.'

I remember that's a thing people care about.

'I'm sorry, I just realised how hard that might be for you. Christmas, I mean. Do you have plans? Please tell me you won't be alone?'

'It's cool. A few friends have invited me over to their various places but I'm gonna see how I feel on the day.'

'Okay, as long as you're not alone – unless you want to be alone.'

We ponder our alone-ness together.

'How long are you going away for?' he asks.

'Just over a month.'

'Wow.'

'Do you think you'll still be here when I get back?'

'I'm not sure.'

Aeons pass.

I put my head on his shoulder.

'I'll still be here.'

A phone call.

Romy.

I'm driving home from Coogee.

'Hey, Rom.'

'Is grief horn really a thing?'

She's never been big on salutations.

'Is what a thing?'

'Grief horn. Getting super thirsty after someone dies.'

Wow.

'Jesus, woman, buy a girl a drink first.'

God, I love this woman.

'Yeah,' she says. 'On reflection it's probs uncool to ask your fragile friend about bereavement fornication.'

'Especially when that friend has just scattered someone's ashes,' I say, laughing.

'Oh fuck. Sorry, I forgot that was today. God I'm a dick.'

'It's fine. I mean, you are a dick, but it's fine.'

I need petrol.

'So, how'd it go?'

'It was nice, a bit anticlimactic.'

'How so?'

'I don't know, these things always have a tinge of "Really? Is that it?" You build up the gravitas and symbolism and then, it's over in like thirty seconds and you go get breakfast.'

'Well, it is the most important meal of the day.'

I laugh.

'At least there was no blowback,' I say.

Beware the wind, future ashes scatterers.

'Oh god,' she says. 'Does that happen?'

'Yeah, apparently it happened a bit with Eva's ashes.'

'Noooooooo. But that seems kind of appropriate for some reason.'

'That's what I said!'

At some traffic lights, a very handsome man crosses with a very handsome dog in the truest display of people who look like their pets I've ever seen.

'Did her son sneak in with you?' she asks.

'Nah,' I say. 'He let us do it without him 'cause it's what she wanted.'

'Sounds like a good guy.'

I pull into a servo.

'So …' she says.

'So what?'

'Grief horn, is it real?'

'Yes.'

There's something deeply poetic about crying at a petrol bowser.

A week before I leave on my trip, I get an email. I've been accepted into a Master of Creative Writing for the next academic year. Though I was ninety-nine per cent sure I'd get in, it feels good to have it in writing.

I got into uni.

Mazels!

As I try to cram everything I own into one suitcase – because you never know when you might need a blazer cape – Julia Louis-Dreyfus jumps into the bag, lies down and stares at me with pure disdain. She knows.

'I'm sorry I can't take you with me. But you'll have fun with Romy.'

I try to move her a few times, but she swipes at me until I give up. I'll do it later. Last-minute packing is a hot kick of adrenaline and I've never done it any other way.

Plus, now I can squeeze in one more baths hit before I go.

I'm in the pool, saying goodbye to the crabs.

'I'm going for just over a month.'

They don't care.

I hear squeals and turn around to find that everyone in the pool is over at the ledge, looking and pointing out to sea.

I swim over to see what the fuss is about.

Dolphins! The fuss is about dolphins. At least ten of them, maybe more, frolicking between us and Wedding Cake Island, maybe two hundred metres away. They're so close we can see their whole bodies when they jump out of the water.

I turn to see if everyone on the rocks and grass is watching and behold a truly magnificent sight. Every woman here is standing facing the ocean and all I can see is boobs.

So many boobs.

Dolphins and boobs.

Mother nature's greatest hits, together at last.

I feel a hand on my back.

'Shirley sent you a farewell gift, love,' says Lynne, putting an arm over my shoulders.

I stand in the water, this powerful healing water, crying silent tears – for Shirley, for Mum and Dad, for Nanna, for Eva – as I watch the pod swim south towards Maroubra, until the very last one is completely out of sight.

Maybe the sadness will last forever, but for the first time since I went to Officeworks to print a note, I feel alive.

EPILOGUE

'Hey, when was the last time we were on a plane together?' Liora asks, as she flops down on the seat next to me and fastens her seatbelt, ever diligent.

'Um, Hawaii?'

I'm busy putting my flight essentials – iPad, fashion mag, headphones, lip balm, face moisturiser, hand cream, life savings – in the seat pocket in front of me.

'Yeah, probably.'

'No, wait,' I say. 'We went to Melbourne that time you and Sean both had work stuff and I was your travelling nanny slash indentured servant.'

'Oh yeah. Thanks for that.'

'You say that like I had a choice.'

I take the menu card out of the seat pocket. The vegetarian meals are never listed, but I like to know what everyone else is having.

'I can't believe I'm not going to see the kids for a week.'

'I can't believe Sean agreed you could leave for a week. In school holidays. And pay for it!'

'I knew there was a reason I married him.'

The plane starts moving and we half-watch the safety demonstration.

'I can't believe I'm not gonna see Julia Louis-Dreyfus for a month.'

'Or Andy.'

I make a face.

'Stop it.'

'Stop what?'

She makes a face.

Then, a crackling sound. A baritone voice.

'Cabin crew, prepare for take-off.'

As we start down the runway, I realise that Liora and I are going to spend the next entire week together. 24/7. On purpose.

'Do you think Mum and Dad would ever believe we're going on a holiday together, just the two of us?'

'Not in a billion years.'

And we're off.

Acknowledgements

Writing this book stretched and tested me in ways I could never have imagined, and I'm grateful to all those around me for giving me the space to lean into that. While I'm tempted to thank everyone I've ever met so as to not leave anyone out, the following cast of legends deserve a special shout-out.

If I've still somehow managed to forget you, I'm very, very sorry.

Foremost, my eternal gratitude to Ariella Roth, for remembering more of our shared past than I do and revisiting it in great, often painful detail; to Ricky Roth for being a rock but not an island; and to Aidan, Chelsea and Annabel Roth, for simply existing.

Thank you to my wonderful publisher Lex Hirst, for asking me if I wanted to write a book and tolerating me while I did; to my dreamboat editor Tom Langshaw, for his gentle guidance and boundless patience; and to Ali Green, Léa Antigny, Kajal Narayan, LinLi Wan, Melissa Snook and absolutely everyone at Pantera Press, for being the best hype crew an anxious new author could hope for.

Thank you to my management team, Emma Woolley and Stacey Testro, for seeking me out, pushing me forward and keeping me in line.

To my copyeditor, Camha Pham, and my proofreader, Bronwyn Sweeney, for their keen eyes and delightful comments; and to Amy Daoud, for the cover of my dreams.

To Elfy Scott, for coffees, camaraderie and indulging my very specific porridge-based needs; Nick Visser, for films, food and fun; Kara Schlegl, for plot-wrangling and her infallible kindness; Lisa Edinburg and Lisa Shillan, for their unwavering loyalty and support; Tim Rigg for making me tea and letting me smoosh all the foster dogs; and to all the foster dogs for smooshing me back.

To Keeradenan Dahl-Helm, Cybele Malinowski, Ellouise Davis, Sophie Mallam, Alice Fenton, Tanya Babic, Sophia Marinos, Angela Bennetts, Chontelle Perucich, Arya Geike, Helen Lovelee, Louise Mewton, Elmo Keep and Dorrie Krahe, for almost thirty years of love and lolz.

To Helen Razer, for telling me to accept writing as my fate and get the fuck on with it; Alyx Gorman, for giving me my first writing gig, and many more after that; Benjamin Law for mucho adviceo; Melissa Leong for supporting and amplifying my work and advocacy; Amy Remeikis for random sweet messages; and to Myf Warhurst for being Myf Warhurst.

To Anthony Levin, for always going above and beyond; Anthony Nemeth for checking in; Josh Meyer for offering the help I probably should have accepted; Tamara Kennedy for walks and talks; Luke Leonard for talks but not walks; Ruby Blessing, for baking lessons and beds; Sahra Stolz for olives, gherkins and beds; Nicole Glavan for fashion, gossip and pictures of Scottish men; Vered and Avi for lockdown sandwich delivery; Greta Gaiani for coffee and risotto; and to Arlene Normand, for free rides and tough love.

To my Hope for Nauru team – Helen, Bec, Anca, Lucy and Tim – for standing on the frontlines with me; Zahra Hashemabadi Barat for true friendship; Sahar Ghasemi for inspiring me always; Imran Abdi for being born; and to Dulce Carolina Muñoz Garcia for solving every crisis.

To Charlotte Dawson, for brightening my world before forever dulling it; and to all the Shirleys, but especially Shirley Solomon and Antonia Williams: may their memories be a blessing.

To Debra Adelaide, for her support and understanding; to Delia Falconer, for introducing me to autofiction; and to the entire creative writing department at UTS from 2016 to 2020, wherein I completed a master's and originally gestated this story.

To Thelma 'Tammy' Close at Create NSW for answering my many, many emails; and to Create NSW for supporting artists, specifically me.

To Rabbi Chaim Perez and the late Dr Igal Augarten, who know what they did; and to the nurses and medical support staff who made the unbearable a bit bearable, and to those who continue to do so for all. PAY. THEM. MORE.

And finally, thank you to the badass 19th-century women who fought for a private bathing space; to the 21st-century trans women who fought for entry therein; and to all Bidjigal and Gadigal people of the Eora nation, upon whose unceded land McIver's Ladies Baths sits. I will remain eternally in your debt.